The Creek

 A catalogue record for this work is available from the National Library of Australia

https://www.nla.gov.au/collections

Title: The Creek

Author: Pritchard, Tony (1952–)

ISBNs: 9781922912763 (paperback)
            9781922912770 (ebook – epub)
            9781922912787 (ebook – Kindle)

Subjects: FICTION/Psychological; /Erotica/General
            NON-CLASSIFIABLE

Any references to historical events, real people, or real places are used fictitiously. Names, characters and events, are products of the author's imagination. The author, their agents and publishers cannot be held responsible for any claim otherwise and take no responsibility for any such coincidence.

Cover design by Peter Harris

Cover layout by Ally Mosher at allymosher.com

Cover images by Tony Pritchard

The Creek

Tony Pritchard

Also by Tony Pritchard:

Canoeing Down the Darling

Paddling Down the Darling

Drifting Down the Darling

FIRST BIT

The Creek is in South-east Queensland, and I know it well. Perhaps not well enough. It is a fast-flowing creek that is pure as the steep rainforest it flows through. It is not really called The Creek, but that doesn't matter because a place of physical and spiritual beauty is pretty much subjective, and who's to say one is better than another. Bet you have your own place anyway. Or maybe we construct, construe, and contrive our own self into a place to suit our own purpose, no matter where it is.

Where The Creek is situated exactly is not made clear, because geographical identification can be irrelevant in its preciseness. Exactness doesn't necessarily need coordinates to warm the heart, because vagueness has its own allure.

The Darling River, which shares some of this story, is in western New South Wales. It is really called the Darling River and I know it well, though maybe too well.

I went to The Creek to live in solitude and to find my real self. Self-discovery is a measure against a known, a known that can be denied, or at any rate, avoided. Which I did. I had wilderness and isolation, surely enough to find a unity within the self. You would think. Some sections are rather cranky, some occasionally crude and disgusting, and some downright rude. Yet all sit comfortably within the realms of the madness of living alone, even with the understanding, and experience of knowing that desolation often comes along for the ride. It's a little anti-social, this linear tale of solitude, and will hopefully be disdained, dismissed and disliked by some men who hate themselves, women, anyone not white, as well as the planet. Real men, unlike the previously mentioned, can be strong and hairy, but will never condone men who are being a dick. Real men will relate to the vulnerability of letting go, the desire to be accepted by the self and others, not to mention the smoking hot sex, which is often hilarious and occasionally a total failure, not necessarily in that order.

Women will love this because they are all beautiful, and they understand stuff that men never will.

While being a fiction, everything in The Creek is almost true. Sort of.

However, the act of remembering gives a temptation towards dishonesty, let alone my tendency toward exaggeration done on purpose. Intentions may or may not be honourable and resemblance to fact is often quite loose and pretty much a product of my imagination, historical events included, so if you find any dodgy bits get a grip and leave me alone. In the many years of solitude at The Creek, you will read stuff about the searching for the true self (which includes discussions with the rational brain and the emotional brain), building a house, maintaining an old truck, multiple observations about the local flora and fauna, and details regarding a few innovative bushwalks. All this stuff has been adapted and are my take, so please don't rely on anything as gospel. You may come unstuck. For example, if you were to use my notes on bushwalks in the rainforest, there's a big chance you would get lost and starve to death.

Some sections are soft and brimming with peace and love for a special girl, and a special place. Just think how good it could be if they could always be combined and reciprocated? There are heaps of big swear words, bucketloads of lustful scenes described in full black and white, a few tears, and a few laughs. This is the story of a personal struggle, a search to comprehend life, and a calling out of the devastating effects of inappropriate attitudes and behaviours towards the planet. Mine too.

TP

2023

Brisbane

Grey to green and some advice.

You really sure you're ready for this? Things aren't adding up here. Like, what will you do for work? Your savings aren't that great you know. And you don't know anyone from around here. And won't you get lonely?

I had two people to help me sort my life out. I had never heard them agree on anything and they were often unpleasant to each other. One was my rational brain (also known as RB), with his advice of me not really being ready, and his '… *won't you get lonely …*' shit, only gave me fear and uncertainty. He was logical, he wasn't helpful, he hurt my head and I hated him.

The other was my emotional brain (EB). Thank goodness I have her to steer me through life.

Don't listen to him for fuck's sake. Give it a go. You might regret it, you might have disaster, you might end up running away in disguise, or maybe, just maybe, you might find the caprice, the giddy, the trifle, the freak, the fancy, the wilfulness, and the wantonness. And you might also find what you are looking for, the stuff you dreamed about. And be yourself without that disguise. Yes sir, you might come here today on a chance of hope, on a dream of hope, with the last good kiss you had years ago, but you might find those answers. So, grab that whim.

I loved her. She was the one constant in my life, the one who understood me and the one I listened to. My rational brain had no idea.

* * *

Grey to green for the first time. I had swapped the grey clay and the grey tea-coloured water of the Darling River for a valley in the green of South-east Queensland. A change of geography and a new search for my true self.

I had left a note on the bank of the Darling River:

Going to a new place
Bit scared.
Might stay for a while
Might come back,
Not sure.

As I headed towards the valley for that first time, on the whim of chimmering chance, of nervous crazy, of seeking the almost unseekable, walking, because my ride had pointed and said, Yep, there's your valley see you later, there were two green perpendicular mountain walls running parallel, and it seemed there was about three feet between them. Two towering cliffs, dense green rainforest spilling over their edges and seemingly no way to get in. What do I do? Go straight over the top, or just crash into those cliffs? Then the dirt track swung right then turned a sharp left into the opening between the two towers, the two dense green rainforest towers – and my new world began.

The valley opened to a creek, known locally as The Creek, and it spoke to me in warm welcoming murmurs on the breeze, delicate fine feathers of touch and a revealing of soft love. And this was only day one. As I entered this new world, this new beginning, I pushed aside fronds of worry, the grey boulders of doubt and the spindly grass that had tried to capture my anxieties like spider-webs. The creek itself was a fast clear creek, its water reflecting needle-leaved river oaks, tall gums and mottled lichen-covered rainforest trees, and lime-green moss-covered rocks. Light was filtered and brought on a sleepy feeling, a slowed-down, I would like to sit here for a while feeling. And it felt right to be here, really so right to be here. My rational brain had done his best to dissuade me from coming here, ending with, *Won't you get lonely*? Well, yes, I might, but this change is worth a shot, worth a whim.

EB-You and I, we will handle any issues of the heart. Old RB should stick to his tax returns, his facts and his organised existence. He has no idea about real life, our life.

I built a house next to this creek, this crystal-clear cold creek that never ran dry, where there were climbing cliffs, tangled strangled roots, rainforest-clad gullies, mountains, and haunting bird calls, where dingoes howled, and platypus played. And I stayed there in the green, alone, for a long time.

The house, which became a home, and there is a big difference, was timber and tin – a typical Queenslander, and most of the material used to build this house home came from an old dairy house down the valley a bit. This old house, which was given to me, had moved off its stumps, and was inhabited by various living creatures and not a few deceased ones as well. But still had plenty of timber that was useable.

How do you build a house? I didn't know. Still don't. Plans? Sorry rational brain, no employment prospects for you, I'm a get-excited and do it person who plans later, and one who searches too much. I was always searching for an elusive butterflied-settled ray of sunshine that let me breathe deeply, and a little ray of sunshine that shone an, It's okay, you're a good person. Searches that seemed to be more than for a life-change event search, but rather a search within an unsettled mind.

At this green place called The Creek, I was searching for my true self, a possible new true self, that I thought was already settled like a black duck in a swamp, but wasn't. He was still flying up there, waiting for the drought to break and sheets of water to appear across the flood plains, before they were leveed away by those who cared little for the natural order. I desperately wanted a true self who understood and accepted himself, a true self that others liked too. But what would a real me look like? And act like? Was there such a thing anyway? Was it stationery, static, or stable? Was it creative, crazy or cretinous? Or all three? Or all six? I searched for a way to become a better person and get love, acknowledgement, and a bit of history to let me know where I had been, so I could be here now and in the future.

I searched, not so much to be knowledgeable about a skill, like building a house, growing vegetables, or even walking in the mountains and feeling the clear green air, but for an inner stability. I had thought then that the life skills were not really a part of this search, which was singular, insular and individular. I wanted an inner peace that brought wisdom. A wisdom that would go beyond wisdom. An inner peace that would give me secrets on how to live and how to be a real man.

I levered twenty huge foundation stumps (each six-feet long) into the three-feet deep holes I had dug with a crowbar and a long-handled shovel. Two each day. The twenty stumps were then levelled. Start from the one who was the lowest, (preceded by a slow double-check that indicated that everybody else was indeed higher), saw him off, run a stringline and mark the everybody else. Sawing a stump off was done by double-nailing short boards across the stump, one on either side– if you use one nail, she swivels, resting the handsaw, previously owned by my grandpa, on these boards and away you go. Ant capping was then placed on each stump. These do not stop termites, which are not ants and are related to cockroaches, but when you later inspect under your built house, you can see if the little suckers had made an earthen tubey-trail around the capping so as to turn your house into mud and sawdust without you knowing. Until you leaned on a wall, for example. Then, after you extricated yourself from the wall, you would crawl under the house and find a tubey-termite trail and politely ask them to go someplace else.

The bearers, 5 x 3-inch hardwood, were placed on top of these ant caps, but they were not nailed because that would compromise the security of the ant capping; if termites get a sniff, they're in. Anchor bolts are the ticket. They secured the bearer to the stump without touching the capping. I anchor-bolted every stump.

* * *

I wanted a mentor, an understanding guide to help me to understand me, who would be there for me, through the good times, the bad times and the times in between. I did have one, sort of – my grandpa – but I wasn't so sure he would be my new-beaut full-time long-term sweet understanding guide, because he was a cunt. But maybe when you have no other, you love the one you're with, cunt or not.

Grandpa raised me and was my early guide when I had none, as in, no parents. I never knew my parents really well because early on they had decided, apparently, to ditch me, to ditch me to an orphanage. Being ditched is a part of life, a part of some peoples' life, I know that, and it's shit whichever way you look at it. I think that's what happened with me earlier on. Don't really know, sort-of want to know, and maybe will never know.

RB-Hang on a tick. There's something we need to talk about ... I asked grandpa who my parents were and why was I ditched but he avoided my questions. He perfected the art of avoidance and dismissive put-downs, often at the same time.

'Christ, you're fucking hopeless. Can't you do anything right? And for fuck's sake, go away and stop asking ridiculous questions that you know the answer to!'

That was on a good day. Then my guts would churn as I waited for the next confrontation. Guidance at its finest. Grandpa had a turkey's wattle under his chin, and his deep-set beady eyes let you know you'd done something wrong even if you hadn't. Even though I knew he was there for me, in his own cranky way, I thought, No, he wasn't the mentor, the guide that I was searching for.

But who did I want? And what would he look like? Where would he come from? *Hey, I've got some really good ideas …* How on earth would rational brain have ideas, apart from how to write a shopping list? I shut him down.

* * *

Some say the grey Darling River country is harsh, but this is a challengeable point of view. Like judging old men who drive open-top sports cars with young blondes next to them. Big sunnies, billowing hair, brown skin, singlet top and shapely shoulders. Her too. The Darling River country is what it is, like most things in life. People pigeonhole according to something they think is valid. Like overstocking sheep there and fucking over the saltbush, or spruiking historical facts from only one point of view that aren't facts anyway. These judgements also suit beliefs that often aren't our own. Or at least, partly not our own. We adopt because we are morons who can't think beyond the rest of the sheep's inane bleatings. Some don't need an annual shearing; some need wethering.

The Darling River country in western New South Wales is a dry place, but to say it as such without the context of its reality is unfair, and way too subjective. Bring on the blonde. It does have a low rainfall, compared to say, the Amazon, most of tropical Asia and all of England, individually or together, and floods that mostly arrive courtesy of Queensland. That's if the irrigators all the way from southern Queensland down to Bourke decide to play ball, even within their allocated rules, which a lot don't. Back in the old days it was called stealing. The Darling is an unregulated river system, meaning, that there are no major man-made storages (except for the massive turkey nest dams the irrigators have. And okay, a few dams in side streams) and therefore no releases to be had to shore up the man-induced, produced and helped-along natural-cycle droughts. Menindee Lakes are down lower and they are another story you and me may not have enough time to talk about. If this is so, which it is, then why is the Darling's water overallocated? Why do irrigators steal and not get consequences? Why are farmers allowed to take flood-plain water? Why is there such a thing as donations to political parties? Particularly from irrigators.

The Darling itself is usually grey. A grey river, cool, calm and collected, hiding fish, mussels and memories, and doing what it's supposed to do. The black soil country around the river is grey, with the occasional towering orange banks that make a stunning contrast. I spent time out there in woolsheds, doing roustabout work and enjoying the fishing. But after ten years I disowned it. Went to live with someone else of a different colour. But what if things didn't work out with my new love and I went back?

'Excuse me, could I come back into your life? Want to spend the night with me? I don't have a girlfriend. Do you?'

* * *

But while grandpa was pretty much antagonistic, dismissive, and in general intolerant, in his shed he was a mellow helpful old bloke. A complete change in personality. An escape for him, but from what? He had a great shed. Talk about orderly. My goodness. The spanners, hammers, screwdrivers, pliers and sockets were all either hung, hooked or clamped onto their shadows. Multigrips, scrapers, soldering irons, cold chisels and hot chisels were in line like marching soldiers. Shifters nowhere to be seen,

'Won't have them near the place. Burr the nut with those bastards.'

The wee drawers were full of pieces of string, ceiling wax, cabbages and kings, of washers, nails and screws, electrical tape, safety pins, hooks, clips, clamps and plugs.

Shovels were called shovels, pigeonholes cooed and the raunchy calendars displayed their smooth, flashy white-smiled sexy post-war buxom allure. The workbench was an acceptance, an adoration and an adulation of God done through the worship of a space designed to link the earthy with the spiritual. Which it did in spades. And shovels. Redemption and confession weren't only relegated to a Sunday. You stood in front of that workbench and you were pretty much straight into Heaven, forgiven, ordained, and blessed. No paints, chemicals or petroleum products were allowed near the bench and death to he that broke this rule. Straight to Hell, and no amount of pass-the-plate bribes would stop the descent. No, He has shown remorse, would save your arse. No, Forgive me Father for I have sinned bullshit, either. The wide workbench only allowed timber and leather. The glory of wood and hide. Break the rule and you were dead, gone and buried.

In his shed, grandpa was laid-back, cool, almost a mentor. Almost. But even in his shed, his orderly world of order, his safe haven of tools, lists and scraps, he avoided my questions. And it took a long while to work out why.

It's a fucking miracle I turned out so sensible and gorgeous.

Grandpa had said, when I was barely a teenager, 'Find out what you can be, and be it.' But I found this confusing, because I didn't like grandpa much, nor trust him with my uncertainties. I now wanted someone else to be my guide.

In one of his shed moods, Grandpa taught me how to saw. He then gave me the handsaw, one that could be sharpened. Not one of these new-fangled high-tensile pieces of shit. He said, 'After you vice the saw between two bits of wood, you get a flat bastard and run it along the top of the points to level them, to create a flat spot on each tooth. Then triangle-file the teeth with 8-10lb pressure, three strokes, forwards only. Do it gently, caress the file in the teeth. Then reverse the saw and do the other side.' I was never sure why he gave this saw to me. Obviously he knew I'd be building a house, but then he never gave me his hand-drills, a set of spanners or a plane. And because I had been a model student, I could now saw a 3 x 2 piece of ancient ironbark with my grandpa's (recently sharpened) handsaw and do a perfect square cut. Without a pencil mark. After I first did this and checked it with a small setsquare, I thought, What a good boy am I, I tried to do it again. But I sawed all crooked. This surprised me, because hadn't I just fuckingwell done this perfectly? Maybe skill comes when you don't focus on it, only when you keep doing it and it becomes a natural part of your life, and of the entire universe, not based on an individual skill, but based on flowing water, on a breeze, on light, which flow when and where they want.

Grandpa taught me how to use a chisel. He said, 'It must be sharp. Wasting your time otherwise.' And to assume it might slip and allow for this. I have seen people, real carpenters too, actually push a chisel one-handed at a piece of wood while holding said piece of wood, with their soft pudgy lily-white inside forearm on the other side laid bare, facing the chisel, waiting to be ripped open. No, grandpa said, Secure the wood, and use two hands.

Hardwood is called so not because it's hard. Balsa is a hardwood. It's all about cell structure and how the tree reproduces. Anyway, the second-hand ironbark hardwood I used from the old dairy house to frame up was a hard hardwood. Made from steel. I had no electricity therefore no power tools. I had to use a hand-drill with a 1/8th high-speed bit just to be able to belt in a three-inch jolt head nail.

I sawed two 3 x 2s to the required length – one being the top plate, the other the bottom plate. Which means the 3 x 2 wall studs, ten-feet long, would eventually go in between and make the frame of a wall. Lay the two plates on their sides together. Mark out both the edges where the studs would be aligned (a two-inch wide mark, every 18 inches), because this means there would therefore be no unstraight wall studs. Separate the studs, scribe across each studly place a mark, one inch in, grab the handsaw and saw, by eye, down to this scribed mark. Then stroke the chisel, kiss it, and say nice things. Secure the plate and chisel from the centre to the sawcut, bevel facing down. Do the same towards the other cut. Then grab the chisel, flat side down. and gently chisel across the remainder of the unchecked scrap off the marked-out section of the plate, taking off small shaves each time. So if the wall was to be twenty-feet long, I would end up with twelve checked out spaces on each of the plates. That's if there were to be no doors or windows.

* * *

Who was I Who am I Who will I be,
What will I be,
Ask me an easy question why don't you,
I wanted I craved and I searched inwardly
For an elusive ray of sunshine of self-understanding and self-acceptance,
Not a full summer's worth was needed, just an early touch of inside spring
Would do
Thank you very much,
And possibly some warmth from outside (I promise I'll wear a hat).
But what is the real self anyway?
Is it now, then, or soon?
Is it a constant, a definitive, a moveable?
And if either, could it get a wriggle on please because
Time's a-wasting.
Did I have any control over it, and if so, how much?
Was I looking too narrowly?
As in, like only just day-to-day?
Are there bigger things at play I was yet to discover?
And if so, did I really want to discover them?
That might come back to the control thing.
With suggested input, I like being in control, and I'm not so sure that I'm
Doing a good job, Which is why I'm here right now.
Are my choices totally invalid?
Should I just be and let the universe have its way?

Is there only one self, and if so does it remain as one?
Or is there more than one?
Will I be handsome?
And do they remain as however many there are?
This oppositeness confused me.
Does having only one self, mean you are boring, and won't change, or at
least consider changing?
Because if nothing changes, nothing changes, and all life changes,
Even if you don't like it or accept it,
Or does one self speak of solidarity, of stability, of great personal
confidence?
But if you have more than one self, does this mean you are exciting, have
Or can change and are ready to change again?
The constant thing again.
Or does it mean you are not solid, you are unstable, and have no self-
Confidence?
And anyway, what the fuck is wrong with that?
Or are these selves interchangeable, as in, you can have one today, but also
Have more tomorrow?
Or have one self for home and another for elsewhere?
Should the true self, a one-self, be a no-self?
As in, with a solid base of goodness, then for goodness sake stop fucking
Searching and just be, and enjoy yourself and your place in the world?
Would this approach lead to a greater connection to a real self, humanity
And the planet?
Is looking for this certainty, the one answer, the one true self in this
Instance, merely a means to come to terms with the fact that such an
Outcome can only be found inside a cow's arse, which is possibly removed
From the everyday?
Will I be rich?
Does proof deride trust?
Does one answer lead to more unending questions and end up bordering on
A circular insanity?
Or, within all this search stuff, what am I covering up?
What am I hiding?
It's a fucking miracle I have turned out so sane and stunning.

I read words of wisdom from the ancients – some of them were ancient, but not all of them. Some were quite young and attractive. But I stopped reading because they seemed too formulated with restrictions and too much of do this, too much of do that. Rules for little reason, except for, That's how it's always been, and, By the way (this being the Greeks), we have slaves and we hate women just because we can. Sometimes some of their advice disguised as truth is a good thing, but sometimes some of their advice that is not disguised is control and needs to be chucked out. Religions, or belief systems if you like, also turned me off. The Buddhists say, No mate, there is no self because the self is controlled by the ego and desire. And if you crave shit, well this leads to attachment and that clinging will get in the way of truth. And if you liberate yourself from worldly attachments, here be nirvana and you will avoid misery, pain and suffering. Fuck me. You detach, you isolate, you avoid, you control the senses, you are devoid. You will shrivel. Hinduism has an interesting premise; that is, you start with meditation and further explore inner strengths and weaknesses. Now that is true owning up. Hinduism seems to be a mixture, although its idol worship worries me. And for God's sake, don't start me on Christianity or Islam. Both are totally fucked with their control, fear, anger, exclusion and the open discrimination, usually of the environment and women. Yes, there were and are more religions, non-religions, beliefs and other subtle mechanisms available to control us, but really? You live you die, with nothing beyond. I wanted the live bit.

I also read contemporary Western philosophy, but stopped pretty quickly with that too, because it's shit that's why. It's full of white male supremacist rubbish. I know that was the language of the times, a, That was what society did then, but these become excuses to justify a practice of submission, control and exclusion. Then, and your choice of now. Which is barely a step above the ancients. Some of them were old, etc. They rarely gave voice to others, particularly women, (or other cultures) and they just railroaded non-Westerners from a narrow point of view that omitted, denigrated and dismissed. Power, imperialism, and colonialism ruled and just quietly, not much has fucking changed. In philosophy, or contemporary society.

Even though I ridiculed all of the above through opposition, non-understanding and ignorance, I knew deep down that there was still a greater truth in amongst all or some of them, somewhere. And I knew, not particularly deep down, that these teachings understood that beyond our daily lives, there is higher stuff way beyond the base details of gender, society and even nationality. Maybe I needed a starting point, a bottom line, that was undisputed by me and spoke of simplicity, kindness and understanding.

And yet, for all their inner searches, these individual choices and denials, a lot of these teachings were way way too forcefully put forward, I might add. I say, you railroad me and do this to make me feel inferior, inadequate or like shit, I say, fuck you. You are only out to impress me with how cool and special you think you fucking are. You may dazzle me with words, ideals, and hope, but don't insult me. Let me relate to me through you, and for Christ's sake, make it fucking relevant. Eventually what I found was a combination of most of the above (with a couple of idols), and these were shared, lived and negotiated with real people. And I did end up with some misery, pain and suffering. I suspect it's called life as it happens. Before I unleashed myself onto unsuspecting genders, societies and nationalities, I wanted to find and be my true self through solitude, a search for my true self through living alone. I had done a bit of this living alone and searching business on the Darling but only for short times in between camping, shearing sheds and towns. This time I wanted years of solitude so I could hopefully use this longer time frame, in the one spot, to sort stuff out.

Back then on the Darling, solitude had often been scary, because it took me to places in my mind I had not been to or even knew existed. And some of these now-being-known alone places had a mixture of fear, savagery, and beauty. With no escape hatch; with no secret opening bookcase and no tunnel from behind the basin in the cell. The fear caused me to question my existence, as in, Do I deserve to be here on the planet? An almost suicidal, Am I worthy? Do I belong? The answer to both was often, Nope, I am not, and Nope, I do not. But I held off because I was quick to realise that death is reasonably permanent.

Living at the head of a valley would give me all the physical isolation I wanted and needed. Stillness of the mind. This one was mine to learn about, to cultivate; to discern the difference between troubled waters and the what is hidden. Could I let those waters settle after a flood? Is this a desolate place? A place of mind quiet except for nature? A quiet that was a still, silent quiet, a quiet that gave me a chance to disengage from external industrial noise, from jabberings, from society's pressure and interruptions. This quiet became a social disengagement, except for my one eventual day a week in town.

And yet, yet, self-righteousness rarely comes with a badge of honour.

I went to The Creek to get away from a consumer society that I hated. I hated its falseness disguised as success, progress, and a comparison of I am better than you, and making me feel like shit as it did so. My choice of feeling I know, but sometimes this choice was limited through power via media, by a promotion through economic and shaming control. I did not belong nor did I want to belong. I had freedom but still the chain marks were evident. My alienation was self-imposed, but I was not a victim, and my personal inverse attempts at independence were chosen with good intentions, intentions that eventually brought me home.

Taxes, gravity and death are not the great levellers of society, solitude is. I read that somewhere. Taxes are arbitrary and can often be waylaid, relatively legally, via other countries and tricky trusts. Just ask big businesses and corporations how it's done. Cost you though. Gravity, think 1969 and we're good. They not only got to the moon, they wandered about. Mass the same, weight different. No levelling here folks. Gravity, got you covered.

Death? Apart from the one-day eventual outcome, death is the most unlevel of all. Think of the fear religions dish out disguised as control, the social avoidance of discussing dying, the individual uncertainty, the politics of euthanasia, and the ubiquitous fake old folks' homes. Death, while being inevitable, separates individuals and families, takes away their dignity and gives power to others. As in, the government, legal teams, the rich, the church, the rellies, the media, the old folks' homes and the funeral providers.

Solitude is that last great sorter-outerer, and although it may have been commonplace way back when, it is now largely a memory within a society that thrives on and needs constant company. Solitude being isolated sounds odd, yet attractive, because it comes with choice. Solitude is being alone but not lonely. Huge difference. Massive difference. Alone is just that; a physical space occupied by one. Lonely can certainly happen when being alone, but it can also happen in a crowd. And that is really sad. A non-connection in a crowded society. Apparently, in the olden days, solitude came as living a secluded, prayer-based life renouncing worldly goods and pleasures in order to be closer to God. Fuck that. The seclusion bit I was warming up to, but the prayer-based stuff was shit. Renouncing worldly goods and pleasures? You mean, like filthy thoughts, gambling, haircuts, fast food, music, judging people, and sex? Not fucking likely son. Or were these renounced items from back then more old-fashioned and subdued, such as, filthy thoughts, gambling, haircuts, fast food, music, judging people and sex? Closer to God? What the fuck for? I was already too close to the bastard. That bastard and his messengers who strived to make me feel like shit, to be unworthy. Wandering the desert alone for forty days and nights hoping for a change of heart never really grabbed me either.

Dear Dad, Ducking out on my own for a bit. Please send food and water. Regards, J.

Dear J., Your choice son. Try to drink lots of water. It's good for you. Particularly in the desert. Good luck. Dad (aka G). PS. Ask the locals for assistance. They are good people.

When you are alone, it is who you really are or will be, because you have the quiet of solitude to help you be at peace. Solitude is a deep essence, it is the now in life, not the future, not a maybe, and it is fascinating within this quiet solitude to do nothing, to be unbusy on purpose. To just sit. No jobs to do, no plans to make, no dreams, just to sit. And be silent. The world will come in because fortune favours the preparer of nothingness. That slight breeze will caress your cheek, the butterfly you perhaps didn't see before because you were too busy cluttering your mind will appear so beautiful it will astound you; clouds will become more alive and you will feel a connection so deep you will become breathless with the wonder of the universe. Solitude. I did not know how living alone for a long period of time would work out, except that it would be a starting point for an exploration of the mind, and therefore I would be free to find love from me to me. Which I could not envisage being available in our current crazy world. Aspirations, hopes and dreams may be the refuge of the insecure, but also rewards for the honest seekers and rewards will come to the seekers of solitude. Because I said so. And I know that reality can interfere with dreams, and that gratitude and resentment are closely related, but fuck it, let's give it a shot.

Solitude let me make decisions without anyone else. Sort of almost without anyone else. This solitude had the company of my two brains, usually a quietish twosome, a beautiful blending of minds, but more often a quite rowdy pair, an oppositional bunfight, a no-holds-barred kill at all costs competitional bunfight.

My rational brain, the one who had tried to talk me out of coming here to The Creek, analysed things, and at times could be fairly realistic in his advice. He was legal, straight, and to the point. However, he was generally a pain in the arse. I hated him to bits. What fucking use was he? His revelations were not related on day-to-day reality, but on some frigging pre-determined responses that were usually based on a logic of, Let's use these assertions to gauge what might be the result, of, Let's reason through our options, of, Let's use data, of, Let's use outcomes. Fuck me. I did my best to ignore or openly reject his assertions, and his total lack of empathy.

And I had my emotional brain. How I adored her! She was reflective, sensitive, could read mine and other peoples' thoughts and feelings, and was so passionate and loving, she made me swoon. She talked way too much for sure, especially about injustices, but she was my go-to, my support, my love. She was a little crazy and she liked to be stroked. The sight of her was worth the price of admission, the rest a bonus. She was my imaginary friend who could bounce, who could agree, yet she could also challenge me to reconsider, but in a nice supportive way. I loved her regardless.

They were not nice to each other. One day, emotional brain said to me, Watch me. Watch me bait him.

EB-Hey RB, the moon is my heart.
 RB-Wait, no it's not. The moon is that big white thing up there.
 EB-The Earth is my heart.
 RB-Bit closer to home, but still bullshit. Your heart is that red squelchy thing ...
 EB-My heart is all of me.
 RB-What are you on about? Your heart pumps blood so shuttup! You are unhinged. Which I could fix with a drill and a few screws ...
 EB-Gotcha! You moron!
 RB-You are an imbecile, a maniac who has no idea about life.
 EB-Me? No idea about life? Fuck me!
 RB-Never! I'd rather ...

There was another who had input that was totally out of my control; my dream brain (DB). Didn't mind this fellow. He would draw events, aspirations and worries together in a kaleidoscope of fun each night. As well as the occasional horny night. I liked him, not only because of what he did, but because I had no say in when and what he did. His advice was loaded with abstract metaphors which I often did not understand. Therefore, I was innocent, absolved, and accepting of whatever he did, yet not accepting because he mixed things up. One minute I was with a gorgeous blonde, the next I was being stroked by a hairy bloke. What a weirdarse he was. The dream brain, not the hirsute one. When my time comes for the big deep sleep, I'll bet my dream brain never dies. There I'll be, laying on the forest floor because some fucking reptile has done me in, and I'll have a grin. 'You see that? He must have died so peacefully.'

But I knew, even with my limited understanding of my confused brains, that it was up to me, the real me (the one at this point in time anyway), to make decisions, every decision, no matter if great or dodgy.

Solitude and I have been friends since childhood. Then, I didn't search, I only survived. A solitude from necessity, but now by choice. And then as now, we still can't work out how long we can spend together, without the fucking eternal internal conflictual rubbish that forces oppositional individuality together in a crushed confusion. Yet when we were settled, as in, being so relaxed with each other to be able to scratch where it really did itch, it was bliss. And that was what I wanted now so I could sort me out, with the help from a relative peaceful existence between my minds. I was hoping solitude would steer me to deeper stuff, to show me how to be there for me. But I suspect I was holding onto the wind, to the light and the sounds that made up life.

And I'm not sure I always had a good grip.

I wasn't sure of what I knew about the self and solitude, but I did want to know what I didn't know. Then I'd know what I didn't know. Then I'd be knowledgeable. I wanted my own story, my own commonness that would become my ideal, and hopefully an unsureness that didn't always equal fraud, and I know I am not an imposter, a fraud, a charlatan. I know I am important to me, and maybe to someone else.

Living alone let me have time to recall, reinforce and reiterate what I did and didn't like.

Birds.

I like birds. Birds remind me of good people – colourful, crazy and emotional. Mirrors are what they are, characters doing day to day stuff. Trees are stationary versions of the same. All different, even within species. They will both die without food, water and love. Like us.

Soil, I like soil. Hands in the soil, deep, rich, crumbly, digging in the soil, sorry little guys if I just ruined your home. Soil can and does give new life, or be there to take it away. As it should be.

Intimacy. Basically, I like sweet talk, touching, stroking, hot sex, cool sex, it's always different, all of them.

I like to fix things, even if they don't need fixing. To build stuff, to create, is to feel an immense inside pride, an, I did that, which gives confidence to do or at least try the next task.

The only light I really like is the stuff that comes from the sun, its mirror and those other twinkling things. Natural external light has rhythms that once embedded, give off an internal light that delivers deep sleep. The other stuff has uses, but too much ruins the psyche.

I like rivers, do I what. And creeks. Apart from the maintaining of life through drinking, there's so much beauty, love, and peaceful music through waves, ripples and stillness.

I like chooks. They are characters, individual idiosyncrasies galore. I love chooks. Their eggs, their meat, their basic scratching. They are worth watching for their squabbles, their soon forgotten routines, their seriousness.

I'm a simple fellow really. Alone is good, lonely is not. I like nice people, kind people, raunchy people.

I don't like some things.

Consumerism. I did not like the political, economic and social ideals of con-sumerism, and that's what they are promoted as, in the West at least, though other compass points of culture are joining the race to the bottom of capitalist consumerism and its eviller twin, advertising. Trickery, tactics and deceit all. They promote and produce excess, debt and hollow people. They are false premises based on a disrespect of the self, women, and them pesky coloured people – whose land has usually been nicked, or misappropriated somehow. Chasing materialistic goods for their own sake rather than for functionality and care for the planet exudes greed, a poisoned greed, an inner crisis, an unsuredness of who you are, a predilection to answer to others' demands for success, beauty and social appeal. Advertisers support this by extending a vote of no confidence in consumers' ability to think as an individual. I suspect the advertiser's dislike of you is based on a self-righteous power-trip, greed of upcoming riches, and a false sense of entitlement.

I don't like religions, governments, most political parties and anyone with a dick, usually all the same gender – though I do know of some people who don't have a dick who are mean bitches (just passing this little gem on to let the outraged aggressive controlling misogynist pigs, aka, most males, breathe a bit easier), put women down in one form or another. They do this either through discrimination in the workforce, in bullying coercive relationships, the justice system, or within society in general. Compliance through fear is not living, nor is fulfilling someone else's wishes based on empty greed and false hopes. A time may come, maybe many times, when conformity, while possibly bringing security, will induce a questioning of the self. A wonderment of, Why do I conform, of, Can I maybe conform just a little bit, but still be me inside and outside of this particular social time? Hopefully.

I was well balanced – I had a chip on both shoulders.

* * *

Grandpa had a wide selection of knives, some of which he made himself. Each of these knives had a specific job. They were so sharp, so razor-blade sharp, so independent and strong-willed, just like the old boy, that if you attempted to use one for something other than its intended purpose, it would twist and slice your arm, and say something like, 'Now put me back and choose the correct knife or I'll really hurt you next time.'

Grandpa could mend anything that was broken and not a few things that weren't. He could untangle fishing lines, he could solder, weld and drill, he could run his thumb along a piece of timber and smile, but when I asked him about why it was he who raised me, he would get evasive and do a put-down.

'So, I hear you made the cricket team. What, were they short of players? Why don't you get out of the house. Go learn French, or build something.'

* * *

I lived in a pigsty for two years while I built the house, an abandoned pigsty. And the pigs' memories, warmth and smells kept me company. A healthy earthy grunty beautiful scent that brought me into the silver shadows of birth, life, death, and beyond. Pigs do that. I slept on the concrete floor in the corrugated-iron lean-to that used to shelter the pigs. One late afternoon I found a snake curled in a circle under my pillow. That's what snakes do when they sleep, they circle. I belted him then ate him. I had deep sleeps, occasionally disturbed by owls and dingoes. I drifted with the owls, but hid from the howling dingoes. Owls hoot and it's mostly a soft hoot, a lullaby soft to float softly with, but some owls screech so terrifyingly that dead people have been known to get up and leave their coffin-home.

'Hey, why has Uncle Fred's grave been opened?'

'Heard a screechy owl I suppose.'

Dingoes scare me. They stalk and hunt in packs and will bite the back of your thighs to bring you down. And dingoes like to howl during rain. The remaining dead people pull their lids tighter. I cooked over an open fire in a sawed-off 44-gallon drum. No refrigeration, no electricity, no running water. And I felt grubby, of the Earth, and slightly at peace.

I liked the being at peace feeling because it was a deepness, a state of now within the mind's glory and in a place that let it be at one. Does the self belong in only one place? Or maybe it doesn't matter because the true self can be itself in many places? Two selfs? In two or more places? The Darling River brought out my best because it was my soul home. A home where my soul lived, not in me, but there, and I could go back and my soul would be there, waiting to greet me. I thought that then and I still do. I think. Maybe one day I'll go back to double-check if it's still there, under the river red gum tree where I left it. My commute from the pigsty to the building site was half a mile. I watched as I walked. A fascinating commute. A choice of, Which way will I go today?

What about along the worn track? Saw a four-metre carpet snake crossing the track. I waited. Because I'm polite. Saw my first brown pigeons feeding on the ground. Tell that to the grandkids. They usually feed in trees. The pigeons too. They, the brown pigeons, are now called brown cuckoo-doves. The grandkids may still have the same name.

What about along the ridge? Hot, exposed, and dry. Me and the ridge. Saw a koala clinging onto a tree trunk. Looked down at me in disdain. 'Why did you wake me?'

What about along The Creek? Saw a tiger snake. Swimming underwater. Already had the bends.

What about through the flooded gum forest? Saw yellow-tailed black cockatoos. So majestic, so gracious, so heavenly.

What about through the blady grass? The roots are edible, the blades can be thatched, and the flower-tops are really good as fire starters. One spark and you're away. Fire also rips through a paddock of blady grass quite rapidly. Blady grass has rhizomes. Cowboys love them.

When I linger on a walking commute, not much building gets done.

But that's okay. There's always tomorrow.

* * *

The mountains here have two sets of clothes, green and blue. It seemed that most things were green. The air smelled like crushed spinach, mint and freshly peeled cucumbers; all resting in a bowl of fresh creek water. Green sounds dripped off the cliffs then rose out of the wet gullies. Catbirds are green, pigeons are green, and the rocks are covered in green velvet. And when the sun was at the right angle, the mountains were a deep hazy blue. Cold, blue naked mountains, waiting for the Earth to get a wriggle on, so they could turn green.

* * *

Building had different days. The days of getting nothing done usually had previous frustrations of rushing to get it done, and these never work. You get nowhere doing that. The days of slow quiet methodical completion, a stop and do one thing, and do it well, were the best days. Fulfilling and deeply satisfying and after I had done a job, a repair or anything not necessarily using a new skill, but just a finished thing, I felt good. Immensely so. I would praise myself and say, I have done that thing, I actually fixed it or built it and I would poke it and touch it, and say, Wow, I took no shortcuts, I worked hard and honest and I did that thing. Now, my ability to cope in the bush is nowhere near what the original people did, it is nowhere near the colonialists, the bushmen and women, I know that. But in some ways, I don't care. Because I will never be that good, not a hope in hell, and nor do I aspire to be that good. I am what I am. I can do what I can do, and I am proud of it. This view has taken me a while; but it is a valid one, and it pleases only me. Others may think I'm rubbish at doing things. I do my best for me according to me. I am my judge.

And there were the building days of singing, singing for the pleasure of being alive, of believing that nothing bad would ever happen, that the day, and the world, would always be a wonderful place. Doing and hope breeding joy. My emotional brain asked, rather quietly I thought, *Is this a part of your true self?* There is a rule of Doing Things and it states that the first time you do that thing (e.g., putting a floor joist, framing a wall), it will take x amount of time. This first x amount of time is made up of deciding when, where, what and how, hardware, hesitancy, tools, timber, a few fumbles and then getting the job done, and can be represented as

x = 3w x 3 h x 2t x f x jd

The second time is x amount of time minus three-quarters of the time you spent doing it the first time and minus all the other shit.

Therefore, (2)x = -0.75t x ft – os x jd

I may need to go to town.

* * *

The town I went to for supplies and some company was around thirty miles away and had been created by bush people (with no reference or acknowledgement whatsoever to Australia's original inhabitants), but had now been taken from them by people who hate themselves first and everyone else second. These takers were businesspeople and councillors who rejected the earlier values, deeds and history. The weatherboard hotels were bricked over, the solid wooden bridges were transformed into hideous overpasses, and the muddy creek beds, full of reeds, grasses, and life, became concreted gutters. The council park was shaved and trimmed, like a horse's mane before showtime. A sterile desert, once beautiful.

I caught the school bus into town, then graduated to a motor bike, a 250cc trail-bike, which was more of a Tony may have to repeat a grade than a Tony will go on to high school comment. The rack on the back held the essentials – chocolates, lamb shanks and wheat. After three accidents, I decided to drop a grade. Fifty stitches up my left shin, a broken ankle, and severe concussion, in that order but at different times, were indicators that I was perhaps not very good at riding a motor bike.

I swapped the motorbike for a 1954 Dodge truck.

The Dodge truck was meant for solid work and comfort, not speed. This was a heavy truck made from steel that would be happy being the outer layer of a submarine, destroyer or a tank. At the same time. I once dropped a ten-foot, 4 x 4, onto the bonnet and it bounced off and didn't leave a mark. If you haven't done that, you have an exciting time ahead. The deep-sided open ute section held a ton. I had some racks built so I could carry long pieces of sawn timber. That I usually didn't drop. Or weigh more than a ton. The faded grey duco told me stories each night to put me to sleep, the silver bumper bar was built to push hippopotamuses off roads and sink aircraft carriers that had chosen not to use its steel. At the same time. The interior, worn tatty and rustic, had one deep red leather bench seat, torn but still alive, pedals that pushed into the floor and disappeared in a vortex of grinding meshes, and a stunning dashboard that clearly showed the speedometer, fuel gauge, temperature gauge and oil pressure gauge. I like gauges. Gauges are your new best friends when you own one of these old babies. It had a column gear stick and three forward gears with low ratios. To get first, start in neutral, come to me and down one. It was almost a low-range four-wheel-drive. However, if you attempted to slip into first when the truck was mobile, the grinding grating of gear teeth would be a gentle reminder that synchromesh was not present.

* * *

Use skew nails, they said, to fasten the four by two ceiling joists to the three by two top plates. But I didn't like skew nails because if you didn't get it exactly right, which I did often, the nail either lifted the timber, or split it. But I discovered triple grips didn't I. A three-sided galvanised bracket with a long rhetorical leg. They come in left hand or right hand, not for the builder's preferences, but for which face of the timber. And when you drive the flat-headed one and a quarter inch gal nails home on all three sides, ten nails all up, the joists, or whatever, are going nowhere.
Ever.

* * *

I did not have an owner-manual for the Dodge, and the brakes needed new pads. A dilemma that could be solved by a show not tell of the six or more senses, and an understanding of uncontrollable and varied emotions, because wheel nuts have feelings. To use a hydraulic nut-turner is evil and needs to be stamped out. Even to shove on a silver plus-sign wheel-brace without a please is not far short of assault. As I gently removed the tyre, the wheel hub and brake pieces, with permission, I sketched as I went (some pretty sexy drawings I might add) and placed the parts in order on a wheat bag. You could have played with my head by swapping a couple. I also removed the carburettor and replaced the needle and seat. Okay, they were a bit higher. Each girl must have her own choices. And adjusted the fuel mix with a thin long-shanked screwdriver. A real screwdriver too, not a Phillips or an Allen Key. Might as well remove my balls as use either of those. What pansy invented them anyway? Phillips Head screws are too soft or not deep enough thereby eventually render their screwdriver useless. Allen Keys change in increments of 0.0005 mm, and this makes it jolly difficult to choose which one. Occasionally on cold mornings, just to spice things up a bit and to make her kick over, I poured a bit of petrol directly down the carby's throat. Try that in your spare time, and if you blow your head off don't blame me. It's fucking stupid and dangerous.

Just how life should be.

When raised, the bonnet of the Dodge was dual-winged, and opened up and inward like a Christmas beetle's wings on a sultry December night. There were days when I was whistling away, leaning down pretending I was a mechanic, and the beetle's wings would move slightly; but there was no breeze. 'Hey,' they would say, 'We need to go for a drive.'

One morning I decided to open her out. See what she could do. I didn't pre-set the throttle because, unlike modern cars, my throttle knob let the truck stay at its predetermined speed until you pushed it back in. So, if I set the throttle at 50 mph, and then braked, I'd be braking at a constant 50 mph. Possible, yet another version of stupid and dangerous.

At 60 mph, she talked to me.

'Oh, thank you for letting me sway to the music, letting me be a dancing queen. Out of time yet never out of time. I love you. And a love like ours is hard to find, let alone keep. I am out of control with you. Please tickle my carby, touch my starter button and spurt me with your penetrating oil. You are wicked for making me dream of you.'
It's hard.

In my recently renovated, refurbished and reconditioned Dodge truck, I went to town. There was a girl who owned a coffee shop. She was tall, willowy lanky tall, and had dark-brown raggedy hair. A, should there be some things in life that shape us that we should always revisit, type of girl. A, sensuous confident quiet deep dark beautiful type of girl. You either love your barista, for herself more than for the coffee though that does help, or you will never return. Coffee shops are like that. I watched her serve, the coffee shop girl. She was happy and content. Each customer was spoken to in either an alto of understanding, a bass of joy and understood pain, or a silent soprano of given genuine love. But even with this extraordinary outpouring and insightful understanding of others' emotions, not to mention singing prowess, she took peacefulness in and was herself peacefulness, too. She whispered her lanky love of not just the Earth, not just the Universe, but beyond them both. She was that good. This tall willow tree of love who made great coffee. She also made leather things, beautiful leather of the Earth things, like her, beautiful, not leather. I bought a dust jacket thing. It was just over A4 size, and at least three millimetres thick. It smelt glorious, felt sensational and I didn't want it to ever end. In town, I bought bags of wheat, beautiful huge rough brown civilisations of grain, and I milled my own flour. I was in Samaria, beside the Euphrates and the Tigris. I wore wheat bags;

leather sandals and I had goats. I turned the handle slowly to grind the wheat coarsely. Mixed it with cold water, olive oil and sultanas and cooked it in a large cast-iron frying pan. The stiff mix was then patted onto not-too-hot olive oil. I adjusted the temperature with small sticks. Flipped the damper carefully. A crusty brown fried damper ready for jam, which had been made by the coffee shop girl. Who came from Phoenicia.

* * *

What is happiness? An end achieved after some length of time involving hard work? Is happiness not a right now and not a maybe when? Is not happiness individual if it's chosen to be so and allowed to be so? Is happiness made up of everything? As in, joy, pain, grief? Does happiness come from the outside? A happiness dependent on the validation of others, of family, of strangers? I think I was having a happiness now but wasn't sure of its inner ratios. Would solitude fix this? Give me guarantees? Is integrity a relation to honesty? Can the self be pure honesty and therefore have integrity? So therefore, you don't steal? What if no-one was watching? Gung-ho lads, let's go. Grandpa had said, Always be honest to yourself and you will be honest with others. Really? That easy? What about telling lies? Can you justify them because others do? If so, where does *that* end?

He also said, Giving is good. But giving what? Money, help, kindness, smiles? Speaking out? About what, why, and to whom? What about pleasing others? Where does that baby end? This huge baby who needs to get off the tit, the formula and its self-importance. Is the true self based on a perceived view of happiness? Of an understanding of the unliked and liked parts that make up one's self? Can any of them be changed, or do they change anyway?

* * *

Sometimes when I had a stockpile of heavy stuff, I commuted in the Dodge. A new way of transporting me, my dreams and some small birds to the building of the house site. A welcome swallow had built a mud-cup nest inside the passenger door, just up on the top of the window ledge. When I would hop in and kick her over, a glorious push-button start, the swallow would fly off, circle round and swear at me. As I drove up to the house, via a steep hill, and a rocky creek crossing, she flew around the truck, swearing and squeaking. After I had parked she flew back onto her eggs.

'Just as well they're still there, you bastard.'

It's pretty intimidating, being sworn at by a swallow. Funny thing was, when I would drive back to the pigsty, she would stay on the nest wearing sunglasses and reading a newspaper, watching me like a Cold War operative sitting in a hotel foyer. When the eggs hatched, her babies sat next to me, all in a row, singing beautiful melodies. From the old dairy house, I transported timber, concrete washtubs and a box of three-inch jolt head nails. I transported corrugated iron, doors and windows. I transported new life, love and hope of nice things for everyone, including those who were welcome.

* * *

I needed some money, so I worked.
I helped dip cattle.
I helped build stables.
I drove the school bus.
I helped out at the local school.
And I worked at a sawmill with a man called Joe.

Cattle. An old bush tale was this; when you mix the cattle dip, you toss a frog in. If he doesn't make to the other side, the dip's too strong. The cattle know what's going on.

'I'm not jumping in that shit. That pile of dead frogs is not giving me a great deal of confidence.'

There's another old bush tale; if you've seen the frog, you're fucked.

I collected oysters to eat. You squeezed a calf's scrotum at the base until it was tight then cut across and squeezed a bit more until the balls popped out. You then either chewed them out or cut the strings that held them in. Dabbed a bit of antiseptic on and released the animal, who at that point didn't want to kill you because the poor fucking thing was in so much pain it was bewildered and could be pushed out through the gate.

Stables. I liked building stables. Horse-people builders are slow workers, and the job gets done quietly and properly.

'Hmmm Pritch, we'd better have a pot of tea.'

Fifteen minutes since we had the last one. Nice slabs of timber, planed, so the rich kid's ponies wouldn't get splinters. Or the rich kids. Nothing sharp must protrude. Queensland hitch the wire to hold boards in place with the twitch hidden on the outside.

Toughen up, get a life, cut the apron strings. Kids too. Working quietly and properly has sounds of beauty and longevity, perhaps even a forever longevity, because working surely and focusly has eternity stamped all over it. The timber never rots, the wire never rusts, and the skill and love are passed on to whoever touches the stable.

School bus. Angus the regular bus driver had broken his leg.

I had a bus licence, so I did the school run. I copied some lyrics. I said, 'Kids, take one pass them on. We're gonna sing.'

'Geez mister, Angus never lets us make a noise. Anyway, how can we sing songs that voices never heard?'

School. I knew one of the teachers at the little school nearby, and she asked if I could come in every fortnight to help. Stuff like spelling, reading groups, mathematics or maybe a bit later, outdoor trips. I liked it with the little kids, and the pay was fair.
Spelling.

'Vase. The man put flowers into the vase. Write vase.'

Say the word, put it into a reasonable sentence, repeat the word. I drilled the kids. I said, 'You must know how to spell. Some words don't have much of a pattern and you just have to learn them by rote. Because, Although, Again, Great, Also, Come. Just friggin do it. I saw Varse, Varz, Vays, Vass, Vasse, as well as Vase. I gave them a sticker for every correct letter. The correct spelling people got a book of stickers. Each.
Reading.

I didn't like round-robin reading because the kids who weren't good readers got embarrassed. So, I would read and ask for volunteers to continue. And I'd stop frequently. 'Look at that! Did you see what the author just did? Who can tell me? Yes Billy?'

'Well, sir. The author has used repetition to create an effect of continuity and emphasis, and to enhance reading pleasure.'

'Billy?'

'Yes sir.'

'What are you doing in year three in primary school?'
Mathematics.

Was everywhere in nature. Or was it that nature was in mathematics? Spirals, rules, no rules, numbers, straight lines, 2D shapes, 3D shapes and patterns. We brought in stuff from the playground and from anywhere. We drew, compared and measured. We made graphs and asked why. We pasted artefacts on butcher's paper and made displays for the parent evening. And I let the kids do it.

'Sir?'

'Yes Billy.' Einstein is on the move again.

'You know the blue triangle butterfly …

'Yes, of course.'

'… Well, the blue pattern isn't a triangle.'

'You sure?' Why do I question this kid.

He brought out a butterfly pinned onto a bit of ply, and sure enough, the turquoise blue was an overlapping stack of sort of quadrilaterals, becoming smaller from the centre to the wing tip.

Maths was also in the kids' daily lives and one morning we went on an excursion to investigate how. There was a cultivation down not far from the school. The farmer grew lucerne hay.

'See those hay bales? They are rectangular prisms. Real ones kiddies. This is maths interacting with real life. God, I'm good. Now, kids, I know stuff, so listen up. Here is your question of the day. Get it right and you're on free time when we get back to school. Each bale has two strands of baling twine around its long side, and I know for a fact that each bale has approximately 480 cms of baling twine. Your job, should you choose to accept it, is to work out how much baling twine would be needed for the whole cultivation? Away you go.' I had them. There is no way they could work that one out. Not even our resident smartarse.

'Sir, sir, I know!'

This could go two ways; either Billy totally stuffs up and I win, or he works this out and I'm shredded. I wasn't feeling real good.

'Well sir, this paddock is 50 acres, and because of this particular good season, it has given 100 bales per acre. So that's 5,000 bales.'

Sacked.

'Now, as you rightly say, each bale needs about 480 cms of twine, so you would need around 2,400,000 cms of twine.'

Unemployment benefits.

'Which would be 24,000 metres, or 24 kms of twine. Or, as some old folk around here like to express themselves, 15 miles of baling twine.'

'Billy, how the hell would you know that?'

'Well, sir, me dad owns this paddock.'

Buried.

'Says he's lookin' for workers too.'

Billy's dad drove the truck, an old Bedford, which looked longingly at my

Dodge when I pulled up. Disgusting. Imagine their children? Be called Bodgies. Two of us were on the tray waiting for the mobile bale scooper-upperer to birth a large Weet-Bix of deep green lucerne. Our hand-hooks for both hands were from the same factory as those made for Captain Hook's left hand. He must have been handy. Watch out for tik-tok. You whacked one into each end and you walked it to its place often using your knee. Neatly. The stack, not me. If the stack wasn't done neatly in correct sequence and solidly, you would have bales tumbling at you. Not me.

I met Joe from a sawmill a few valleys over. He said, 'Want a job?'
  'No thanks. I want to keep all my arms and legs for a bit.'
  'Pay is okay.'
  'Nope.'
  'You'll get a hot lunch.'
  'Not a chance.'
  'Cost price on all timber?'
  I wavered; and he knew it.
  'But won't those saws get me? They're really sharp.'
  'They are fast. That inside saw runs at 90 miles per hour. Sharp you say? When you see what it can do to a hardwood log, your puny arms …'
  'Hey, watch it!'
  '… would be blood and bone compost pretty smartly. But no, those saws won't get you because they are fixed.
  'That's a relief then. I had visions of them running around like hoops, chasing me.'
  'The saws won't get you, but the logs might. And, along with the cost price thing, you can have free firewood.'

At the sawmill I discovered beauty, hard work and a feeling of contribution. Joe was eighty something. He had never finished primary school, had a bullock team at age twelve, and had fought in New Guinea against the Japanese. He was philosophical and devoid of revenge. He was a bushie who was strong and deeply spiritual in a non-religious way. He found his inner peace via a sawlog. He never justified, never defended, he just let the world do what it wanted to do and say. He was total beauty. A true self man who never feared death, logs, or long hours. And he ate eels for breakfast.
  I worked with Joe at the sawmill and I learned how you get a 4 x 2 from a log.

Logs would be delivered to the mill, hopefully butt first towards the saw, in front of the bench that fed the breaking down saw. My initial job, apart from cleaning sawdust from under every hidden place on the planet, and pouring sump oil onto the sloping beams, leading up to this breaking down bench (then down to the number 2 saw) that would eventually move the flitches, was to de-bark these logs. This is way easier if the logs are green.

There were logs, and then there were logs.

Spotted gum had a thick dress which prised off readily with a pinch bar. Alright, if you fucking well ask first, and I say Yes, then you may remove my clothes and have your way. And if I do say Yes, then I too, will enjoy your pleasure. A spunky female, willing to be a part of a mutual pleasure. Is there something in life I've missed?

Forest red gum was a typical example of a man who thinks he's in control. But we all know better, because a male arrogance borne of a tall teetering ego, is not merely a strong attractive arrogance, but a liability to himself and all of his kind.

Ironbarks, gender non-specific, had huge swathes of clothes, rough, tough and raggy. Tight, firm and stubborn, that only came off in torn shreds.

Hoop pines, possibly too young to be undressed, but what the hell, their bark came off in sheaths of creamy-white and streaky yellow, and left exposed, pink-stained teenage flecks of sweet, blood, and cycles of smooth-ness, innocence and purity. Going to hell anyway.

There was a winch. I wonder are these winches totally happy to be there, or are they yet another male fantasy? A wire rope with a massive steel hook on my end winch. I would run this hook out from its surf lifesaving reel, go under the log, then hook the hook back on itself, so any pull would lock it in. As I automated the wire rope in, I chocked the log as it crawled up the ramp, left, right, and occasionally straight, until its frilly low-cut blouse, short skirt and tray of beverages were in place on the steel benches. Were they just a willingness to be a fantasy, or a raunchy decision to be a true-self erotic woman?

Joe. There he'd be, that massive pinch bar in his huge mitt, as he and the wedged-sawlog headed for a couplet-death in a massive two-metre sawblade spinning and screaming. An eve of destruction. He'd be kneeling there beside the log, adjusting and tweaking the wedges and wee chips of wood. And there I was, a beginner, green as a navel orange in February, hanging onto the wooden lever with two hands that either stopped the bench or let him become sliced meat. And did he yell out, Stop! at the last minute before he would become a sliver of corned silverside? No, he just raised an eyebrow. I'm fine Joe. Thanks for fucking asking. This was merely the breaking down of a log and while being risky for Joe, and somewhat scary for me, was the first step at the mill in the creating of a piece of sawn timber. The huge flitches, those semi-circles of death (the trees, not us) were slid down oiled 12 x 3 joists and chocked ready for the inside saw.

The inside saw, the one that spun at 90 miles per hour went to another level of noise and danger. Joe would slide a flitch onto a trolley and rest on the bench, just before the screaming saw. He would sight along this 30-foot hunk of timber and say something like, 'Hmm, this one has a woofle. He will spring to the left because it was from the western side of the mountain in some rocky country.' The first cut was usually just to make a straight edge, then the gauge could be set to say, 4 inches. I too had a trolley, the same as Joe's – a weirdarse old-fashioned Western movie type of trolley on railway lines. This trolley was pushed up next to the bench and as the two-pieced newly-sawn flitches came at me, at first one thin one thick, I had to gauge the point of balance of these fuckers and move the trolley back toward me at this balance point as I hung onto the end of the two flitches. If I didn't judge it correctly, the flitches would fall either toward the saw or on top of me. When a flitch hit the saw, the high-pitched scream was deafening, almost literally. Not as high as some cicadas scream though. 'Hey Joe! I need earmuffs!'

'WHAT? Speak louder, will you?'

The arrivals that were supposed to spring left did so. 'This bastard is tight, and he will pinch so watch him.' Which would be more Joe's problem, because a pinch against the saw often meant the flitch would grip the saw and come back at him at high speed. Although if I were quick enough, I could belt a wooden wedge in to open the cut. Joe's instruction if this were needed was, 'Quick, hit him with an oomphreguy!'

One morning we stacked some sawn timber on a trolley, 6 x 2s off an ironbark. I walked to the side of the trolley. Joe was instant. 'Quick! Get behind the trolley. Never walk alongside, the timber might fall.'

And he said to always assume that a log aint going to do what you expect it to do. He said, 'They have a mind of their own. Assume one will roll on you and get ready to jump. The saws won't get you, but the logs might.'

* * *

There were venomous snakes at The Creek. Plenty of them. The browns and tigers I could handle. I understood them, where they lived, and while being wary, I felt okay. They usually knew you were coming and would slip slide away. The odd one would get aggressive but still, avoidance was fairly easy. However, the death adders were another story. They were not aggressive, because they didn't need to be. They do not, will not, or even fucking attempt to, move out of your way, especially when they sense you or feel a good vibration. Death adders lay there, all curled half-hidden under leaves, wriggling their skinny rattlesnaked arse-end bit to lure prey. And not move while they wait. Quiet chaps really. Probably be nice pets. I nearly trod on three in the first year. A fat green-patterned one, curled on a wallaby pad. As I was about to step on it, I did a step in the air like a coyote in a cartoon. Second was next to the rabbit-proof fence which at that point of its life was the New South Wales-Queensland border. The last one, a grey version, was threaded in amongst pasture. No, it's all right, you stay there, I'll go around.

* * *

Does a real self need approval from the outside? From family, friends, work team, your current gender preference, or from society's expectations, goaded by the media? I say yes. To a point. And only to a point. The energy from Others, their acknowledgement, their validation, their praise, call it what you like, only a percentage is needed, and I can allow or deny how high or low this might be, but I was unsure how much of my self I needed from these Others. Or does all oneness come from within? The self as an independent, with no donations, party rules, just the self as pure because stuff from within radiates warmly like the orange rays in the cut trunk of a forest oak, because when the sense of self-worth emanates from within, life unfolds in a powerful way, especially when you live in solitude. Like Old Harry the hermit had done.

Old Harry had lived in a cave. This cave was in the corner of my block and occasionally I would go and sit in there, just to pretend. Harry was a vegan and story has it that after World War 1, in which he got injured badly in the trenches, he took an objection to all killing. He would not even wear leather boots or belts. He grew corn and ground it to make meal which he cooked in the coals. He drank grog though. Did he what. If I cashed in the amount of sherry bottles I found near his cave I would be able to buy a new ute, a block of units and have enough change to never need the old age pension. Mind you, if I went through a war, not even one that was supposed to end all wars, just a normal garden variety war, and ended up with a steel plate in my scone, I suggest I would need some form of mind-altering in order to cope. I have seen photos of him. Long-sleeved white loose-fitting shirt with the sleeves rolled up above his elbows, long twill trousers, bush hat and a beautiful face framed by a full white beard. But it's his eyes, the eyes of beauty, that make him. The eyes of peace. The eyes of a real self.

He had helped find lost people in the rainforest on many occasions, and had been a guide in the rescue of survivors from a plane crash. And apparently, he had pet snakes. Death adders.
Why would you do that?

* * *

Rain.
The Darling River country has an annual rainfall of around 6-8 inches. And that's being generous. One year at The Creek I recorded 100 inches of rain. That means everything was growing, even a few things that should not have been growing, including sawn timber, rope and canvas. If only mildew was edible. The ground oozed water, mud and blood, if you stood still for more than say ten seconds, a vine would entwine itself around you rather quickly, growing left to right, that's if you were looking in at the person being entwined. That year, when The Creek flooded, several times, it didn't roar, it screamed get out of my way without asking. It removed huge portions of its banks and rocks were tumbled down like monstrous grey ice cubes along the brown swirl.

I kept daily weather records. Rain, wind, clouds, air stillness, birds, insects, and when and where the wind came from. The wind was pretty much unpredictable and often gave no signs it was coming. It just did. A still night could roar, an October day could bring hot blustery flying bark days and a powerful wind could blow into a storm, not from behind it. The wind brings personification at its worst. An angry wind, an unsettled wind, a restless wind, a violent wind, a hot bastard of a wind, a penetrating wind. Typical male-characteristics. A gentle wind, a biting wind, a harsh wind, a feeble wind, a merciless wind, a wet weeping wind, a frigid wind. More male characteristics. Bastards need to reconsider a few responses and choices I'd say. Me too. Is not wind just wind? And doing a fantastic job of removing loose bark, dead leaves, dispersing seeds and perhaps annoying people? Maybe winds share secrets, and can be soft, even lonely? Personification at its best. Clouds are puffy white balls, cosy enough to sleep on. Yet can be rebellious black thunderheads, lines of green death or streaky hopeful lines. Or just water vapour doing what it's supposed to do. Air stillness is an opposite to wind without the gender-based descriptor. A black to white, a Ying to Yang, a sibling to sibling. Stillness talks. It says, You may die as you try to breathe my air-water. It says, My stillness may give crispness to your life. It may say, Hmm, if I were you, I'd be watching those green clouds out there.

Birds.

I had no radio for a weather forecast and newspapers were pretty much out of date by the time I read their predictions anyway. But my goodness, the birds knew some stuff. If the plovers called out at night, it would rain within two days, regardless of the time of year. If the yellow-tailed black cockatoos wailed and cried as they flew above the ridges, even on a crystal-clear June morning, I would bring the washing in. The koel, a cuckoo, is known as the storm bird, but I'm not so sure. They are migrants from Indonesia. From the Australian point-of-view, there's a lengthy stay in a prison right there. The male is black (add to previous comment) with a red eye. He pisses off currawongs and crows while she ducks in and lays an egg. She is a sort of blotchy-brown with white spots patterned sort of girl who does the heavy lifting, in her spotted Doris Day dress. And sings about whatever will be and stuff. They do this during, not creating, the storm season in late spring. Let's not lock them up. Please let them eat the daisies.

Insects.

Before rain, crickets squeal and ants build mounds. Frogs croak loudly and often. They're not really insects but never mind.

Rain.

The set-in rain came from the South-east. There is a huge factory back there, that produces low depressions of sweepy scuds, black fast clouds, and rain on top of the rain. When the rain came from the South-east, you knew you would have some serious falls. The late spring and early summer storms came from the south-west. They started away out there somewhere, somewhere in a distant hot swirly place, and the suckers moved really fast. Some strong winds, some hail, and a smash of heavy raindrops that would bruise a horse. The rumbles rumbled, the booms boomed and echoed, and Mordor wavered. The swifts hawked, the dragonflies flitted, and the creek shimmied. Sometimes three of four storms would follow each other. 'I'm better than you,' they challenged. And they often were. The rain was so fast and heavy, it hissed through the trees in a clear, grey, see-through manna, it smelt fresh and was renewable, renewing and renewed. Its patterns were uncertainty mated with your dreams. The drip tip leaves did their job, and the leaf mulch said thank you. If it were daytime after a storm, the orange rocks would shine, the leaves would sparkle and the valley would sing. Insects too, after as before. And the smell of the earth became pungent and fresh. The summer rain was hot and happy. The winter rain was cold and lonely. The rain that trees on top of the plateau made was mystical. These trees suck the water up and release it out of their leaves in an invisible process called voting below the line. These trees breathe out around four politicians per hour, three Royal Commissions per election year, and two irrigation lobbyists per water licence (those not purchased at inflated prices, that is). A typical rainforest tree. And because of the density of trees, not to mention tree type, wind, soil type, temperature, humidity and take-away the last number you thought of, the water hangs around and forms clouds, white clouds, funnily enough called cloud rain. Sustainability at its footprint finest. Recycling at its local best. A danceable tapestry, a misty picture, and a beauty to behold.

* * *

Hardwood weatherboards along a wall can be long heavy suckers. If you don't fix the first one correctly, all the others up the wall will be out of plumb. A spirit level, a stringline and a bit of spit are handy to start. From then on, all bottoms must be level. Nothing better than having a wall full of level bottoms. And be careful as you nail because weatherboards overlap, and you must go through the base of the outside one and through the top of the inside one as well. Get it wrong and you split the inside board which is underneath the one you just laid and nailed. Cut the ends plumb to meet at the centre of a wall stud and the next row end should be staggered so as not to weaken the stud with splitting nails. At a corner, one will end flush. His ninety-degree (possibly) mate will stop short to allow a length-of-the-wall three by one and half inch piece, which will project to cover the end of his other mate.

* * *

I met Henry, a local bushman who chopped lantana with a brushhook. He lived down the road and came up the valley to chop the lantana, that ubiquitous introduced shrub that invades any cleared area on the planet. You should see the eastern side of Antarctica; it's not widely known, but it's loaded with lantana, as it had done so quite successfully in the valley. He wore thick leather gaiters up his shins, made by the coffee shop girl, and said they were to protect him from snake bites. Henry rode a horse up the valley each day to where he had finished the day before. He rode an old baldy mare and led a creamy pony, which was being broken in. His old red kelpie tagged along. The back of Henry's neck was brown worn leather, streaked and creased from aeons of burning sun, hard work and neglectful Akubras. This leather wasn't a quarter-inch boot leather from a cow hide, this was a thin pliable kid-glove type, and when Henry leaned forward, his leather neck stretched tightly, and the hidden creases were white. Maybe he should lean his head forward and sunbake occasionally, just to even things up. His beautiful, rugged hands were subtle sculptures of strength. They were soft sandstone, they were Michelangelo's marble, and they were quietly confident. His long twill trousers that sat low on his hips and stayed thin and long, forced me to buy several pairs; and my God, his wool vest twisted me into spasms of copyness. His clothes suited his wiry figure, a figure that spoke of hard labour that always produced the salty odour of the bush. He smoked a pipe. Now, I'd do anything for love, but I won't do that. He sat quietly and stroked the tobacco like he was making love to it.

He asked me, 'Where you from?'

'Well, I'm not really sure where I'm from. I mean, somewhere.'

'Confused eh? On the run?'

'What? Hell no, just a new start. What about you?'

Henry had some newly-relaxed tobacco pressed in his pipe, struck a match and cupped his hands around the pipe as he drew a breath. 'Well now, let's see. *I'm* not on the run – unlike someone I know. Not this time anyway. And no new start either. I'm goin' home directly. Which is about three miles down the valley. Me and my missus Lena. You better come down one day and have a meal with us while you decide where it is that you come from and why the police are after you.'

I remembered everything about Henry when I first met him. This was a bit weird for starters because mostly the first time you meet someone new blurs into the following years, but I remember feeling put out, even a bit annoyed. I didn't want to meet anyone who lived close by yet. I wasn't ready. I was only ready for life on my terms, my solitude terms.

Lena was a bush cook. A no-nonsense bush cook, who never humiliated anyone else, ever. She was so nice, so humble. We had corned beef and white sauce, mashed potato, peas and pumpkin. That was it for mains. Then hot deep yellow custard and thick whipped cream. I was ready for a sleep.

Henry said, 'Would you like a sweet sherry?'

I said No thanks, and knew why.

Henry said, 'When you move to a place, it takes a while to fit in and for the locals to get to know you.'

'Really? How long?'

'About seven years. By then people can see what you're like.'

'Seven years! You're kidding me! That's ridiculous.'

'Maybe. But if you're accepted, you know you've earned it.'

'How do you know like, if you've been accepted? And who makes the final decision?'

'No-one in particular, it's just something that's said one day. Not to you of course …'

'… of course not …'

'… it's, well, just talked about.'

'Where?'

'Oh, at the pub, in the town, in the bush and on the phone.

Henry was an Australian bushman on a horse. He had been born there, many years previous, which may or may not have been distressing for his mother. He was an extension of the animal. There was no bouncing up and down, no pretention, nothing fake in the way he used the reins. He moved like a sinuous upright cobra about to strike, but not really going to. He was the man of natural beauty, the one who was the epitome of archetypes, the model for sculptors and the reason Australian history books were written. He also smelt like a horse, a strong sweaty white frothy pleasant smell, a smell that made me dizzy.

Late one day, Henry said, 'Want to ride the old baldy mare while I test the pony? She's a quiet old thing, the old baldy mare.'

Do I want to ride the old baldy mare? Listen mate, I taught the man from Snowy River how to stay in the saddle, I showed Breaker Morant what to do, and I gave classes on how to talk quietly to horses. However, I have retired from such dangerous and strenuous activities. 'No, Henry, thank you for asking, but I do not want to ride the old quiet baldy mare.'

As we rode along, I suggested to myself stuff I might like to address at a later date. Like, insecurity, manhood, false beliefs, and in general, how to stop being a pseudo-brave dickhead and stand up for myself. We walked the horses up a spur, all loose reins, just talking horse talk and me pretending to be one of my former students, who, at any given point before, during and after lessons were way more skilled than me.

Henry yelled, 'Look! Up there! It's those bloody steers I've been after! Let's get 'em!'

We did indeed go and get them, and I died three times doing so, because the old quiet baldy mare was an experienced stock horse and would not be headed. Over boulders, through lantana, down and up gullies Henry pushed her while screeching with laughter. It's hard when you don't know you've been had.

But I'll get him back.

Henry and Lena lived at the head of the valley, pretty close to the mailbox where I posted and collected my letters, and they had chooks. They kept them locked in during the day. 'Too many hawks, crows and goannas. Besides, we want the girls to lay their eggs in the nest, not under a bush somewhere.'

Each afternoon between sunset and dark they opened the gate. Then stood watch so the girls didn't go near the vegetables. If Henry and Lena were a bit late in opening the cage door, the chooks would picket, rattling steel mugs and tin plates across the wire.

'What do we want? Let-us-out. When do we want it? Now!' they chanted through megaphones, which we purchased using membership funds which were left over from a junket. If Henry and Lena were late for a few days, the chooks would forget about their late arvo release. Because chooks lose habits quickly. Their long-term memory is shot; too much weed when they were chickens. Unlike union officials. Memory I mean.

* * *

I was horny, all-the-time, as in, every day. Girls it was, with glorious smooth shapely legs, full breasts, and a provocative mound. I had a continual lust that often interrupted my days. And nights. I had despicable designs and dishonourable intentions on the coffee-shop girl and indeed we were close, but we were the friends who would never go to the next level. To move into that territory would be wrong because it just would be. Mind you, I never asked, 'Excuse me, would you mind ...'

It is a weird thing, like checking out your sister, or your sister's friend. You might think they were spunky, delectable, rootable, but you make one wrong suggestion, and you are dead meat. Others you just get to fuck hard straightaway.
Like a girl called Joan.

We met in town, a chance meeting that exploded. She said, during this first meeting in town, 'Hey old man, want to spend the night with me? You know, have a raunchy good time?'

No-one has ever said that to me, like ever. And what was with the fucking old shit anyway?

'Well,' I said, as I wiped the dribble away, pushed my stiff cock lower, and tried not to sound too nervously inexperienced, nerdy or too pervy old, 'Well, I have a girlfriend.'

I didn't. Why the fuck would I say that?

'You haven't answered my question. What do you reckon?'

Don't you love it? You get a proposition, you waver, then end up being easy.

She was hot. Black hair, black eyes, big forward-facing pointy tits and curves enough to make you wank for three weeks straight. 'Okay, I mean, yes thanks, I mean please.' Or something like that. My rational brain had words. *Hey you. What the fuck do you think you're doing? This will only end in tears. Put it back in your pants and get out of there.*

My emotional brain, however, was of a different opinion. *Hallelujah! About fucking time! Give it to her son.*

I ran my hands through her coal-black thick shaggy hair, I held her face in both hands and kissed her, full and soft. She oozed a hand down my tummy to my cock, and left it there, sort of a soft firm, but a just right soft firm I was screaming for, but it was a contained scream, one that said, Holy fuck, I love it when you do that. I gently put my hand down her pants and as I did so, she opened her thighs.

She said, 'You okay with that?'

'Actually, I am quite okay with that. Probably the same as I am with your hand on my cock.'

My emotional brain said, *At last I get a look in. Isn't she fucking hot? My goodness let's get some more of this!*

After our first session, Joan said, 'Can we do that again?'

'Sure, give me a minute.'

'Not right now as in right now. I mean at another time.'

We made a deal. Based on her extreme horniness I might add. I thought I got horny, Jesus. Each week when I came to town, we wouldn't go out, we would stay in and root like rabbits. The deal was, signed with a wet handshake, that I could have my way with her any time I wanted to, and this included but was not exclusive of, me feeling her gorgeous tits from behind and then getting her to kneel on the bed while I entered her from behind, all the while watching my stiff cock slide in and out. Her part of the deal, apart from her having any personal pleasures after or during when I had my way, was that she was to be able to come to me, at any time, and say, 'Could you please kneel and kiss my pussy?'

And I would then say, 'Oh, alright, if you insist,' then do so. I loved kissing her soft pussy. Sometimes I would gently slide two fingers in, curl them and stroke downwards. And she'd fly away. Fly to somewhere else that wasn't in travel guides, psychology text books or manuals with instructions on How to Pleasure Her.

When I said I felt guilty about my fantasies of submission, she said, 'Hah, wish you had more.'

I did. Lots. One was based on memories of a prostitute.

'So,' Joan said, 'You want me to wear high stay-up sheer stockings, a short tight skirt, no pants, a blouse that is half-open and shows my tits, *and* pretend I'm a hooker?'

Oh God, I felt bad. 'Well, sort of, yes. Actually, that would be nice. Sorry if I …'

'Just checking. I'd love to.'

My rational brain was not happy. *Excuse me? I hope you two are planning to be married. I mean, this is a bit disgusting.*

* * *

When I was ten, grandpa took me to a strip show, the Dance of the Seven Veils, which every young bloke should have the opportunity to watch. The anticipation, the urgency in my pants, and the stripper's smooth white skin were mesmerising, and that was even before I went inside the show tent.

'Roll up, roll up, who wants to see this beautiful young maiden take her clothes off? Roll up, roll up.'

What do you do with a constant stiff cock? One that decides when and where it will appear.

* * *

They were standing or sitting in doorways, wearing unbelievably short tight skirts, and my heart was thumping loudly, because I knew, I knew that this night was going to be the night. You could choose, you could actually choose a girl to fuck. After some wide-eyed wonder, and this let me tell you, is what I call window shopping, I walked up to a stunning blonde, I'm guessing early twenties, wearing flat shoes, stockings, a tiny tiny tight red stretchy skirt, and a low-cut blouse that showed nearly all of her breasts, full, white and proudly firm, and asked her how much. She said six dollars.

She closed the door, I undressed, and she stood next to me. She took my hand and ran it up her stockinged thigh and under her skirt. She then lifted her skirt, an inch at a time. What a start to my career of lust, a wildly erotic start. I can see her job description now; *Must be able to drive a fifteen-year-old youth wild.*

With her skirt all hitched up around her hips, I could see that her stockings finished high up, just staying there with elastic, and there was a gap at the top of her thighs where they met her pussy. And she had no knickers on.

Hitched up short tight skirt, stockings, no pants and a cunt; the world as I knew it changed forever that night. Finished; never to be seen again.

Her light-coloured pussy hair was fine and I could see her open lips; soft petals, gentle and sweet. My God, a real pussy. It was such a wondrous thing to see. She said, *This is your first time*, and it was a statement, not a question. Wonder how she knew? Some people are just so insightful. And no, I did not lose my virginity that night; I know exactly where it is. She placed her hand under my about-to-burst tight cock, her fingers facing towards me, and stroked me up and down with a sort of soft slow stroke, mixed with a couple of tight grasps. How on earth I didn't ejaculate just then I'm buggered if I know. She then undid her blouse and exposed her beautiful white breasts and placed my hands over them. She led me over to a single bed, lay down with a pillow under her bum and opened her thighs slightly. She bent her knees back, so her cunt was sort of raised, and as I lay on her, she guided my throbbing cock inside her. The moist slippery tightness, the slow movements in and out, her smell, the warmth of her smooth skin and the tightening of every muscle as I shuddered, made me dizzy with pleasure. I stood up feeling dopey and light-headed, and she laid there, hands behind her head, legs still bent back and open, letting me see her, all exposed, glistening and soft. She smiled an enigmatic smile with her eyes, like that lady in the painting, reached for my hand again, this time leading it down between her thighs. She placed my fingers in between her slippery pussy lips, and swayed her body, up and down, and our hands moved in time. As I leant down, she placed my other hand on her breasts and we both softly caressed her full curves. She then closed her eyes, not that I was looking too much into her eyes just quietly, opened her mouth and her breaths become really short. Then she gasped and closed her legs tightly on our hands, and tensed her body. She spasmed a few times and then totally relaxed, looking all sleepy. Knew just how she felt. I was currently in worship mode, and suspect I could have stayed right there a bit longer, for example, three or four weeks. Her flat tummy, her pure white softness, her curvy thighs in smooth stockings, her mound, her soft pussy, all so beautiful. My cock was tight again, and the second stiffy is always harder than the first, all blokes know that, but this business venture didn't include a two-for-one offer. Best six dollars I ever spent. She kissed me full on the lips, a long soft kiss, and I walked out into the night.

Put my clothes on first.

* * *

Joan said, 'I want to be your slut. Is that okay?'

'Hang on a tick, I'll just check the diary.' A slight pause. 'Okay, I'm good.'

Has there ever been more welcoming words to a male, like ever? '*I love you,*' doesn't cut it. '*Hey, want to get married*?' Please.

'I will lay back with my legs open, knees bent, I will let you put your hand down my pants any time you want, I will kneel down for you, I will tease you with my tits.'

Oh alright, if you must.

The things I have to do.

'You don't mind?'

'Mind what?'

'Me saying I want to be your slut.'

'Well, no. No I don't mind. To be honest, I find it fucking amazingly erotic. Women may fall for the badass, but men will always desire the slut. And I feel so good as a bloke knowing you are my slut and that I can stroke you softly, fuck you whenever, and that you really want me to do this and that you enjoy it too.'

'I like it when you have your way with me. I really do. I like to submit to your cock. Or your fingers. Man, you know how to finger. And your mouth. Jesus! You drive me nuts. But you know, it is not degrading to me, because

I am a strong woman. It is my choice, too. And I know you are a real man because even though you fuck me hard, quite often it seems, you can also fuck me softly. And you know when, you just know. Your hardness, your tenderness, they make me want more. You are caring and never controlling. Besides, and don't you ever forget it, you are my bitch.'

Joan looked glamorous. Her long, luscious hair was cut short. A spunky cut, thick and black. Her striking face with those dark eyes and darker eyebrows, accentuated her freckles and pretty mouth. Red lippy, small ruby earrings.

'My God, you look stunning.'

When she opened her long coat, she was wearing thigh-high boots, stockings and a short skirt. Fuck me, I was back in red-light heaven. I have been in nine brothels and this girl was better than all of them together. And she was mine, and free. Her blouse was partially open, the girls' day out. Full, pointy, and upright. Gravity not acknowledged, straining with a desire to be kissed, lightly. She sat and lifted one leg over the chair arm. And that skirt rode up. Smooth thighs, electrically smooth.

And no pants.

She was spectacular and fuckable.

'You want a hooker? Well, here she is.'

It's easy when you know you've been had.

* * *

I don't like nails much, I like bolts. Nails say, Even though we can hold own and then some, we are only good on little jobs, like floorboards, wall boards or kitchen cupboards.

Bolts scoff at such menial naily-tasks. Bolts (and their accompanying washers and nuts) say, We mean business. Bolts say, Stroke our nuts and we will love you forever. I get that. The veranda 4 x 4 hardwood posts were cut out top and bottom; to fit the 4 x 2 floor joist and the 8 x 2 top rail. Two ½ inch bolts for each touch. I never used cup-head bolts because their heads bite in okay but if you want to undo their nuts they tend to spin, particularly any that have seen weather. I used ½ threaded rod and cut it to size. I even put these in as 10-foot cyclone rods on each corner, and beside each door and window. All nuts were tightened with a spanner, not a shifter. Might burr the edges.

Thank you, grandpa.

* * *

Joan had firm smooth light-brown thighs, solid and powerful, but ever so shapely. And a thigh gap that led to a beautiful mound, a mound that projected an invitation. One morning, wearing a short loose mini skirt that was more mini than skirt, she sat low on a chair opposite and opened and shut her legs as we talked. Then put both her hands between her legs and gently rubbed herself. Then quietly pulled her skirt up higher to show her mound. I went nuts and raced over. It's hard when you don't know you've been had.

I said, 'What if I unscrew my cock and leave it with you so that you can have continual pleasure for the week I'm up in the mountains?'

'That'd be cool. But how will you pee?'

Naughty, and clever.

* * *

Australia has roads. This may be a revelation to those who live in our crowded cities, but it's true. I have seen them. These roads are ostensibly there to enable ease of local access, community safety, and the really important one, economic viability. But these reasons are pure bullshit. Australia's roads are there to enable a rite of passage that is unheard of in quite a few western countries – it's called the road trip. There are stacks of western countries are around twenty miles across and fifteen miles long. An Australian travelling on roads in these countries would call this commuting. Or a trip to the corner shop to buy some milk, bread, and a paper-bag full of red frogs. The Australian Road trip rite of passage asks of you, Can you handle the long hours of driving, Can you exist on servo food, and, more importantly, Can you maintain your vehicle. The rewards of a road trip are many – new places, freedom, independence, and self-confidence when you either repair something or other, or when you finish and are still alive and in one piece. Road trips reinforce the entrenched Australian values of government wastage, pure innovation and family bonding.

Grandpa came up, saw me running checks on the Dodge, and went, 'Hrumpf, where are we going in that?'

'We are going for a spin grandpa.'

The border-control gate between Queensland and New South Wales was so high-tech, so contemporary, it made future facial recognition, data-scanning and inappropriate frisking seem like a virgin's birthday party, a milk-run of options with the gold-top indicating, This one has the cream. There was one dark-blue uniformed-man to uphold the values of equality, the Aussie traditions of, Don't come the raw prawn, and Fair suck of the sauce-bottle. His job was to stop scrub ticks from crossing an imaginary border, and although this would be a challenging task because the little suckers are hard to see, he was diligent, efficient and knowledgeable. Grandpa and I had driven up the range to this state border at the start of our road trip. The border-control man's duties were carried out with a wave through and a blown kiss from his guard box as he read the racing guide. Then he noticed that the Dodge was boiling. This brought him alive. Alive enough to put down the form guide and his sharpened pencil. He was beside himself. 'Hell mate, look at that steam! You'd better pull over and let her cool for a bit.'

But he didn't understand a four-cylinder flat-top that runs at almost boiling point, basic physics, or an outstanding mechanic when he saw one.

I said, 'Nah, she'll be right.' And as I had been cleared for travel by border control, customs and been given a few reasonable tips in the upcoming daily-double, I eased down the other side of the range in second gear, because I knew that going down in a low gear cooled the engine quicker than letting it stand still with the engine turned off. Grandpa was impressed. I knew this because I heard a grunt. He also didn't know that I was genius Welch plug man. Not many grandpas know this about their grandsons. It's a shame really. As we drove through the green countryside, bouncing along as if we were in a mouse cartoon, there was a loudish bang and the old truck shuddered. The temperature gauge went through the roof. Golly gosh, we said together. I am a gauge watcher. I rarely watch the road ahead or use the mirrors, I just drive looking at the gauges. Crazy if you don't. But I knew what was going on. I was a hero for a day. I pulled to the side, checked for road safety, chocked the tyres, opened the beetle's wings, removed the remnants of the blown Welch plug, wiped the hole with my shirt tail, and used the wet and dry from my back pocket to scour the edges of the small circular hole. I pulled a brass Welch plug from my pocket, left side, wiped it on my shirt tail, new section, positioned it convexly, got a cup-head bolt and hammer and belted the Welch plug into place. Put a nut on the bolt first so I wouldn't stuff the thread.

'Grandpa, kick her over and bring us a bucket of water, will you?'

Doesn't happen often enough I can tell you.

We played a couple of games. Seeing as we were travelling through dairy country, the Cow game was perfect. We each counted how many we saw on our side, and whoever ended up at the final destination with the most cows won. When you passed a bank, you could bank your cows at five percent interest. However, if you passed a graveyard, your cows were doomed.

Grandpa said, Let's play I Spy. I was in. Me first, he said. GLN. What the Fuck? Grandpa's Left Nostril. See what I have to put up with?

Hot farts were not only allowed but encouraged

At the end of our trip, Grandpa said, 'Hmmf, 'spose you did a good job.'

* * *

Joan said, 'I have something to tell you.'

'Fire away.' I've had these before and they rarely end well.

'When I have my period, I get way more hornier.'

Is that even humanly possible? Who knew with this girl.

'I have to drain myself of pleasure until my lower tummy aches empty. I have to keep hauling out the orgasms otherwise I can't concentrate on anything.'

'I'm good with that.'

'What about the blood thing? You okay with that?'

This one ended well.

* * *

Henry said, 'Did you know death adders came in pairs? Always. So maybe you were lucky when you jumped over one.'

'Really?'

'Not sure if you mean the pairs, or your athletic ability. Anyway, Old Harry kept death adders as pets.'

'So I heard. Why would he do that?'

'Because he could. I also heard he trod on one. You know your wool vest?'

I felt a twinge of being busted for copy syndrome coming on, which included a missing serve of self-confidence. 'All yours for the special price of four-dollars fifty, only available for today, because when you buy it, you will look amazing, just like the other bushies.'

'Don't wash it. Ever.'

'Hah! As if I would do that!' Pause. 'Why not?'

'When it gets sour, hang it over a fence for a bit.'

'Of course, that's what I'll do.' I still wasn't sure why I would do that.

'The wool vest will shrink.'

'Thanks, mum. Hey, whatever happened to Old Harry the hermit?'

'I found his body. All puffed up with a bite mark on his ankle.'

Henry asked for a lift into town. 'I have an appointment. You got room?'

As we drove into the town, I found out stuff about Henry. He was so old school; he was there before the old school was built. A generation that knew a depression and a World War. He lived in our place of dense green and even denser skies that were blue, so blue that they hurt your eyes with their intensity; a place of mental and mountainous isolation with clear memories and clearer water; of wilderness and incessant hot rain; and of peaceful sunny winter days and black and blue nights.

And he was the same age as my grandpa.

'Now, I can see you don't understand the scrub, and I'll tell you something, you'll never beat it, even though its struggle over you is predictable. If you don't destroy it straight away then it cannot be owned. If you stay still long enough, one of them vines will use you as a ladder. No sir, it's a bloody bastard of a thing, I've seen it ruin good men. Even kill some of them. You take the day Splinter Johnson got caught up in those bloody water vines. We was felling some scrub up in Stevenson's top paddock, next to a gully, and Kevie, that was Splinter's real name, had a Cedar almost ready to go, and we pointed to the vines and said, 'What're you goin' to do about those?' but he reckoned it'd be okay. Well, when the cedar went, and the bloody monster had three thousand super in him, it took those vines as well. Trouble was, them vines was attached to a massive fig. And you know what them figs is like (I didn't). Them vines wrenched the fig out by the roots and flung poor Splinter, chain saw and all, across the gully. The last we see of Splinter is him flyin' through the air followin' the cedar and the fig.' Henry looked down and tended to his pipe. 'Still haven't found him.'

Henry paused and looked straight ahead as if he were addressing the single-paned windscreen this time, having given up talking to his tobacco. 'Then there was Bertie Johnson, Splinter's cousin.'

'Yes Henry, met him last week as I was driving through South Australia. Same day that I met Splinter Johnson.'

'Well,' Henry continued, 'We were up the scrub one day and Les was having a piss and the poor bugger leaned too close to a Gympie Stinger leaf. Now I've been brushed by one of them leaves, and I can tell you it's painful. So, when Les gets stung *down there*, you should'a seen him hop!'

And Henry roared with laughter, thumping his thighs and coughing pipe smoke everywhere.

On the way home, with Henry pretty much off his face, the ute lurched to the side and straight away I knew I had a flat tyre. And by the way the front end was swaying; the flat tyre was on the left side at the rear. I stopped on the gravel beside the road in a safe enough spot to do what had to be done. Henry reached under the seat and brought out the wheel brace. 'I've got this.'

He opened the door and immediately fell out into the gravel, and little wafts of dust rose from beside the opened door. Henry staggered up, as the dust settled around him.

I think I smiled.

I smelt revenge,

I sensed payback.

I felt power.

The Dodge, like most small trucks, had opposite thread on the left-side wheel nuts. However, Henry wasn't aware of this because he was a horse man, and as he struggled to loosen the nuts, he was actually tightening them. I watched in fascination as his face went deep red from the extreme exertion he was applying. The veins on the side of his neck swelled beautifully, in a wavy pattern like a deep purple river in flood, and once he farted from the strain. I felt a little guilty. I mean, he was a nice old fella and I didn't particularly want to be blamed for his death. On the other hand, revenge is a form of purity, of emotional release.

'Bloody rotten bastard. Who tightened these nuts last? A fucken gorilla?'

After he had suffered a bit, I asked innocently, 'Them nuts should be bloody easy. Hang on a tick, which way are you trying to turn them?' But as soon as I mentioned this, he knew.

'Something is funny here. Wait a minute ...' and as he forced the brace the other way, the nut jerked loose. '... You mongrel, you knew that!'

I roared with laughter. 'Never mind the never forgetting the fucking Alamo you old bastard, never forget the baldy mare!'

* * *

'He comes in every month and stares at that one painting. Nothing else. Doesn't check out the Impressionists, the Cubists, or the nudes, he just stands in front of that Darling River, and dreams.'

A return bus to Brisbane and back is a long day. A long exhausting day, making me long for the cool purity of The Creek, but still worth it though, because I get to see my old river. Except this time at the gallery, my painting was gone. They had taken away my painting, 'The flood on the Darling 1890' by Piguenit. It was gone. My once-a-month city excursion, ruined.

'What do you think he'll do now it's gone?'

The other girl, also dressed in the gallery uniform said, 'Maybe for his next visit we show him a different Darling painting?'

* * *

Two scientists in waders, sitting next to The Creek, recording data. 'Hi,' the boss said, 'This is my offsider, Julie.'

'Do not drink the creek water,' said Julie the offsider.

'Right.' And isn't it a nice day, Julie.

'Its E. coli reading is too high. Someone's pooping in this creek. This is bad water.'

Thank you very much for that. Been lovely talking with you. Are you fucking kidding? I have drunk from the Darling River, from puddles, and have sucked on the end of a hose, and I'm still alive. The water from The Creek, which only ran through the rainforest before it got to me was the purest on the planet and I drank it daily. What were they talking about?

'Would you like to come up for a cup of tea?'

I forgot I had a snake on the table, ready for the pot. A long, red-bellied black snake.

'Oh,' the boss said.

'Goodness,' Julie the offsider said.

'Yeah, he was caught in a fence. In a bad way. Had to dispatch him.'

* * *

Brisbane. No Darling painting, still. I went to the desk. 'Hi, where can I find the Darling painting?'

'I'm really sorry, it's still being restored. But we found you another one. Come,' she said.

She took me to a small room that had a painting by Ludwig Becker, the artist on the Burke and Wills expedition in 1860. The painting was called 'A Darling bend.' Jesus, who are these foreigners? We get a Frenchman and now a German who both get the old river. My once-a-month Brisbane trips had meaning again. Landscape is more than just a certain place like mountains, rivers, plains, or whatever. More than a culture, more than politics, more than a memory. It is experience and yet it is beyond experience. And when an artist can take you there, especially where you've been, it keeps the scene in your head every day. Maybe a redefinition of character? 'Thank you. May you and your children be blessed.'

* * *

The sandpaper fig grows next to The Creek, and is so called because of the rough leaves which cabinet makers line up to buy. It can grow in drier places too. Caterpillars hack its leaves. Birds eat its fruit. The flower of the sandpaper fig is found inside the fruit. And wasps, who pollinate the flower, can only mate inside the fruit. That is a bit creepy for starters. The figs have cameras in there. A female fig wasp recognises the scent of the exact species of fig tree where she was born. She squeezes into the fruit via a tiny hole, damaging herself in the process. After she lays her eggs, she dies. That's tough. Male offspring are born without wings, mate with female offspring, and then die. Insect incest has guilt.

The white cedar is not a poor cousin to the red cedar, not at all. Maybe not as straight and millable but with a bit of help, it could be though. Nonetheless, a beautiful tree on its own. Grows to over a hundred feet and spreads accordingly. One of the few deciduous trees in the rainforest. Reshoots with small lilac and white flowers that smell honey sweet. Also found in several other countries and known as the bead tree, the pride of India and Persian Lilac. The dangly bunches of berries turn yellow when ripe, and are toxic to mammals except for flying foxes. Birds love them: brown pigeon, pied currawong, king parrot, and crimson rosella.

The black bean grows up to over a hundred feet tall, has dark green glossy foliage and red and yellow flowers that grow off the branch. Pods are huge and contain green seeds with a brown skin. The old mob used to eat them. With some preparation.

Grass trees aren't trees. The black trunk, which is really compressed leaves, green spikey needle-type leaves, and a long flowering stem, grow up to 4 metres, phallically protruding. Which can take 20 years to grow. They grow on the dry slopes and can live up to 600 years. Imagine the crowds at a This is your Life show for a grass tree? Need a big studio. Grass trees aren't a grass either. They are related to lilies.

Stinging trees are a tree. And can grow up to a hundred feet tall. They also grow in dappled sunlight, as in, they colonise breaks in the shade. Their leaves have tiny hairs and if you touch one, the pain is unbearable, almost literally. It is like being stung by thirty wasps, being burnt by hot acid and being electrocuted, all at the same time. Wonder how much the researcher got for that info. Probably still in rehab waiting for the expense's claim to come through. I was aware of the stinging tree but still managed to cop it. I brushed my thumb against the leaf of a sapling, and the pain was certainly intense. Adding to the wasp, the acid and the 240 volts, was the feeling that someone had belted my thumb with a hammer. Three times hard in the same spot.

* * *

Mobs of crested hawks, a blue-grey bodied barred-breasted raptor, rock up in September. A couple will call, swe-chu, swe-chu, which translates as, 'Hi Tony, just passing through. See you in January.' This pair returns and does spectacular aerial displays. The hawks then renovate their old nest, high up in a flooded gum along The Creek.

Paradise Rifle bird. Usually a top-level rainforest dweller. One morning a female landed on a partially opened banana bell and picked. I was going to hunt her, but noticed she was picking in between the newly formed flowers. These birds dance well and both sexes bend their wings in a sort of curved semi-circle.

Grey goshawks often mate with a white goshawk. I heard their young children ask, 'Who was here first in this country? You dad, or was it mum?' When you see a white goshawk swerving through the trees you're not sure if you just saw a bird, or the ghost of one. They are a stark white, and outlined with a 0.4mm fine-tipped black-ink pen.

Whip birds. Zip amongst the low scrub. Brown, white face patch and a crest. The male calls a whip-crack call, just like stagecoach drivers make. The female answers, 'crack crack.' Sometimes the male does both calls. Other male species have also been known to do this at nightclubs, footy games and while fishing with mates. It's like, 'Hmm. I can't get a chick, so I'll just pretend I'm cool.' The male whip bird's call is a pebble dropped into a rainforest pool; it is fluid beauty; it is a plunk of secretive sharpness.

A mystery bird. A winter early morning call in the dry gullies, eerie and haunting. A two-note pure whistle. I love to identify birds, to understand, but I left this gully caller as a mystery. To identify it would be to take its magic away, to lessen its link to ancientness, its etherealness, its pureness. No Agatha needed, just a mystery I didn't want solved. Mystery bird was a poet in an unknown language. To understand poetry, you do not need a translation, because verbal expression is beauty in any language and is as much imaginative visual as it is verbally visual. The physical and spiritual are joined in sorrow, sadness, beauty and inspiration. Maybe some secrets are best not shared? Or maybe they are best not discovered in the first place? Imagine how many secrets and magic there are out there, waiting to not be discovered? This place is not just new left-alone magic birds. This place is

The Creek, The Creek of magic. And magic is a special thing, a special thing that has a special something that is often hard to name specifically. A hard to pin down, harder to explain feeling that is human, is land, is natural. I soon realised that The Creek was magic. Like, really early soon. And I realised that this magic does not need a name, does not need or want, a name, an analysis, does not need its secrets dragged out because to leave some things as magic keeps the magic. This magic was spiritual, health-giving, deep-breathing, and asked you to consider the planet, and why you were on it. It was a magic that combined the emotions, the physical and the mind, a magic that asked you to think about the past, the future, and the now. You could feel it, powerful yet beautiful, like an invisible wave. Everyone who came to visit said so. It was the landscape, they said. The mountains, they said. The Creek, they said. It certainly was some or all those, but it was also us who were here, too, us who carry a fine line between magic and madness. A magic carpet ride for you and me. Maybe the outside magic was a way to connect to the inner self? And a way to give a whole lotta lovin' and happiness?

* * *

Peter was an ex-dairy farmer, now a bush carpenter, and one who used old-fashioned tools. No apprenticeship, no formal training, no nothing. A stocky bloke, with white hairy legs and eyebrows, full of respect, politeness, honour and a sense of always doing the right thing, which he did. A generation gap of solidness that should be kept alive, promoted and taught. Put in apothecary's bottles, stored in a time-capsule, and hand-scribed with those coloured-first letters like you see in ancient texts.

He came up to help me build things that I couldn't. Which was quite a list. He saw my handsaw, and he said, 'Now that, is a nice tool. Which has been well looked after.'

Peter was a really nice bloke, a sweet sweet man. And a brilliant carpenter.

I had framed the house up to the ceiling joists, but I did not know how to set rafters, how to cut plumb against a ridge board and how to cut a birdsmouth where the rafter met the top plate and make the rafter true at both ends. Peter came up. No calculator, no preset ratios, no cos, sine or cosine. No textbook, nothing fancy. He had a large steel setsquare, a pencil and a handsaw. Full stop. What followed was something akin to Giza, Palmyra, and Athens, the Taj, Hagia Sofia and anything you might see in Rome.

He worked out the pitch, the overall run, minus the ridgeboard width, divided the adjusted overall run by two, cut a ridge post, allowed for an overhang, and cut to his pencil lines. Peter mumbled lots, as he wrote all his measurements down on a piece of wood in an ancient number system.

He mumbled, 'Nine-foot eleven and fifteen-sixteenths. Six and three-eighths divided by two.'

I have kept the piece of wood Peter used to do his calculations. It's a cultural artefact, a mathematical treasure, from Peter, the bush carpenter.

* * *

'Hey Joan?'

'Yep.'

'I'm sorry.'

'Sure. What have you done now?'

I told her sorry because I was trying to resolve, reconcile and make amends to her mob. Not her exactly, or about me exactly. Living on stolen land and feeling like I didn't belong.

'Well, Pritch, you are genuine in your extravagant, though perhaps misguided, display of remorsefulness and sorrow, but …

'But what?'

'… fuck off. But hey, thank you anyway. I get it. You are beautiful.'

* * *

Peter the bush carpenter said, 'Tony, you know when cyclones come and blow a roof off?'

'Yes Peter, of course I do.' Happens to me all the time; it's just fucken awful.

'Well,' he said, 'a lot of the time it's not just the roofing iron that blows off by itself, it's the battens that lift because they are the weak point, the fuse of the roof so to speak. So how about we screw your battens down as well as your iron and you should be apples.'

We countersunk three-inch coach screws through the three by one and a half hardwood battens which were resting on the newly birdsmouthed cut four by two hardwood rafters which were triple gripped to the centre of the Earth, and then prepared to lay the roofing iron.

Peter the bush carpenter said, 'Let's have a splash day.'

'Hell yeah Peter. I'd love one.'

No idea, me. Limited bush intelligence. Happens all the time, and at times hinders my day-to-day understanding and future personal development. I think the title, slow learner, would be applicable.

'Today we will get that roofing iron on. This will look impressive. As in, a lot of work done.'

'Right. A splash day.'

'Correct. Compare today, for example, with a future day of doing trim around windows.'

'Hell, an awful experience Peter.' I was starting to get it.

'You would measure, cut, remeasure, cut, swear, and ask why some idiot had not squared the frames beforehand. And if you didn't belt your thumb or get a hernia, you would think you had done okay. Total accomplishment for the day? Two windows trimmed. If you were lucky.'

I got it. We screwed the roofing iron to our recently secured battens. Every line along each batten was screwed. Huge proper two-inch self-drilling roofing screws. The roof is still there.

Thank you, Peter. Love to get to know you and your family better.

* * *

I was telling Joan about Peter and she was inquisitive. Not in an, Oh, what an oddity, way, but in a way that spoke of experience, and perhaps more than a little care and attention.

'I bet he's really old-fashioned. Mutters to himself, yeah?'

'Wow, that's him to a tee. You know him?'

'Puts the pencil behind his ear, stuff like that. Yeah, I have come across him in town a few times.

* * *

On the final day at the pigsty, the welcome swallows put on a party. The babies, who had now grown up, said, 'You helped keep us safe and we love you. Bring a plate to share Uncle Tony, and we'll party into the evening.'

It's hard making moth, beetle and wasp pies let me tell you. They cooked me muffins made from straw, dead beetles and mud pellets. I was grateful and humbled, but thought of their little sticky mitts in the muffin mix and we all know where kids put their fingers.

The snakes said, 'Hiss off and don't come back.'

I said, 'Ha, bitches, I leave the pigsty to what's left of you!'

The owls enjoyed the party so much they stayed up all day. The dingoes didn't take part. They just watched silently from the back ridge. Give me the creeps that lot.

There was still work to do on the house but it was home now regardless. My first one. Not so much a control or ownership first-one feel, but a deep inner connection to the earth and life. My stability. My mess. My choice of personal things.

My place of solitude.

It was time to lay the 3 x 1 floorboards, which may seem odd because I was already living in the house, but it's not because I had laid planks to walk on. Besides, the breezes coming up from the cool earth gave me an idea for later. Recycled tongue and groove ironbark and red gum, and because they weren't end tongue and groove, which saves bucket loads of waste, I had to be assiduous, even careful. I would have to cut their overlapping ends to meet back on floor joists, alternate joins to reduce splitting of the floor joists. I had no mechanical floor cramp to squeeze the floorboards together. These floor cramps have so much amazing strength they are used to turn aircraft carriers over in drydock. I would cut and lay four full lengths of 3 x 1, lay a dummy length, whack a sharp chisel into the joist touching the dummy one and lean her in. Nail the outside board because when it's secure, so is everybody else inside her. If you stick the nail into a jar of fat it helps it penetrate the timber. Even better, run it through your hair.

The nail.

Peter was right. Trimming windows was not a splash day, it wasn't even near getting fucking wet. Nor was hanging doors. Heavy awkward bloody things, heavy because I built real doors, not poofy ply rubbish with cardboard in the middle. That's not a door, slut, this is a door. Hanging a door by myself was a chore, but a fulfilling nice one. Hinges on the door first. Tick. And using proper wood screws I might add. They have a thicker gauge at the top, and are of course, real screws, not Phillip's head. We're still hand drilling all holes don't forget.

After you checked that Yes, the recently fixed hinges did indeed open the way you wanted them to. Do not laugh about this.

Position the door

With blocks, nailed in pieces of wood, luck and spit. Tick.

And flattened newspaper underneath to allow space for swing. Tick.

After the door had been hung, there are the architraves.

First, I chose two long 4 x 1 hardwood boards for the sides.

These have been lightly sanded but not planed

Because I want to see the mill saw-blade curved marks

And like most timber I use, I want it smooth but still rough under the smooth.
Run the plane down their edges to knock off the burr,
Forty-five-degree cuts at the top, done with a tenon saw, which has fine teeth.
Spirit-levelled upright and tacked in place down low only (You'll see why.)
On either side of the door.
And because I had watched Peter,
I didn't measure and cut the top shorter horizontal piece that will go above the door with forty-five degree ends to match their vertical mates.
Yet.
I cut this top horizontal board, square cut both ends, just a bit longer than it should be,
Gently lift forward the two vertical long chaps,
(Which have been tacked in, but lower. See previous.)
Slot in this top horizontal piece,
Plumb it horizontally,
And pencil in where it has to be cut.
Then cut outside the pencil mark.
If you were a carpenter and I was …
As in, a bit rough,
Maybe even clunky
Would you come with me anyway?
The two ensuing cuts
May not be exactly 45 degrees.
One might be
But it doesn't matter, because anyway they will mitre in nicely and no-one will ever know their precise angles.

An argument.

Tenon saw vs grandpa's saw.

'Ha, I may be smaller, but I don't have a wobbly arse like you. I am trim and terrific, and I have twelve teeth per inch and you only have seven. So there.'

Grandpa's saw stayed silent.

'And I have a top reinforcement to keep me straight and true. You don't.' Silence.

'I, get the job done. I, am built for speed. And I am pretty cool.'

Grandpa's saw cleared its throat. 'Well, yes, you are way more sturdier, you are indeed faster, and you look soo much more trimmer …'

'I knew it! I'm better than you!'

'… but a reinforcing bar? It stops you from having any depth, literally too. And yes you do have more teeth, but this is detrimental to your future because the fuckers are high tensile and can't be sharpened.

Silence from Tenon saw.

But grandpa's saw wasn't done. 'And you are a small-minded vindictive cunt.'

Locks a different kettle of fish. I say fuck locks, especially fuck deadlocks. Those dangerous fire-engulfing stupid dumbarse inventions. 'Excuse me, does your house have deadlocks on both sides of the doors, windows and chimney?'

'Kidding me. Think I want to burn alive?'

'Well, your premiums will be higher …'

'On second thought …'

I invented wooden latches that could be opened from both sides.

Locks?

This place of being was my first one.
That first one I will always remember fondly.
I bet you have one too.
A place of deep inner feeling
Of stability
Of my mess
Of my choice of personal things
My first one
My place of solitude had
Three rooms,
Mine,
The spare, and the Other.
Mine
Was small,
Tiny even.
Had a small cupboard for clothes,
Just a few open shelves.
It had no bed,
It had an alcove instead of a bed
With a kangaroo hide on some old floorboards, a pillow and two blankets,
And I slept well because of and with.
Double windows opened me to the world

Of quiet noise, cool breezes and the occasional moth.
Even though moths are soft,
They still hurt when they bump into your face.

The spare room had a hard wooden bed, a desk and chair and some windows. The walls were 6 x 1 silky-oak, roughly sawn, not sanded, and laid horizontally. It was a much bigger room than mine and had double French doors that opened to its own verandah. Guests would stay and I wouldn't see them for weeks. Or months. Some I never saw ever again.

The Other was the kitchen lounge living. And I did live there. I dreamt on the lounge, I wrote letters at the slab table, and I cooked on a stove.

My stove was called a donkey. A variation perhaps on the real wood-fired water heater donkey, which is a 44-gallon drum with a fire underneath. A donkey is a must for the discerning solitary person living in the bush. They are loving and caring. And like for most of us, they like to be treated nicely. My donkey was an Everhot 204 combustion stove and was gentle and giving. A donkey will give you warmth, hot water, slow cooked food and love. Just like any good partner should. Combustion stoves don't give out high levels of heat like, for example, a pot-belly. Combustion stoves are not meant to. They are insulated to keep the heat in to make hot water and to keep the oven ready. Roast vegetables need 400 degrees so it's forest oak for the firebox, thank you very much. Although I believe olive oil to be at the top of the food pyramid (plus for soft skin, gut balance and world peace), mostly I used lard to roast vegetables. I couldn't be bothered par boiling potatoes to give them a start. For God's sake, put them all in the bloody oven. Spuds first because pumpkin takes way less time. Chokoes aren't so good to roast. They are mostly water and will roast accordingly, i.e., turn to green water. Although in a really hot oven if I left the skin on, they held together okay.
I rebricked the firebox.

After I cleaned out the old busted dirty white bricks, I placed the new heat retaining pure-white jigsaw-pieced bricks loosely in place, in order of number. Some wouldn't snug in so I had to use a rasp to trim their edges. The cement sets quickly so you must be sure. Of course, the water jacket is left bare. The heat needs to make that water move up the ¾ inch copper pipe into the 44-gallon drum then keep recirculating until it's all hot. No pumps needed to access the hot water; gravity is enough.

The inlet pipe at the base of the 44 needs to have a one-way valve. The hot water must not move up the source pipe to the 1,000-gallon rainwater tank. A plumber told me that the ensuing airlock of cold and hot would cause an explosion.

Nothing worse than an explosion in your airlock.

The 44-gallon hot water drum needed a pressure release valve. I used a long copper pipe extending through the roof. With a shepherd's crook end. Which I covered with gauze wire. Because if the mud wasps block it, you may have 44 gallons of hot water in your lap. Mud wasps have been known to shut down 747s. They fly in through the open windows and sting the pilots. Mud wasps build nests in the sensors and the plane's systems give either no data or incorrect readings. After the new bricks, you must light the stove with kindling and let it burn out. This seasons the new bricks with a short sharp heat. Then you're okay to go. At night, I adjusted the four levers. Flue, oven, hot water, and firebox. At daybreak I opened the air flow to the firebox before I opened the door and added some sticks. The coals must have a chance to glow before the door is opened otherwise the house and your lungs will be full of smoke. And you and the house will cough together. Then slide the coffee percolator over to the sweet spot which is just right of centre.

And smelt the aroma of history, travel and dreams.

At the second-hand furniture store in town, the lounge set had arrived. It was from a deceased estate and consisted of a three-seater lounge and two chairs. It was a Genoa set. Genoa in Italy has given us Columbus, focaccia, pesto, jeans, and Paganini. Now I don't know if the Genoa lounge originated there too, and I didn't really care because a Genoa lounge is worth ten of all on the previous list. Soft, yellow, and brown, and when you sit in one, you are obliged to stay there for at least a month. Without moving. They are that good.

I said, 'I will buy the set please.' The man said, 'Well, hang on sport. For starters, it's just come in and hasn't been cleaned, and besides, you don't even know the price.'

I said, 'I will buy the set please.' And I grinned like if he didn't sell me the set, right then and there, I would stab him.

Henry helped me unload and he looked at the lounge and then at me. And repeated. I said, 'Alright, alright, you go first.'

We weren't talking about sitting on the lounge, we were talking about what was inside the lounge. A deceased estate and a lounge that hadn't been cleaned can only mean one thing; there would be stuff that had fallen between the cushions.

Henry took the farthings, the halfpennies, and the pennies. I got an opal brooch, and a letter written from Papua New Guinea in 1944. It was a soldier's love letter to his sweetheart back home and after I had read the first few lines, I decided not to read any more. I'm okay with voyeurism, I actually don't mind it, but this was different. This was too intrusive to be leered at, too personal to know any more. Maybe Henry got rich cashing in those coins?

A table
A solid slab table,
Built by a grandfather and his grandson.
This table and its memories
Will never be moved by anyone.
Ever.
Some timber was sawn roughly
Some was retrieved from the dirt.
Wooden pegs, mortise and tenon
Held it together.
A local bushman noticed some semi-curves on the top slabs and said,
'I'll fix it.'
He turned up with his chainsaw.
At right angles
The screaming blade swept back and forth,
Echoing screechingly off the hoop pine VJ tongue and groove wall,
Chips of wood fling through the air
Like angry wasps
Which were still being discovered fifty years later,
Behind books.
Paper wasps.
I sat at this table, the one that helped me write letters, and the large window in front of me gave me the ridge opposite and inspiration.
And I cried because I could.

I had a bathroom, and it was outside the house. It was below the top tank, so I got a slow gravity feed for the shower. The bathroom was a slab frame bolted together. The walls were wire-netting festooned with vines, ferns, and epiphytes. The floor was a concrete slab and drainage went out through a channel and into a two-inch poly pipe, which I shifted to water assorted bananas, oak trees and grass. I used only pure soap, no shampoos or conditioners, and no doors.

* * *

My house faced south because the slope gave me little choice. But I liked it anyway because I looked directly at a three-thousand-foot-high ridge which was six miles long, a sort of elongated flat-ish mountain top, which I stared at every day. Which changed nearly every day. Its shadows became furtive and hid secrets; its soft yellow light, its thick yet thin white mist seeped through the high-levelled trees, like lost ghosts wending their way to a haunted house.

Flocks of pigeons, tiny specks in a bundle, would swirl and dive like a distant swarm of bees intent on starting a new hive. After a storm, sharp outlines of leaves, rocks and soft yellow grasses would bring breathlessness and possibilities, tall red cedars and spreading rambling figs were miniature toys, and I thought, one day, when I'm ready, I will go up that slope, right to the top, just to see what I might see.

On the therefore back northern side of the house I planted deciduous trees because the winter sun needed an entry. The tall dense ironbarks further back behind me were almost as tall as the sky and gave a security borne of insecurity. East and west existed only in name. They gave glimpses of what might be, but you had to climb higher to see these.

Under the house I planted ferns because of my non-floorboard-breeze knowledge. Depending on the time of year and day I sprayed these ferns with misty water and the coolness would infiltrate the house via adjustable slats. The evaporation would create its own lower-temperatured weather pattern. No wind, clouds, air stillness, birds or insects. No rain like the canopied-recycled white cloud, just a non-humid coolness.

* * *

I had chooks. Twenty-five. Sold eggs as well as the green pear-shaped vegetables from vines. The ones called choko. I counted one chook missing. My favourite orange bantam. Twenty-two days later she came back with eight chickens. A six-foot, red-bellied black snake slithered into the pen, searching with his tongue and his memory for a small feathery plump snack. I waited near the door with a first aid kit. He screamed out of there with an orange bantam hen on his arse.

No chook pen will ever stop a carpet snake. You may have cyclone wire the first three-feet to stop the wild dogs from ripping their way in, you may have strip-netting tacked onto the bottom to stop rats, and even make an effort, a well-intentioned though largely pathetic effort, to stop carpet snakes with half-inch netting, 4 x 1 boards and covered deep holes with sharpened stakes at the bottom, but you'd be wasting your time. Better to have a sign saying, *Entry this way.*

* * *

I could see trees, smell trees, hear trees, touch trees
I could see life, smell life, hear life, touch life
I could taste anything and everything
I could touch the Earth's memories
because my chest was full of the deep breaths
deep deep breaths that stayed in my chest
and gave me settled thoughts occasionally sparked by a crazy adventure.

The steep slope opposite the house, the one I saw out of my south facing windows every day, the one I knew I would climb, called out to me. It didn't say, Hey Tony, climb me, I am ready. It said, Hey, are *you* ready?

A slope you say? How about three-thousand feet of sheer rock faces, gullies, and open dry forest hopping with kangaroo grass? It had no walking trails and straight away I got excited. I was certainly ready for this adventure.

I left a note on the table.

Going up the slope opposite
Be back tonight
If I'm not
Please look after the chooks
And watch out for death adders
They come in pairs you know.

Holy fuck it was more than exciting. I was on drugs. Legal, real and natural; the best kind. It's better this way. Each step, each step made me strong and warm and aware. Looked down too. Whoever said not to? No idea. From my perch, one slip meant at least a 1000-foot fall, bounce off some rocks, slam into a couple of trees, fall another 1000 foot and possibly land in The Creek. If I were lucky. Not that it would matter much by then. But I could read crumbly rickety rocks, slippery steep grass, and I knew I could look down. My turn to have no idea, full of fear, but doing it anyway. No compass no map no nothing. Along the ledges, up the crevasses, and onto the false top ridge, through the lawyer cane, raspberry vines, stinging trees, and onto the real top ridge to emerge into the high-altitude subtropical rainforest, where I could walk freely. And pray. No wait, I don't pray. And in the understorey, amongst the ferns, the regent bowerbirds, the lyrebirds, I stopped, and almost prayed.

There is an awe that comes when you are the company of heroes. They are usually good looking, superbly fit and somehow above us admiring mortals in both appearance, word and deed. You might ask, 'How could I ever be that stunningly gorgeous, that articulate, that brave?'

When I walked through the rainforest, with its tall magnificent massive trees, shafting their way from the soil phallically into the heavens, the soft light angling in with beams of yellow, blue and white, the dead leaves wafting down onto mossy roots, the ferns, the fungi, the lichen and the litter, I felt the awe. Good looking alright, healthy, strong, and beyond the realm of the day to day of paying bills, commuting, worrying or searching for abstract unreachable concepts like Who the fuck am I? A pure contemplation of a wild and raw place, a mouth-opened wonder, yet a wonder attainable in a strange way. Free from space and time, not reachable through space and time, but reachable only through the mind. A place, not other worldly, a place between worlds. Take your shoes off Tony, you're on holy ground. A mystical, beautiful and heroic place. I knew then that landscape can indeed define us, shape us, and take us wherever we want to go.

* * *

Making a garden in an unfamiliar environment is tricky. All the things you had used before in say, western New South Wales, may not be applicable. Newer bugs, heavier soil and crazier weather. I started with chokoes before graduating to other vegetables. Chokoes will grow in Antarctica, the Sahara and on the summit of Kilimanjaro. At the same time. Grandpa grew chokoes over his outdoor dunny. A green world of cool captured children, of sheltered shady nuances, all done while you had a poop. I grew so many over my dunny and along the fences, I picked and sold two bags full each week.

Summer was a poetry in motion, a poetry that encouraged hot tight slippery sex. Not just me and Joan. We didn't need a particular season. The thunder's deep rumbles excited the insects to perform a sex-crazed frenzied dance of death. Fair way to go out I suppose. Like the male antechinus in my ceiling, continually mating until his heart gave out. A reasonable way to end it all. Despite these unfortunate death sentences and defensive garden forays, I loved summer's hot set-in rain that filled the reservoirs of earthy continuity. Summer gave me zucchinis, cucumbers and climbing beans, and frikkin bitey March flies that sense fresh blood like crazed vampires. Their sting was like a nail gun let loose on any part of your exposed body. In the rainy summer, the vegetables were so prolific, I had to use a brushhook to get into the garden. The harsh sun cut branches like death's scythe. It bit the grass in a vampire-inducing witheredness and sucked their green blood in daylight hours. The bugs, worms and birds were numerous and varied. I let them be, because they always left me enough.

Autumn deceives us by making us believe it doesn't exist. In South-east Queensland at any rate, and seeps into our psyche like mud through a sock. It is mostly balmy, even a hottish pretend balmy. Perhaps spring's reverse, though not as contrasty sharp, or suddenly dry. Autumn longs for an extension of the previous slutty wet season rather than leading us into the icy maiden of winter in its deception of horniness.

Winter was clear blue, was crisp, was Antarctica when the trees captured the sun.

I grew carrots, peas and parsnips, slow, sedate and solacious. The vegetables, too. And yet, winter was a trick, because winter here was not really a season, but an aberration of summer. An aberration of sweat and wet inner thighs which may groan their way towards you at any given minute.

Spring is a sort of new, a new sort of. I mean, in this part of the world, when spring has no snow to melt, and only a few deciduous trees to contend with, it can be a fucking searing ninety degrees. And you long for a crack boom storm to hurry you into the summer rain. While I waited, I planted rocket, bush beans and tomatoes.

Grate carrots, zucchini, sweetbucks, add salt and pepper, an egg, a bit of flour and cumin (or fresh herbs) and drop small bits into hot olive oil. Squash them with the stainless-steel egg flipper. Turn when applicable.

* * *

Trees.
Koda.
A deciduous tree with thick large dense green leaves. Can grows up to sixty-feet. Has clusters of yellow berries. A solid, strong tree with attitude of

confidence within itself and its appearance. Ask anyone who has seen one. Hairy Walnut.

Has big red balls, rust-coloured hairy stems, no shaving to be seen here, move along. Grows to 60 feet.
Bleeding Heart.

Oh God, haven't we got enough of these bastards? No, you can't keep little Mary in because she hasn't done her homework. A pioneer species, i.e., takes over areas that may or may not belong to them. Grows up to thirty feet and its leaves, sort of shaped like a human heart, turn bright red when done with life. And they always hand their homework in on time.
Frangipani.

Fast growing, I mean really fast. You transplant a seedling, move away quickly. Small white and yellow flowers, delicate, like their sharp, sweet scent. What is scent? How does it travel? Why do some scents go further, stay longer or are stronger? Get back to me please. If a scent comes off the frangipani flowers and there's no-one there to smell it, is it still a scent? A scent sent to transcend. A scent meant to make memories. When you walk towards a flowering tree in the springtime, you will either be drawn towards the flowers like you see cartoon characters drifting in the air towards a burger, or you will collapse. There are no other options.
Forest oak.

Rough fissured bark, grows on the driest slopes, never along The Creek. A sort of sparse understorey but also its own person. A confident tree that uses little of the Earth's water resources. Burns hot, hotter than ironbark, coal or nuclear fission. Trust me. Has outward spiralling rays in its orange wood.
Lilly pilly.

Has survived several name changes but they are still ubiquitously common. Red or even purple berries acridly edible. Is grown widely as a hedge in Brisbane.
Silky oak.

Tall, really tall, big-reaching branched rough-fissured trunk. In October the leaves, rather large (leaves mind, not leaflets and it's a huge difference because leaves can be made up of leaflets that look like leaves) fall, and the new sort of isolated showy orange hanging blossoms are edible. For humans as well. You have to push the honeyeaters to the side. The sawn pink timber is divine. It smells, feels and looks wet. Stop it. Easy to seed. I planted 500 so they would be my pension fund. Not a hedge fund, a tree-fund. Funded by me. Silky oaks are also grown in western New South Wales towns. And do well.

Cheese tree.

Substantial. Less than 60 feet. Yep, they produce wee cheeses, little round Edam-like cheeses. Edible? Only by brown pigeons, orioles, figbirds, king parrot and currawongs. Cheese trees will sucker if the roots are compromised. If you so much as look as their roots, they sucker. When you go for a bushwalk and you walk past a cheese tree, well, on your return, there will surely be stacks of cheese tree suckers. 'Ha! You trod on one of our roots before. Saw you.'

Socketwood.

You have to see this to believe it. The branches will pop out under pressure like a hip joint under stress. A natural ball and socket joint. Used in orthopaedic surgery. The trunk has that typical white and green sort of flat lichen and moss rainforest look. Almost a sassafras smell. The leaves are serrated, so much so you can cut bread with one. The new leaves, like a lot of rainforest trees, are small and red twice a year, then turn pale green then dense green. The new leaves are pinky-red because the tree can't, or won't, produce enough chlorophyll, and maybe, just maybe, they do this on purpose to stop predators. I may have made some of that up.

Tamarind.

Can grow to 120 feet. I have seen them thus. Needs perfect conditions, yes, but who wouldn't grow so well under a subtropical umbrella? The late spring fruit is edible but will turn your mouth inside out like eating an unripe lemon. Large leaves and leaflets. Its Asian relative produces more savoury fruit, but let's not take away its beauty, its stature. Just because you're not as sweet doesn't mean you aren't valuable or important or acknowledged or appreciated. I love you, native tamarind.

Foambark.

The leaves contain foam which apparently stuns fish. The yellow outer sed pods make you itchy. A handsome tree, with a trunk full of the white lichen.

Finger lime

A long bright green fruit when ripe. Pops when broken. Yummy tight bubbly taste. Slowest growing bush on the planet, but should be grown commercially.

* * *

Birds.

Lewin honeyeater.

A thickish call, chipchipchip. Has a handy warning call for snakes, cats, your local member and other unwelcome guests. After a while, you can tell

the difference in who might be coming by each call.
Spangled drongo.

Black mermaid tails all. They come in the summertime from under the ocean. Chickachick, plus their squirrelly sound.
Cicada bird.

Elusive shortish grey and black. A continuous call, which at first is a cicada, then becomes so repetitive and consistent that you don't hear it. Straight into the subconscious for retrieval when you hear it forty years later when you are away from the forest.
A cuckoo.

Trilling down the scale softly. With a fan-tail. An olive-backed oriole. A visitor, who says, Twiddly-twiddle where are you?

* * *

First light. I never once woke blinking like a wombat emerging from its hole. I used to, but not anymore. I've seen them do that. They head straight for a greasy hamburger. I woke awake, and always with a stiffy. Every morning awake with a stiffy. A hammer handle, a rocket, a one-page travel guide to enlightenment.

'Nothing better than waking up next to a horn Tony.'

'Thanks hun. I agree. You should see what I do when I wake up not next to but with.'

'You are a little bit disgusting. Thank goodness. What *do* you do?'
Rhetoric at its best.

My fantasies for masturbation were simple, and it was a fun thing to do. And necessary. I mean, I was seeing my sexy girl once a week, but I craved more. And not only did masturbation feel nice, and was preceded by the pleasures of fantasy, it gave the pleasures of physical and mental release, and one that got the warm fuzzies moving in the brain. But it also kept me in trim, so to speak. I would lean over the side of the bed, groan and unload. Don't tread there. There's a big pile.

Sometimes Joan and I would give each a hand job. Didn't mind this, though no-one can do it better than yourself. There we'd be, fully naked and feeling all touchy and sensitive. Soft facing cuddle, lightly touching, hot breathing, no need to say, Do it this way or that way, because we knew. A roaring hot horn and sliding lips. A few thrusts and soft grunts and we'd double-up and spasm. Sometimes we'd do it to ourselves while we touched each other. Now that was better than doing it by yourself alone.

First light. The kitchen would be set up, ready.

Kindling, the coffee pot, the chooks scrap bucket.

I used to dry the eggshells just above the stove then crumble them into the bucket but stopped doing this in case a clever chook liked the taste.

You don't want chooks picking at their eggs.

If one did, the news would spread like wildfire straight after a hot January dust storm.

'Hey Henrietta, you want to eat something really tasty? Know where I can get lots too.'

Deep sleeps, unloaded horns, coffee and happy non-confused chooks. Life at its best.

Straw brooms are amazing.

They may kick up a bit of dust, but they are vigorous agents of togetherness and an association of history. Long-handled straw brooms are items of social inclusiveness and reform. I have seen photos from the end of World War 11 of stacks of French people sweeping their streets with straw brooms. And laughing as they did so. Now there is not only joy, not only cleansing of the footpaths. but a sweeping away of what had just happened. I had a long-handled version and I got stuck into those floorboards. When I had done, I got down on my hands and knees and scrubbed those floorboards. I got satisfaction from an intimate hands-on, knees-on, thorough scrubbing of my floorboards. Then throw open every door and window and let the air finish the job.

* * *

I mostly saved my piss in a bucket. Diluted it and poured it under a citrus usually. Otherwise, I pissed wherever I was. Over the verandah rail, in the garden or up in the forest. To poop back at the pigsty, I had dug a hole up near the forest, laid two planks longways and squatted. Tossed in a cup of sawdust, and covered the hole with a sheet of tin. Squatting to poop is brilliant. The body says, This is a nice way to unload. No pushing, no grunting, just a squat. When I went to poop, I went to poop. Don't get in my way. No crosswords, magazines or bills to pay. Whoosh, out it would come. Big, fat, long, light brown and all done. My ribs sticking to my backbone.

At the house I built an outdoor dunny and it had a pan – a good old Aussie thunderbox. Which I then had to empty when it was full. It wasn't as satisfactory as a hole in the ground, but was practical in the rain or at night. Occasionally, I moonlighted. Far away from the other side.

One of my first chores for grandpa was to tear up the Daily Telegraph into ragged squares. Some newspapers are shiny and smooth, some are a creamy sort of rough. We had an outdoor dunny with a pan. But no soft-arse toilet paper, only newspaper.

* * *

Grandpa had said, 'You'll always have a girlfriend if you can dance. I'll teach you then you practise with a chair.'
  Pretty much right, the old boy.
  'Lead with your left foot, always.
  The man leads, always,
  Even in a sequence dance,
  The man leads, always.
  In rock and roll, you really need to know how to lead, always, and do so frigging quickly.
  The girl starts with her right foot, always.'
  I got a pine chair,
  They're lighter, always.
  'Keep your fuckin' back straight man.
  You're not digging ditches.'
  I could do a slow waltz, and I could hear the music in me.
  Grumpy old cunt bastard, always.
  He drank bitter beer and followed the racehorses. Once he kept a month of my pocket money.
  'I need it. Give you back double after the Cup.'
  Double it you old bastard? How is that going to work?
  His horse won and I ended up wealthy. Bought two houses and a block of flats. Paid his debts, but grumpy, always.

Yet every now and again there was a glint of respect. A glint, mind. He came up to The Creek occasionally. Pottered about. One night we were sitting at a little fire, just looking. He said, out of the blue, ''Spose you turned out alright.' Don't fucking hurt yourself you old cunt.

* * *

I had no radio, no TV, no refrigeration, no electricity. Kerosene lanterns gave me light. Which I didn't really need because when it got dark, I went to sleep. Sometimes I would light a fire outside near the verandah and sit and stare at the flames, the coals, or the nothing that was beyond. In the pitch-black there is a nothing, but this nothing is an everything. Of course, this depends how you see (or don't see, cause it friggin' dark), or what you'd like to see when you think you see something, or a nothing that you imagined. Beauty will come in if you let it, as will fear, as will worry. Depends which one you want. Choose well. Within the beautiful bright blue-black, the heavy black blanket with sparkling sequins, I imagined there would be the wild beasts, stealthily creeping through the forest looking to kill me. But I was always safe sitting next to an open fire, because evil can't come near a fire. Man-made light may bring social benefits, but real light brings primal security. And you can use it to cook.

Thinly sliced carrot and cabbage. Put to the side. Same thinly slicingness with the wallaby. Heat the pan until it screams. Add oil. When the oil was about to ignite toss wallaby in. Add fish sauce. Add chopped garlic, ginger, green eucalyptus leaves and quickly stir. Three minutes. Pour on top of carrot and cabbage.

While eating, toss dead eucalypt leaves, dried sage and lavender onto the hot coals.
Smell deeply
And feel healthy.
And safe.

* * *

I like letters. I'm a big letter writer. Six-foot three. All the letters I wrote I was meaning to send. Every week day I walked the three miles to the mailbox. Three miles one way. Every week day at a time that suited. I posted and I collected from a white box whose door was secured with a latch and a bent nail. The joy of collecting letters was my social highlight at The Creek. Letters were more than a link to the world, or a part of it, they were deeper beings who gave a connection on different levels to emotions, senses and a deeper security. I could get a letter from an old Darling River friend and feel the old river and history and memory and longing; I could get a letter from the coffee shop girl and marvel at how we were so close and free and open; I could get a letter from grandpa and celebrate how far away we were from each other.

* * *

Turmeric, ginger and garlic, all chopped small sort of. Drop in hot olive oil. Bubble, hiss and sizzle. Add finely chopped tomatoes (rich-tasting Romas, ripened on the bush) and simmer down. Add finely chopped Italian parsley, coriander and spring onions. There's a sauce for anything.

On and in the stove, I cooked using cast-iron. The heat transfer was slow and complete, yet can be fierce if needed. Washing up was easy; boiling water, then pop the pot or pan back on the stove to dry. And of course, as everyone knows, you mustn't put a pot with a wet bottom onto the hotplate because you end up pitting the cast-iron hotplate. But not on top for long because cast-iron, as well as causing pits, can burn. Take it off, and when warm to the touch, wipe some oil in with my hand. Just like the rest of us, cast-iron likes a feed and a good feel.

I built a cupboard to store vegetables in. A heavy-duty gauze base, sides, shelves and top, for airflow and to stop insects, rodents and/or possums. A good airflow staves off mould, mildew and mange. Helpful for the vegies too.

* * *

I was given a horse. This lovely giving person obviously did not know about the baldy mare episode, and I didn't let on. Pride. He, the horse, was just that, balls, and all. And I thought that each weekday from now on, I could ride a horse to the mailbox. And pretend I was a real bushman and stuff. We'd just plod and I'd hang onto the reins all loose like I knew what I was doing.

A plod of casual bullshit. A loose rein of false projected ego, and an inside self of trickery that said, Nah, I'm cool.

I walked to his place, a few valleys over, to pick up the horse, and rode him back home. On the way we got up to a canter. Once. Which is fine. I didn't want fucking Phar Lap on a farm. As we sort of canter galloped, I was a bushranger.

'Comeon, trusty steed, don't let the bastards catch us. We are murderers, madmen and outlaws. Take me to safety. Take me to my love who is waiting!'

And as I looked behind at the pursuing police, the hundreds of pursuing police, a branch hit me in the chest and knocked me off the horse.

After I had started breathing properly, and had fought off the thousands of police, with my pistols, sabres and slingshot, and went to leap on my trusty steed, I happened to notice that he was nowhere to be seen.

No wonder Ned Kelly was captured. No wonder Ben Hall never made it.

Wild Colonial Boy, Gilbert, Captain Moonlight, you name them, all let down by a fucking horse.

* * *

Joan would be waiting for me. Thought I got horny. Strewth. Lust that is accepted without judgement is a wonderful thing. It lets confidence blossom, and it asks that you give all. Not to mention, have a sweet, lustful, safe, horny cum. First up we would gently touch each other, sometimes naked sometimes not. After about two minutes the urge was uncontrollable. Rip clothes, grab whatever flesh was nearest.

Who would cum first? Bit of a toss-up really. But it didn't matter.

Accepted lust no matter what.

After the both-quickie,
We became close.
Meaningful in the silence of talking,
Without talking with silence.
Madonna and the whore,
Jesus and the boy slut,
Together
We'd drift off
In a warm drowsy nap.
Stir, roll about …
Throw an arm over,
Then wake
And make
Soft wet kisses done slow,
Rearing to go
Slippery and tight,
Harder with swollen controlled fight.
A deeper pleasure, not as frisky or urgent,
Or quick.

'You like stroking me?'
   Nodded.
   'For lust?'
   Nodded again.
   'But for other, too?'

'Lots of other too.'
'I like.'
'Both?'
Nodded.

Joan said, 'Just one thing mister.'

Here we go. It's never just one thing is it?

'Yeah, only one?'

'I don't want to marry you. I don't want to fall in love with you.'

'They all say that. But that's a fair call. I wouldn't either. I'm unreliable, I stink, I tell lies … you name it.'

I think she was just getting in quickly before things got too cosy or maybe they were already too cosy and she was giving notice. Maybe she was fed up with clingy men; maybe she wasn't rapt in me; maybe deep down she was a lesbian.

I said, 'Don't worry, my sweet, I won't be asking, or wanting.'

* * *

The horse was a fucking homing pigeon. I walked over the seven valleys to collect him. He looked up and said, 'Oh, it's you.' Then continued eating grass.

I did not feel the love.

As we plodded the 300 kilometres back to my place, I said, 'Listen cockhead, you do that under the tree trick again and I'll send you to the fucking glue factory.'

The fences were secure, the gate was locked, and I had paid all my taxes, but the bastard still found his way back home.

From then on, I walked to the mailbox.

* * *

The track to the mailbox down the valley went high around a contour. One time on the way back there was a woman slumped on top of a two-hundred-foot rock face overlooking The Creek. Slumped, head in her hands. I thought, she is either dead or about to be.

'Hey, how you doing?'

'Oh, hi. Yeah, good thanks. Just thinking.'

Of what, when to jump?

'Nice creek you got here, magic creek actually. Did you know that?'

'No, I didn't. Thanks for that.'

A pause. Fairly comfortable, not too long.

'Just having some time alone. Need it. Do you like spending time alone?'

'Nah, be a bastard I reckon. Hey, want to come up for a pot of tea?'

She said her name was Wendy, now renamed Rock Girl About to Jump, shortened to Rock Girl, and she was exhausted, mentally, because of life and her job. 'All I do is get up each morning, shit, go to work, come home, then start again. The pay is okay, but the people I work for aren't nice, nor is home stuff, a home stuff with a controlling partner. I needed to sit awhile in the bush. What about you? I can see you live here alone.'

'I do live here alone and prefer it because I don't like crowds, un-nice people, domestic awfulness, or working for the Man. I am happy here.'

Rock Girl lived in Brisbane and worked in a top-notch real estate office. 'They don't care about the clients. They just use tricks and half-truths. Do you ever get lonely?'

'Sure.'

'Then what do you do?'

'I cry a lot. Sometimes ride it out, or go and talk to someone, about anything. Stare at trees and stuff.'

We paused for a bit and she stared into the mountains. She was a tall strapping red-head, a striking presence, her shoulders still held back in a strong confidence. 'Thanks for the tea. And the talk. I feel a lot better. Can I come back one day?'

'Sure you can.'

'Be my shout.'

* * *

Chipboard in the kitchen is like giving the keys of the cellar to a drunk; it is like giving greasy food to someone on a diet, giving politicians a credit card, giving priests access to choir boys, and it is like giving mining companies environmental approvals. All oxymorons of distaste and inconvenient untruths; all temptations of evil given the tacit almost unwritten winked half-legal green light. I understand that chipboard has a laminated sealed exterior that is waterproof, kidproof and possibly bombproof, but water is sneaky. Rarely does what it says it will do – like drunks, fat people, politicians, priests and mining companies. Or supposed to do. See previous list. All the joins and all the areas that have been cut to say, insert a sink, always leak. And there goes your chipboard. One day you will plop a pumpkin down and

the whole shebang will collapse. And cupboard doors need hinges, and drilling and screwing into chipboard is like motorbike riders. Temporary. I built a hardwood frame. Checked out and bolted with easy access to the plumbing. The benchtops were 10 x 2 tallowwood, the cupboard doors were 3/8 flooded gum that had previously been sump-oiled. Now, after planing, they were a smooth pink with dark edges.
I could safely drop pumpkins.

* * *

Joan and I lived thirty miles apart. We each had our own lives and would come together for sex but also for friendship. It was nice spending time with Joan. I could say what I really believed. And there was no, This is how you should act, Tony, You should think like this, Tony, Your self should be like this, Tony, Why don't you change, Tony?

If she had, I would have been out of there. (And missing the smoking hot sex.) No, my self, my current self, was good with her. And I never commented on Joan's life, no judgments, no advice. Just us together. Because friendship, and that smoking hot sex, can last a lifetime.
No matter what it does.

One morning Joan said, 'Why do you like it doggy-style so much?'
'It's a fantasy, it's a little submission and …'
'And what?'
'… I can see my stiff cock sliding in and out of your tight moist pussy.'
'Hmmm, I'm good with your fantasies, and the submission too, but could we use some mirrors, so I can see your stiff cock sliding in and out?'
'Yes, of course. We'll set it up.'
'Or, I can sit on your lap facing outwards in front of my bedroom mirror. Might be a lot easier. And quicker.'
'And I could then reach around and gently part your pussy and stroke your pleasure button. And look over your shoulder.'
'I'm in.'
'You know, when you wear those short tight skirts, I go nuts over your gorgeous thighs and I wonder how far up your skirt I can see.'
'Without getting busted?
'Sort of.'
'You're sick, Pritchard. But if I had swimmers on, you'd see more.'
'Ah yes, but that's different. With the swimmers, it's accepted and

allowed that I would see more. But with the short skirt, it's sort of naughty and I'm not supposed to see up your dress.'

'Would you like to?'

'Speaking of swimmers, some women have no idea how to dress. Have a look at this lot on the fashion pages, will you? They call themselves the A-List? My God, no fucking idea.'

Joan was fascinated that I could be so judgemental, and catty. Not to mention understand so much about female fashion.

'How do you know about this?'

I catted on. 'A boob-tube? Really? It pulls her breasts down and looks dreadful. She is so pretty, a longer dress, possibly soft and flowy with red with black patterns, would suit her figure. And that one? Jesus, such a high waistline totally destroys her lines and makes her arse look bigger than it is. And what-the-fuck is that!' I hammed it up, and was enjoying it immensely.

'Okay cowboy, how about one day you tell me about a dress I might need to wear to a special day?'

'You are on my precious. Anytime. For a small fee, of course, to which we will discuss the terms and conditions of later. You just need to tell me where you will be going.'

One morning, Joan wore shorts.

'You don't want to let me have my way do you?'

'Because I'm wearing shorts?'

Shrug.

'Watch this.' Joan sat down and the leg bit went all baggy. 'See? Go for it tiger.'

One morning, Joan had on a skirt. 'Is this too short?'

'Well, no. But I guess it depends where you're going.'

'This?'

'O-kay.'

'Or this?'

'Wow.'

'What about this. Too short? I'm goin' nowhere …'

'No, you certainly are not. Come here.'

I loved going to town, yet I hated the real estate firms who falsified, who spruiked, who lied and tricked, just like Wendy had explained. 'They say things that aren't true, and they omit things like, if a place had termites, or a highway was possible, and they nearly always lie about the proposed price.'

I hated the bankers who pretended to care for community, the bankers who broke the law, (who might get caught and pay a fine that you and I really pay), the right-wing cunt farmers who poisoned anything that wasn't connected to their little-dicked hatred, who smashed trees, the lawyers who talked in circles and thought they were virtuous, the councillors who promised empty truths just to be elected for their own benefits and big heads, the state and federal politicians who blatantly lied in shit-smooth grabs and won, the economists who have but one focus and it isn't humanity, and our preferential fucked-up voting system where who I voted for may be changed.

The number of arseholes seems to rise exponentially according to the previous occupations. Some mutate and infiltrate corporations. Some swap roles when they see the writing on the subway walls. I feel better now. I loved going to town. It reminded me I needed to go home.

Economics is not always an automatic saviour, release or reason for being. The opposite maybe. The uniformity of compliance and unchallenged obedience from Western society is fucking scary. The system fucks us all over and spoils things. It spoils it within what we have, what we should have and they don't need to do this because we have it all. Now. Everything we need.

'Oh, it's not us,' they say, 'We work hard to get what we have, and we are just a part of a system that keeps growth at 4.5% annually and provides jobs. It's all about the economy man, the economy that must always override the environment. I think we are doing well. A few more percentage points, a few more dollar values and a few more appropriate advertisements.'

Fair call, but how long can you keep up 4.5%? You dickwad with your divisiveness. All I see is you stealing from the world now, and destroying our future world. A game of greed and deceit using fear and insecurity to control. But it is their fear, a fear of being their real Self, because that would mean they would have to fucking think for themselves.
No, you don't think, therefore you fucking aint.

Occasionally, Friday came around in two days, time does that, and I shuddered at the thought of town and stayed home, but mostly it was nice day, except for the noise, the crass and the justified.

'Acknowledge blackfellas? Sure I do, the poor bastards. But I didn't do anything wrong. I justify my forward existence away from any bad deeds; therefore, I am innocent. Therefore, I don't need to acknowledge it. Fuck, they're doin' alright anyway. Look, there's one now. See, she looks alright.'

The unintelligent town man's reference to blackfellas. And a black woman, whom I knew reasonably well.

Way too many therefores for me.

Discrimination of the culture, the group, the individual, for its own sake, is rife. No, don't do it. Decency is good, the opposite is fuck you. People are people. It doesn't matter where you're from. People have beauty, intelligence, voice, dignity … But not the discriminators, who are a mob of fucken short-sighted racist fucken pig cunts who are constantly looking for an enemy, a made-up enemy of the moment because they are not successful in love, life and within their self. They hate the planet and themselves, not only because they've all got little dicks, can't woo without the derogatory, and are an insecure fucken mummy's boys who are not yet weaned, who suck on the tit of no ticker, of no thoughts of their own, of no idea about people, culture, the planet, and that we are all one and who cares if we are fucking black, Asian, or refugees. We are all different yet all the same within the difference.
We all love, we all aspire, we all care, and we all deserve respect.

* * *

occasionally
I hated their hatred
their anger
their arrogance disguised as confidence
their bravado concealing their fear
occasionally
despair hits me like I was
tranquilised
anaesthetised,
a successful operation of despair
here, take two of these twice a day
occasionally
which way to go
which way to be
occasionally
I wanted to be

consumerised
conformatised
conventionalised,
you'll need more than two pills twice a day for this
yet I wanted to belong
I wanted to be like them
secretly not even secretly
I felt not so much unloved as not belonging
not belonging yet not wanting to belong,
occasionally.

* * *

I felt loathing against those who weren't nice. To those who put others down because they can, to those who aren't accepting or acknowledging or at least a smidgeon of understanding. To those who take without giving back, to those who are destroying the planet. Must tell Wendy about all this.

And yet, I had a nag. Nags came from my rational brain and were a reminder that I was either a false piece of shit, or I needed to heed this warning. A nag is a worm that wriggles toward our truth, a worm from behind there somewhere that does not and will not go away by sheer avoidance, a worm that says, I am within you, your deepness, a reminder that something is missing from your conscience and your day-to-day, and there's a big chance you are a fucking dickhead, so get a grip. I chose to ignore the nag, knowing that he will haunt me forever unless I acknowledge him and deal with the issue.

Tony, ignore me at your peril. You are denying your convenient double standards, those blatant convenient pretend guilt-free freedoms, the Yes, but it's not me, as you reap the benefits of years of civilisation, hardship, wars, colonialism, beauty, rape, torture and murder. You lecture, you rant, and you do not do what you say. And you do not put back. So, stop it will you?

But I lopped its head off with a self-righteous on-purpose karate chop, as I topped up with fuel, kero, and put some money in the bank.

* * *

I was thinking, Joan, you're my girl,
And I love you,

I love your lust
Our us and our together us lust.
But, my sweet, is there more?
Are we enough?
And I felt a little bad for thinking so,
Now there is confusion that does not come from a lacking
Of whatever is wanted, or maybe missing,
It comes from somewhere else.
An else above me
And what little I know,
From me.
In town.
To see my Joan.

She said, 'Hey, you are different today. I can tell. One day tell me why. But
hey, it's nice to see you. We like being together yeah?'
'Yes. You mean rooting?'
'That too. But I feel relaxed with you.'
'Our menstrual cycles will be in sync shortly.'
'Doubt it. You're way overdue.'
'You're right. And I'm overdue to be more kind to you. And yes, it is
really nice being together.'

And then we hugged,
Deeply.
Nothing more was said
Nothing needed to be said.
Probably ever.
Because deep friendship can last a lifetime,
No matter what.
No matter a wavering, no matter of a different today.

'Ever wondered why we aren't making babies?'
'Sheesh. All the time ... No, not really, I just assumed ... Okay yes, I
have thought about it. Maybe one of us is infertile?'
'You're bullshit.'
'I pull out every time?'
'Please.'
'I use condoms?'

'Jesus, spare me. You wouldn't know one if it bit you on the arse.'
'You win.'
'One day I might stop taking.'
I had no response.

And I was troubled
Because even though I loved my town days,
I really loved my town days
Despite the Others who pissed me off
Despite an awakening of a misguided self-righteousness
My new, I am superior.
I loved my Joanee, my fresh dairy, my sweet-hit chocolates, my coffee shop girl,
But I was troubled.
I was troubled because my thoughts weren't true of me, what I really believed,
And therefore, was I not true? Was I not my true self?

* * *

Peace and harmony, all through us, all the time, is not to be expected surely, because the us are corrupted by others, but mainly by ourselves. But can the not unexpected be a constant peace and harmony and sharing within love? Forever? And save the planet as a by-product of the us, no matter who we are and what level of peace and harmony we may have, or strive for, is pollution? Oceans, soil, forests, air, rivers, our bodies … Can we, as a species, a planet, accept less to curb this?
What can one person do?

* * *

I like letters. Kindness comes in letters.
'You knew. I could tell that you knew, but you were kind enough to let me find my way through you. I feel much better. Thank you. See you soon, Wendy.'

* * *

Joan said, 'So. You like coffee I hear?'
Jesus. This is small town gossip at its best, this is talk over the neighbour's fence every day, and this is perhaps not direct spying, but fucking close to it. Or was it all done just to reinforce a belief?

'Yes, she does make great coffee.'
How long before she would mention Wendy the Rock Girl?

* * *

Wendy the Rock Girl called in. 'Hey, can I stay for a bit?'

I nodded. 'Sure you can. Please come in.'

'I wrote to you, yes? I brought things.' She was so lovely, so genuine. I made us tea and we shared her pastries. 'It's so nice up here.'

'Not bad I suppose. Yes, your letter, thank you. You doing okay?'

'No. I'm not.' She breathed in deeply, savoured her tea. 'I'm going to leave him.'

'Big call. You scared about all this?'

'Yes, a little, no, a lot, but I don't care. He will get angry, he may beat me, again, he will take all I own, but I know, I will be free.'

Tears squeezed themselves out, and slid quietly down her sweet melancholy. And yet within this soft sadness, she still had a smile. A relief, a release, and an entry into a more peaceful future.

She came into my arms. 'Thank you so much for listening to me, for helping me feel good about me.'

'Any time. Keep in touch?'

'I would love to. Actually, I'm thinking of moving into town. See you in there.'

* * *

Henry's dog was an old red kelpie named Fergus. A handsome boy who noticed me. Anyone who is handsome and notices me, I want to pat. He accompanied Henry every day he rode up the valley to cut lantana, that noxious invasive shrub.

'Henry, can I pat him?'

Asking because for starters, he was a working dog. Secondly, because he wasn't mine.

'Yes, and when you do, start at his shoulder.'

I did, and Fergus grinned. Not at me, he was eyeing off every mouthful Henry made from his salami and pickle sandwich.

'Henry, don't you feed him, the lazy little shit?'

'No, why would I do that? You think he's lazy? I loaned him to an old bush mate who worked him too hard and now he overheats. Fergus, not the idiot. He must have little sips of water like a chook. Or run away and sit in The Creek.'

'Mustn't have fed him either.'

'Correct. Fergus is also not particular about whom he mounts. Have you noticed?'

I had. Fergus humped any and every dog that couldn't run away. And I mean dogs, not just bitches.

'Not catching is it?'

'Nor is it compulsory, so we're right for a bit.'

Henry tossed Fergus a piece of sandwich.

One of Australia's narratives belongs to its dogs; thylacines, dingoes, cattle dogs, kelpies, including Fergus. I met a man who had patted a thylacine. He said, 'The bastard turned and bit me on the arse.' And that is why you have to ask before you pat, and then start at the shoulder.

Thylacines aren't dogs, I know that. They are marsupials.

* * *

Art and science occasionally get married, but they'll never have children. Because together they are sterile, just like the offspring of horses and donkeys.

I had a hydraulic ram, the result of a newly wedded art and science couple, and a couple who weren't told about the no-kid thing till way after their honeymoon. Art, who is female, then said, *What? No kids? I am out of here.* Science, who is male (you know, the usual mix of arrogance, privilege, entitlement, inappropriate aggression, an inability to discuss emotions, or in fact, an inability to discuss anyfuckingthing to do with conflict, fairness or another point of view, particularly one that is female, or in fact, any gender other than his own, or people who aren't white) said, *Fine, see if I care. You come back; I'll punch you.*

See? Told you.

But science's male counterparts, the ones who have real balls, spoke up and said, *Hey, he does not speak for all of us. We might be physics, engineering, mining, we might be machines, but we want children too. And we don't punch women.* But they were not respected, in this instance, because they had a dick, and were therefore deemed threatening to her. And rightly so. You want the girl, you want Heaven?

You fucking well leave her alone.

A hydraulic ram is pure female art and should not have married Mr Science. Told her too. I said, You are too beautiful for science, too serene for science, too sweet for science. You should have married a male tradie. He will love you for you. He will adore you forever. Tradies are like that. Pure art that is pure male yet with a feminine side that is adorable.
All male tradies out there, you now owe me.

The hydraulic ram is a simple construction that pushed water uphill using energy from falling water. It is a water pump that uses no electricity, no combustion engine, and no cock.

This is how it works. Redirected creek water runs through a two-inch galvanised pipe to a cemented 44-gallon drum which gave a ten-foot head over fifty feet. The ram was a large hunk of cast iron shaped like a cardinal's hat that is bolted onto a rock. The force of the water shuts a valve on the bottom side of the ram. The water hammer, the most amazing and powerful force on the planet except for lust, just ask the cardinals, archbishops and priests (for starters, then move on to sports' coaches and a sprinkling of cops, nuns and teachers), strikes back up through the down-coming water and finds a weak spot; a seated valve at the base inside the sealed cast-iron ram. This forced a squirt of water up into the compressed air inside the ram. The squirt is forced down, which slams shut the valve it just opened. The squirt is pushed up the delivery pipe to a tank. This released the hammer effect and the whole process starts over. At two-hundred and fifty-foot head height I got four hundred gallons a day. Every day. It never stopped. Four hundred gallons of creek water every day, plus rainwater going into the same tanks.

Science, for all its innovations, is destructive and invents and leaves death way more than it saves lives. It is forceful and logic yes, but it is never, and I mean never, sexy. Science rarely cares about people, as individuals because surely the individual, the one person, is the smallest group and surely this one person has as much right as a group, or a community, or a society, or a culture, or a race, or a country, or the Earth, because when it does try to give understanding through its flawed one-fucking-sided perceptions, it alienates through its rigid dominance. Through its, You who oppose me are whacky.

Art in all its forms, and in all its earlier peoples, can bring the human species to a place of reconciliation, general understanding of others, and world peace. Think oral stories, literature, dance, music and the colour and form of visual art. Their sensuousness, their pure love, and their depictions of raw sex. Is there something else I have missed?

Our collective histories are art. Confusion and division at times for sure, but pure beauty and community belong within art and civilisation and no matter what your stance, they can lead us towards international peace. Art by itself, if it chooses, can make pretty children.

They are called Gods.

Thank God for art and females. That's all I got to say.

* * *

Plumbing fittings are male or female, based so on human genitalia. Let me guess which gender started this.

'Yairs Fred, I'll just have two male iron pipe threads and half a dozen female iron pipes thanks.'

'No worries, Kev. What, are you having a fucking love-in or something?'

Can't remember the last time I saw a thread in a pussy though. My cock hangs right to left. Which is an undoing thread. Unless you're on the left side of a truck. The plumbing world is inclusive and voted well. Female one end, male the other; almost a negative action versus an affirmative action. Hermaphrodite maybe? A female elbow, with an inside thread each end. Lesbian. A fitting with outside male thread on each end. Gay.

'Yairs Fred, I'll have two queers, three gays and a trans today thanks.'

'No worries, Kev. I can get you the first two, but I'm clean out of the last one. They're all in the workshop having work done.'

All of the above are dodgy calls because they mix sex with gender. Which are way different.

Just ask Joan.

'Do you ever fancy a threesome? As in, me and you with a girl?'

'At the minute, that is not high on my fantasy list, but I guess it would be pretty exciting. And because it would be with another girl, I wouldn't feel threatened or intimidated by a male who was better looking, as fucking if, or possibly had a bigger cock, same comment, and stuff like that. I'm interested I suppose. Why, you have someone in mind?'

'No I don't. But I do have fantasies about it occasionally.'

'Okay, when the time comes, I'm in.'

On forms to be filled in, there's a wee box that says, *Sex.*

Hmmm, let me see, *Last Friday at 0800 hours.*

Why would you need to know that? Thought I was merely completing a

driver's licence renewal. Joan would pull her black hair up and stick in a long wooden pin, perpendicular like. She had to be careful going through doorways. I thought she might use it to stab me like you see in the movies. Her neck was gracious like a gazelle's, strokable like an Egyptian pharaoh's and with her hair all wispy and uncontrollable, was damned arousing even without the sex. And when I did stroke her neck, softly, when I did kiss her neck softly, and one morning when I said softly, 'Hey you black girl I love you.'
She turned and gave me the most beautiful kiss ever invented.

* * *

If you run your water pipes inside a wall, or under a concrete slab, you need your head read. And your psych report would read thus:

'He is erudite, compassionate, and skilled.
An honest, hardworking, loyal tradie,
Yet obviously not qualified to work with pipes,
(Regardless of his, or her sexuality).
Is mediocre, ordinary and even second-rate.
And basically, has no fucking idea.
Get another plumber.
Rather quickly.'

All pipes must be visible and therefore accessible. Wasting your time otherwise. Heard someone say that before. Three-quarter inch copper pipes clamped together onto walls,
Are sensuous and beautiful
No matter what their gender/sexuality (not that it is anyone else's business. Except for those the pipes choose it to be).
Copper pipes that have elbows are ice-skaters going around a corner, forwards or backwards.

Regardless, they are the fit bodies.
The hand in the crutch
The toss into the air,
The melding as one to get a perfect score
With a Bolero,
And they are electric wires on a winter's day,
Humming, stretching and singing
Like Glen Campbell.

The Creek

I stroked my copper pipes often,
And I liked their joins to be coupled with olives and nuts,
And few slices of Serrano ham.
A bit of compound smeared under the join,
Thread tape the same way as the thread,
And tighten with two spanners,
Leaving a bit of thread just in case.
Soldered joins are for those still having their head read.

'Is true, resolute and solid.
However, this person has not responded to the remedial sessions,
And will therefore have to redo the plumbing course.
That will be $2,000 thanks.'

* * *

To town
In the Dodge.
Down a gravel road, early, a crunchy slow gravel road,
One laned, exciting and aware.
A windy gravel road that might throw you over its edge,
Which it has done to others before who were excited but not aware.
Past dairies,
With long swinging blotchy pink bags.
Soggy wrinkly after early morning,
Tighter on the way home.
Opposite of mine.
Waving to Danny and Vicky, Sid and Ray, Brian and Lorraine in their
cultivations of
Corn, lucerne and oats.
Pumpkins for sale
Another roadside attraction.
Huge Queensland blues
In a trailer
Next to an honour box.
They're honourable.
Then it's your choice to be so.
One house had no electricity wires.

A father and son lived there. They had cows and calves, no pasture just grass, and carried cream cans in the back of their black 1940's car. Which had running boards that extended into mudguards. Rumour had it that they use kero lanterns. For inside lighting, not in the Chicago car.

In town.

The corner shop had bulk foods. I brought my own containers and paper bags in and bought brown rice, red lentils, and the Earth. At the hardware shop the nails were weighed in pounds, any tools were placed to the side and their tags saved. A young person wrote all the costs down on a piece of paper not unlike a small version of butcher's paper, and then added them up, with the carry over numbers all above the sum.

Please God, save me from barcodes, and give me people who work at a pace then lets breath give extra life and give meaning to a transaction, to a purchase, to a sale, to life.

In town.

Joan said, 'Want to show you something.'

'Again?'

'Yep.' She stood up, spread her legs a bit and lifted her skirt.

About now, she had my full attention. My psychologist says I'm making fair progress.

She pointed and beckoned me to kiss her pussy.

She said, 'Go really softly, yes, yes, that's it. Oh yes, that's it alright. Hmm. Oh God!'

I was enjoying it too, don't you worry. The giving of pleasure, and the acceptance of same. And I was stroking my cock, too, don't you worry. I pulled her pussy lips gently with my lips, gently yet firmly. Then ran my wet tongue up and down her softness and her little button of pleasure.

'Oh that is so nice! Where did you … Okay stop stop; and I'll show you the something.'

Joan lay down, bent her knees back and started to rub her clitoris, easy at first then frenetically. Me, I continued stroking my cock and denying my latest medical assessment.

'Oh Oh! Watch this watch this!'

She urgently straightened her legs, tightened her muscles steely tight as she kept furiously rubbing. And she grunted and pushed and made noises in her throat. Her face turned bright red, flecks of spit scattered from her lips and she screamed and spasmed and flopped up and down, wildly, flaying her arms. I thought for a minute I'd be tending to a corpse. With a ton of explaining to do.

'GOD! That was good! Hang on a tick I get my breath …' She drew in deeply a few times. 'Last week after you went, I was still horny …'

'Really?'

'… and because the edge had been taken off it took me longer to come. But when it started, I tensed like I just did, and holy smoke it was powerful. I held my breath, I tightened my leg and tummy muscles and I pushed down, hard, like I was trying to have a pee. Then the orgasm started and rose like a dolphin coming up vertically from the seabed. When the dolphin broke through the surface, she smashed the pleasure barrier. Booom.'

'That is amazing Grace. Can you do something with this?'

Foreplay at its finest.

* * *

Wendy had moved into town. She started a brand-new real estate office. This was weird to me, because I hated real estate agents, yet I certainly liked Wendy.

* * *

I tried Joan's method of tightening muscles, pushing, and holding the breath to reach orgasm, and my goodness she was right; it was powerful. It's not like you can do without a partner, it's the opposite.

It enhances your partner.

And if she is understanding and safe to you, it enhances the pleasure by ten. But the edge must be taken off, otherwise it's just a stinging hot pleasure of ejaculation done as quickly as you can. Joan was understanding of me. And I was fortunate.

* * *

The barber was an old bloke, ginger hair, long sideburns, who read girlie magazines while he waited for a customer. I did the same while I waited for the barber. A reciprocity of tits. He knew my usual short back and sides and leave the top please. Just like my grandpa's. And don't touch my beard or I'll bend your fingers. I liked the stability and confidence from my regular barber, the links to my heritage, his lame jokes and his Product he swore by, which was shit. It was a fake-smelling smooth paste that could be used instead of cement to fix a corner post. But he had consistency and I had security.

One day, he wasn't there.

A young woman said, Bonjour. Ça Va? and led me to the chair.

I said, 'Where's the blue fella?'

She ignored, and gowned me up.

Then ran her hands through my hair. Several times.

'What eef I treem 'ere, and 'ere, theenn that bit there, and broosh the front thees away?'

I said, 'Ce serait doux. I'm good with a short back and sides. Be gentle though.'

Her hand spidered the top of my head and she controlled me with a soft pressure. I don't mind being controlled with a soft pressure. An assertive, understanding, strong, but gentle control, as she scooped the cutters up and back.

Her swarthy Frenchness was curvy smooth, her black chopped scraggy hair was sexily alluring, and she leaned into me. She brushed her pert breasts and her red lips into my dreams. Long black eyelashes, green cat eyes, and no bra.

'Could I treem your eyebrouse?'

If you keep leaning into me like that you can cut my fucking head off. The hairdryer, the hot hairdryer, followed by a thin spiky brush took over my reason. I became untrue, deceitful, I became loose, open-legged, and hers.

I said, 'I will leave my wife and children for you.'

'No fanks, I already 'af a girlfren'.'

When she rubbed my head and face with a warm face towel, stroked my neck, and scrunched my hair, sort of roughly, I also mentioned, that if she was interested, I would be her sex slave forever.

She said, 'Wif my girlfren'? Pardon m'sieur, mais, tu es Francais?'
Her name was Georgie.

* * *

Joan said, 'Woo, nice haircut. You are lookin' good. By the way, slut, it's my turn.'

'Again?'

'Could you paint my toenails?'

'Yes I will. That's it?'

'That's it.'

That wasn't it.

I was to sit next to her and lightly lean across her legs as I painted. I still carry vivid images of looking up the shortest tightest skirt ever invented. A tee shirt had more respectable manners. Her choice, mind. She would lean her head back in an ecstasy that comes with being stroked, being in control and having a fantasy come to life. The girl had no pants on and no self-control. I was quite okay with all of this. After two nails she opened her legs.

One morning she had me painting from in front of her sweet toes looking up the same shortest tightest skirt ever invented. A singlet had more decency. After one nail done, she opened her legs and bent them back. Pants previously removed.
Why would she do that?
She knows I have no self-control.

I said, 'My turn.'
    'Again?'
    'You know how you shave your legs …'
    'Hmmm, I do,' she said, stroking her shiny legs right up to where her curvy thigh gap was, her enticing kissable thigh gap pretty close to heaven.
    She knew I had little self-control.
    '… Well, could you shave your pussy too?'
    'Sure, I could do that.'
    'Then I can stroke and kiss your gorgeous smooth mound. And your pussy lips. My God, they are so delicate and soft …'
    'There's more?'
    'You're onto me. Could you also let your armpit hairs grow?'
    'Kidding me.'
    'No, the French beauties in the sixties had armpit hair.'
    'In case you've missed something, I'm not French and it's not the sixties.'
    'Damn, I knew it! You're too black. And I'd better change the calendar. But you are spunky, and you do love me …'
    'Oh please. Tell you what, I'll give it a go. There's still more, isn't there?'
    'Just one more. I swear. Could you not wash for a few days before I come in? Please?'
    'You're a disgusting sick puppy. And hey …'
    'Hey what?'
    '… what do you mean I'm too black? You watch it buddy. Speaking of hairy French armpits, you watch out for that hairdresser chick.'

* * *

On hot days at The Creek, really hot days, my sweat dripped like water off a melting glacier that wasn't supposed to melt yet. My singlets become saturated and had white stains from my salt, or whatever it was that sweated out. Shorts and no undies. I never wore underpants. What a waste of the Earth's resources they are. Undies hurt my groin, undies keep the sweat and salt in, and when you have that mixture, you have a rash, a raw red fiery rash. I ran my thumb between my thigh and my balls and smelled maleness, humanity, the earth and the Earth. This beautiful a smell should be bottled. No chemically made perfumes that you must have simply to be a part of the cool people. Try an Aussie male, say, around thirtyish, shorts and a blue singlet, sweaty as hell. Probably a tradie, the beginning of a beer belly, hairy as a wild animal. No young skinny things strutting and pouting, with secrets, just a real man.

'Here you sheilas, get a load of this.'

And he would wipe his thumb and then draw in a deep, satisfying sniff. 'Girls, settle. Take a number. You can buy this in recycled stubbies or old Vegemite jars.'

The fashion worlds of Paris, Milan, New York and Brisbane would never recover.

Must tell Joan.

* * *

Hoop pines grow green cones,
And if these fall on your head, you will probably say, 'Ouch,'
Or something similar.
Though not as loudly if the fallen cone was from a Bunya pine.
Which are not found at The Creek.
And these, and possibly your head, turn brown in the summer.
Seeds are layered in these brown cones, like a dry-stone wall,
Are a flat seed with a sharp point,
With sides like glider possum's skin flaps,
And on strong windy days they peel and scatter.
Exceedingly fast rotating seeds dispersed across
A brown sky with whirring clattering dry-stones.

* * *

One week between drinks I did not masturbate. This was way more fun than I thought. I had sexy thoughts to put me asleep as I grabbed my strokey cock,

but stopped before coming. In the first-of-light mornings, I had to get out of bed quickly or else I'd trip. Overall, a nice soft pleasure without the happy ending. Touching Joan the first time after this was electric, full of sparks and insatiable pleasure, that needed to be speedily satiated. My cock screamed, 'Let me be me! I want to find my true self!' A shared eroticism that is accepted no matter who comes first is a gift, an honour.
Joan had said she would try the same.

One morning, after I knocked, and I liked that as a respect, I liked the not taking for granted, and I liked the honour of politeness, Joan said, 'For Christ's sake, get you fucking arse in here!'

I like honour, I like respect, but fuck me, I like in my face pussy better. And anyway, non-politeness shared and accepted is a good display of manners. I took a quick look into her glazed eyes and I thought, Here we go. Her skin was glossy, her lips were full, her limbs were loose. She lounged on me. She lifted her skirt and leaned her glistening sex on me. She groaned even before I touched her.

'You know how you said you didn't masturbate one week? You fucking idiot, and why would you do that? Well, anyway, yes I gave it a go too. So fuck me will you?'
Life's tough when you know you're about to have someone else.

Joan said, 'I now have regrowth. And I don't mind it. It looks a bit slutty.'

'Open your legs and show me?' I said, a little more demanding than I would have preferred.

'Oh, alright, you pushy thing you.'

'Sorry sorry. Wow, that is indeed a bit filthy. May I please stroke?'

'Hang on, after you've just insisted, I open my legs and show you everything, now you're being Mr Polite? Fuck you Pritchard, get your head down there and kiss my pussy.'

* * *

I needed some money, so I worked.

I pulled the tassels off corn as I stood on the front tray of a tractor.
I painted houses and sheds.
I fenced.
I picked up sticks from paddocks.
I helped at the local mechanics.

I tidied up at the plumbers in town.
At the sawmill with Joe.

A certain breed of corn needed to be fertilised only by a certain other breed of corn. I know, the world has moved on from, Let's just grow a crop of corn. And new corns need to be tested that they be true. So here I was, helping someone else to be true. A true selflessness of true self. Must admit, it was exciting. Not being at the forefront of agricultural research which may or may not save millions of lives, or aiding a true self to be realised, but at the forefront of a moving tractor, grabbing tassels and removing them so they could not be fertilised because one slip and I would be the fertiliser.

'Where's Tony?'

'Oh, he'll be back a bit later, He's still out there helping the corn grow.'

I painted houses and sheds. And I knew what I was doing because grandpa taught me. 'No,' he said, 'You cannot just paint that on top of that. You must first peel off the old paint with a paint scraper, then sand, maybe linseed oil, a bit of spot primer, sand, some undercoat, sand, and two finishers.'

These were the good old days when water-based paints were the new kid on the block and oil-based paints ruled. And linseed oil was second in charge. Beautiful oily linseed oil, so smooth, so luxuriously smooth. A smooth like no other. And the bare newly-sanded timber cried out for it.

If you rush and take short cuts when you fence, the world condemns you. The world says, 'You what? You didn't stay that corner post properly? Strain that wire correctly? What sort of dickhead are you?'

By its very nature, highly-strung wire, its pills, its psych appointments, and its own pre-disposed self-analysis, must adhere to its own wire-mindfulness. You rush, you die. If you don't go carefully, high-tensile wire has a habit of springing back and removing your head. Not to mention not doing a fence line correctly and having to come back five years later and do it properly. That's if you still had a job. Or a head. The corner posts, as thick as overweight telegraph poles, had to be dug in 900 mm. And to make them plumb was easy. No spirit level needed. One would stand back a bit, squat and eye the post. And perchance you set it in crooked, well you merely indicated that, No, my post is plumb, it's the ground that's out of whack. Each corner must be stayed. As opposed to not being able to move? Go and have a cup of tea. If there's a corner, the stay must split the angle; if there's just one line of fence, the stay must line up with the line. And a stay must be a long massive hunk of wood, either blocked in the ground with a flat rock or, in the case of walking the line, its base must be at the base of the last, or first, fencepost. And it must be checked into the corner post, not too high, not too low.

Picking up sticks was a tough gig. Bend, pick, straighten, and toss the stick into a moving bin. The paddocks had to be cleaned for those dead-straight cucumbers, those only slightly bent bananas, those money-hungry supermarkets, and those privilegedly fooled precious shoppers.

The back yard at the plumbers was a mess. The tradies returned to base and dumped their shit everywhere. These tradies were gorgeous for sure, but were not the ones to marry, so move on art girl. I went hard at it soon as I got there till I went home. No breaks. I resorted, repacked and restacked. The pay was ordinary, but I got cost on pipes and stuff.

And I condemned the disrespect and the dishonour of work shown by most of the tradies. Surely a job is a job? A job to keep, to be true to, to be respected as a true worker, and an inner thing to know that, Yes, I have done well today?

At the sawmill. Joe's humour was drier than a ten-year drought. A local brought in some hoop pine logs and was all Hail fellow well met. I moved to the side, out of range. As he leaned against the mill corner post, with his arms folded, Joe killed him. 'You sweep them up with a broom? Better go away and replant them eh?'

When freshly milled, red gum smelt like rancid butter; spotted gum was yellow and clear; tallow wood greasy, and bloodwood has blood rings.

One searing-hot morning I was up on the mill roof, helping Joe replace some rafters.
'Jeez, this is hard work.'
Joe paused for a bit. 'Well, if it was hard work, then your arsehole would be sticking out so far you could cut washers off it. Maybe you'd better check.'
I didn't look around.

When the mill was slow, I went with Joe to his scrub block to plant grass clumps and chop lantana. His scrub was a hundred acres and was literally next to the high-level rainforest above The Creek downstream from me. Some of his scrub was cleared with pasture for his cows, some was eucalypt forest and some was natural rainforest. It had steep gullies, lemonade springs, rock-candy mountains and a huge patch of rainforest teeming with king parrots, lyrebird and topknot pigeons,

King parrots are large and long. Not as fatbig as a white cockatoo but bigger than a rosella in a sort-of rosella shape. The male is bright red with green wings. Noisy buggers but in a nice way. Not raucous but melodically noisy.

Prince Albert lyrebirds are found in the border ranges between Queensland and New South Wales. They are a chestnut-brown, rufous russet-coloured bird, more like a chook than a chook. Except for the silver tail that can go over the male's head. Which shimmers. Mesmerisingly so. Roosters can do some nice shimmies too, with that lowered wing thing when they strut, but they can't do that, they won't do that. Albert often goes to performing arts centres where he dances and sings in Languages Other Than English. Expansive, melodic, rachety, metallic, sharp, rickety and sugary sweet. Laughing kookaburra, king parrot, satin bower bird, currawong, catbird, yellow-tailed black cockatoos, whip bird, wonga pigeon, Lewin honeyeater, rosella; and I found out, they can also mimic a 1954 Dodge truck.
Some men will do anything to impress a female.

The sprawling strangler fig trees bears a yellow-orangey coloured fruit, and this is sought after by many species of bird, including the topknot pigeon. A fat grey bird with a dodgy haircut. Hundreds will descend and gorge on the figs, and squabble, flap about, and even hang upside down like fruit bats. Joe told me that he has seen, just before the arrival of the pigeons, over twenty carpet snakes in the fig tree.
Waiting.

* * *

If you don't start something because you think it will take a long time to finish, well, the time is going to pass anyway, so what the fuck – make a start anyway. And if you don't start something because you think it will be too expensive, too difficult, or that you may stuff up because you have no idea how to do it, well, what the fuck make a start anyway. Avoidance is not a valid reason to not live life. I learnt that off Henry. I think. Not the nomination of Henry, but my whether I had learnt it or not. I had a vegetable garden, and I wanted an orchard. I wanted fruit trees of many varieties and even different varieties within a variety. Healthy fruit, organic, independent, and exciting. The best site for an orchard was just to the west of the house. It was close, had protection from winds and storms through a forest on the western edge, and it was a flatish area with a gentle slope for drainage. The site was also chock full of lantana, crofton weed and tobacco trees, all introduced rubbish.

To clear this and build fences, would take me at least a hundred years to accomplish. I would need several sharp brush hooks, posts, wire, netting, timber for a gate and the fruit trees themselves. This was a daunting task, a massive task, an almost too difficult task, and I did not know how to do it. I needed a cup of tea and a lay down.

But a start it needed, because a start on a daunting job can add up to a finish, and it can diminish most known avoidances, and just maybe, these small starts could give joy, inspiration and success. Or at least a start takes you a bit closer to the chequered flag of life, to the came away with the two points comment, through the deep satisfaction that is given during the process of completion.

Joe and his D4 bulldozer said they would push the rubbish away from where I wanted the orchard. He said, 'No payment. Work it off at the mill.' Back in the old days, I used to lay in front of bulldozers. Now I stand behind and direct them. Joe pushed the lantana, crofton weed and tobacco trees into a huge pile, clanking his way around, the bulldozer rearing up almost vertically to do so. He said, 'Wait till winter then drop a match in it.' I did. A savage scary angry orange flame with black smoke. Little critters scrambling in all directions. Fork-tailed kites sending me thank you cards.

I used a one-man crosscut to saw down my corner posts from up in the forest and dragged each one down with a rope over my shoulder. One per day. On the steeper sections, the fuckers skidded faster than I was dragging and tried to take me out. I used 2 x 1 wooden stakes in between the corner posts and worked extra in town to pay for netting and tie wire. I used 12-inch strip netting at the base of the three-foot high netting to stop wallabies and bandicoots from pushing under. I used 6 x 1 hardwood to build a medieval gate that required a solid meal before attempting to push it open. It took a while, but then, so does life if you don't live it; and now I had my orchard.

Avocados.
The fruit does not ripen on the tree. You store them on the tree until you're ready. Which saves heaps of cupboard space. So how do you know when to pick the bastards? Size maybe. Darker colour if they are Hass. Bit of trial and error really. Pick a couple, put them in a paper bag to capture their

ethylene which helps the ripening process. If you add a ripe banana to the mix for God's sake don't light a match. A ripe avocado has a yellow centre and a green edge and the taste is a buttery yellow nut flavour. I had several varieties for several times of the year.

Persimmons.

These days they won't turn your mouth inside out if you bite a green one. In the old days you'd see people walking around with awful looking mouths. It's horrible when they try to speak. Heaps in Canberra. Several varieties will be ready at different times. Some turn rotten. Like in Canberra.

Custard apples

Are not individually economical to eat, as in, there's a lot of seed stuff. But the natural side bits are so floury-sweet, sugar ants will follow you around. I had two varieties.

Citrus.

I like citrus. So many different varieties. The Creek wasn't the best place because of the heavy soil, but they coped. Mandarins, navels and lemons. That'll do.

Mangoes.

I removed the first flower set in case of cool weather. A wide tree up to twenty metres. I pruned the top to encourage branching so I could climb up and get the fruit. The smell of a ripe mango, that you have grown is up there for the world's best sweetest smell. I grew strawberry mangoes and lemon mangoes. The tree self-pollinates. I do that sometimes too.

Figs.

I had a purple Turkish, which was lush. I also had a white Mediterranean. This fruit went from light green to light yellow when it ripened.

Stone fruit.

I tried early bearing stone fruit to beat the summer fruit fly. What a farce. What a friggin waste of time. The Queensland fruit fly will beat you hands down. I tried a deterrent I had read about. I pissed into a tin and hung it in the peach tree. After a couple of days, it was so revolting, so potent, that animals in neighbouring countries leapt off cliffs to avoid the stench. Fruit flies got bigger from drinking it. Had parties, got pissed. I buried the tin so I could sleep at night, then ripped the trees out and burnt them.

* * *

Bulldozers.
Rusty yellow clanking,

Scarring-white rocks with their blades,
Splintering trees with a sap-inducing smell,
And shattering their splintered aromatic bodies.
Gouging the earth
Ripping the earth,
With their caterpillars.

'My name's Tony,
I like bulldozers.
And I want more.'
'Wooo, that's hardcore Tony. How long have you had this problem?'
'Since yesterday.'
'You sure you're in the right program?'
'Isn't this Hypocrites Anonymous?'

* * *

Cicadas screeching in the ironbarks down The Creek a bit made sounds that were just below the pain threshold. Mine not theirs. After a few hours I would have hearing loss. Like working at a sawmill on the inside bench without earmuffs. The males of three or four different species will often sing together to attract a mate. Their calls come in waves, undulating painful waves. This is where the idea of karaoke came from. Then they all stop at exactly the same time, like a lead guitarist who gives a nod to the band. The combination screeching is also to deter birds that prey on them. After I walked through a screaming bunch, now currently deaf, and they all had pissed on me, I must admit I didn't feel like eating them either. Double drummers, green grocers and yellow Mondays. Over seven hundred species in Australia. Imagine if they all got together. All our birds would migrate to New Zealand.

'Hey,' they would all say, in different whistles, hoots and screeches, as they approached customs, 'We accept all your cast-offs and let them be known as Aussies, so now it's your turn, please let us in.'

* * *

To do nothing is sublime. A sublime that goes above and beyond, beside and next to and occasionally underneath. It doesn't mean to neglect the looking after of animals, the vegie garden, fruit trees or general maintenance, it means that after all these are taken care of, you are free to sit and stare into the void of your mind, via trees, ridges, rainforests, or whatever choice of things you'd like to stare at. It means that you are free from society's shit, from your anxiety, from the what was, accepting of the how it is, and this lets you become ready for the how it might be. You need these might bes. They are hope, they are dreams, and they are exciting, and they are always eternal. To do nothing is sublime within a freedom borne by an emptiness that is not empty. It is an emptiness loaded with a fullness, a fullness of emptiness, an emptiness that has gentleness, and as everyone knows, gentleness takes a while to master. And when everything comes together, it is pure bliss. The first few minutes can be fraught with the day-to-day, the usual suspects, but after a bit, the gentle of the soul kicks in and you are immediately at peace within the self and you know that you are not wasting time, but in fact you are gaining time. This time you are gaining is a full, un-time time, one that makes the world turn more slowly, that makes space and nothing sublime. A sublime yes, of an inner quiet, an inner peace that cannot be lost, stolen, purchased or traded. I liked doing nothing. Absolutely nothing. A sit and stare, a total trance, a spaced-out , eyes open I like what I see out there, eyes closed I like what I see in there. A niksen, a nothing to do nothing, is not hard work being idle, not an idle of hard work, not a lack of strength, skill or what needs to be done, but an idle borne of choice.

And when I did something calmly after the do-nothing time, this calmly became a something, which was one step about a nothing.

I swam in The Creek. I submerged gently into The Creek. Immersed in its icy waters, rebirthed in the cool, within the hot heated summer. Let the healing take the cuts and scratches away, let the cooling ease the mind. Let me have a recalibration of the mind, a resetting of that day and all the forever days. I could see my pale puffy lip face, leaking bubbles and floating upwards hair as if I were looking at an underwater photo of me. No soap, ever. No towels were harmed during filming either, because when you drip dry, you become cooler. Your dick may shrink but you still become cooler. It was slightly differently in the winter. Hibernating dick then. The still pools ran deep and were just above freezing. They were so cold that one day I saw some penguins.

* * *

There were crowds of crowded hoop pine seedlings along a fence line. Most rainforest trees have shallow roots, but not hoop pines. Hoop pines have a tap root that goes down for approximately one-hundred miles and therefore can be hard to transplant. Pulling up such a taproot requires immense strength. I removed two and planted them in front of my house. Took a while. Threw my back out twice.

* * *

'Why did you choose me?'

'You mean, because you're a whitefella? I'm going to slap you, you know that.'

'No way did I mean that. Yes, alright I did. But please don't slap me.'

'Alright, I won't. Yet. And anyway, who says, just because I'm black, I have to choose black? The world's a big place you know. Anyway, bitch, you're white, aren't you? So why did you choose black?'

'How do you know I'm white? Anyway, you can't do that.'

'Fuck off, I can't.'

'I like you.'

'Because I've got nice tits?'

'Hell yeah, you sure have. And you're sexy, but you're fun too. And you're a nice person. Can I go now?'

'No way. Just getting warmed up. I suppose you're alright. You're a bit rough around the head but you'll do. You're not a bad root either. But hey, you treat me nice and I do love you.'

Not sure that went so well.

* * *

I needed some money, so I worked.

I mowed lawns,
I cleaned yards,
I fixed gutters,
And I did an insurance job.

Mowing lawns was peaceful despite the noise. No glasses no earmuffs but still peaceful despite never seeing or hearing ever again. A sort of trance with a green smell that made memories and the lawn even. A four-stroke could be set to be a low soft gurgle, whereas a two-stroke, God love 'em, are all yelly and screamy. Up and down then across to make an even mow; grandpa taught me this. Everyone wanted the clippings as a thick mulch around their trees, but they pack tightly and stop moisture getting through, so I scattered them. I had regulars and used their mower. A couple of little old ladies made me scones to take home. At a couple of places, I used their push mower, no motor. That was tougher. A couple of real estates asked me to be on their books for lawn mowing and odd jobs. I said No thanks, I'd rather let a brown snake bite me.

I loaded palm fronds, old tables, rusty wire, anything, in the back of the ute. The dump was just north of town, and I nearly always came away with more than I dumped. Lumps of timber, valuable solid timber, wire netting, garden pots, and even old ports full of sepia memories and musty books.

Gutters were a bit tricky. Some were beyond repair and had to be replaced. The best way to replace a length of gutter was to run a stringline along the fascia, angling down towards the downpipe, mark where brackets would go, then screw them on. Next, join the entire length of gutter and drag it up onto the roof. The, using ropes and a bit of luck, lower it into place on the brackets.

I was recommended to an insurance company to do repairs by a friend of a friend. He accepted a job on my behalf. I intend to find that person and kill him in his sleep.

Insurance companies are on par with real estate and banking. And politicians, CEOs, and the share market. Liars and leeches. I said I will do this one and then see. The holy see.

Mrs. Kruger's house. Mrs. Kruger had a head like a box of oranges. A rich German with a yard full of BMWs. Probably got her money from stolen artworks. Just warming up, settle. Her house was brick and tile and the garden was so neat you'd think it was a pony going to the show with its mane all trimmed and its hooves painted black. I had the job of replacing her old Hill's Hoist clothesline that was mashed in a summer storm. An insurance job. My first. And last. As I drove up to her house, the neighbour's sneered, the dogs barked, and I hit the gutter and blew a tyre out. Mrs. Kruger was waiting, leaning against the red brick wall, her arms folded like a Kraut sergeant who knows one of her privates is back late from his weekend leave. Where'd he'd been stealing Picassos. For her.

'It's around the back,' she snapped.

Nice to meet you too.

The lawn, or turf, was so bloody perfect you'd have sworn the Immaculate Conception was announced there but when I finished gouging out the wrecked clothesline, it looked more like the Great Barrier Reef than Nazareth.

And all the while she watched.

I sweated, and she watched.

I concreted the main pole in and had to come back in 24 hours after it had set. I seriously thought about not coming back. I could picture the old girl still there, arms folded, waiting for me. There she'd be, a Teutonic fuckin' skeleton, waiting by a busted clothesline. Tensioning the wires on a clothesline is a disheartening job. You pull this way too much and it bends the arm out of plumb. You don't pull it far enough that way and it goes saggy and limp. After two long days of hard yakka with a very interested onlooker, I was ready.

'Mrs. Kruger,' I said, 'She's finished.'

She looked at me like I had typhoid, cow pox and leprosy.

So I spun the mongrel around. It was going well until it hit the wall and tore a huge chunk of brick out. While I stared in horror, Mrs. Kruger didn't move. 'Fix it.' she said and walked inside. I removed the end caps, hacksawed 10 inches off each arm, wound the unneeded wire up and shoved the end caps back on the arms. I packed up rather hastily and was about to escape when the old girl came out.

'Give-me-the-spare-wire.'

I found the bastard who recommended me, and I killed him. I found the dickhead who ordered the wrong size Hill's Hoist and killed him also.

I didn't accept the payment for the insurance job.

I felt dirty. Maybe the ones who cheat need forgiveness too?

Not for them,

I hate them.

For me.

* * *

'How did you know so much about hookers?

'Wha'?'

'Don't give me grief, Pritchard.'

'Because I've been with a few?'

'How many?'

'Oh, comeon!'

'How many?'

'Six.'

'How many?'

'Alright! Eight.'

'Wow.'

'You would have loved it. They were all stunning and way more than sexy. Way more than erotic. It was always hot sex, always slutty, a bit dangerous and …'

'… And, pray tell, just why would I have loved it? You think …'

'I don't think. I know. You love out of control cunt, you are fucking smoking flaming hot, you are a real woman, your thighs are so fucking desirable, you open your legs beautifully, you know how to be sexy without trying, you are … that do?'

'For the minute. Come here, will you?'

She moaned as I fucked her fiercely.

That one went well.

* * *

Old male water dragons, three feet long, lay longways on branches at night. Legs dangling. Leopards learnt from them. Water dragons climb in the stem of a cordyline like a kid monkey-climbing, and eat the red berries. Old male water dragons wear high-vis red chest vests, and furiously vibrate their head, to show any males and females that they are boss and available, in that order, which is like youth lowering a 1967 Holden, or youth wearing bright orange socks.

Old male water dragons jump from high places and land chest first with a force that would kill a hippopotamus or seriously dent a 1967 Holden. Younger male water dragons also move an arm up and down, to talk to each other.

I like water dragons.

Gannets learnt from kookaburras. Gannets fold their wings and smash-dive through the water; kookaburras dive beak first into the ground with no insect or worm thing visible.

Kookaburras have a steel-plated head with industrial-strength shockies.

From the same steel mill that built the chests of water dragons.

Kookaburras are kingfishers but don't need to live next to a creek. They use hollows, or drill out a termite's mound to breed in. They will eat snakes, baby birds and most things that aren't secured to a fixed object. Gannets learnt from kookaburras, but they see their prey, and their entry point is softer.

Spoonbills use probe detectors in muddy water. A sweeping movement not unlike a platypus's. Platypus use electricity in their bills (not yet privatised.

Poles and wires cost extra. And will continue to rise on a regular basis), to detect movement and energy.

Oh, but I'll just keep still, Says the crayfish.

Oh yeah? And stop your heart too?

Platypuses are in The Creek. I saw a few, but they were more common down a bit away from the rocks and toward the earthen banks. They swim so quickly. They swim in a weaving pattern, then dive. If you kept still, they carried on. One movement and they were gone.

* * *

The word dandelion is French for lion's tooth, *dent-de lion*. Apparently in the old days there used to be lions running around Paris looking for *dentistes*. The plant has a yellow flower on a longish thin green stem, say six to eight inches long. These yellow flowers follow the sun, and if you listen closely, you can hear them turning, although this is more hour hand than minute hand. I suspect they are actually mechanical, with amazing flywheels, ratios and cogs situated in the stem. Honeybees land on these flowers to access the nectar, but because these flowers are on such a long thin stem and the honeybees are so fat because they just don't know when enough sweets are enough, these flowers bend under the extreme mass of our overweight bee. What happens next is nothing short of astounding. The bees are pole-vaulted into outer space where they become satellites. Look ma! Satellites! No son, they are merely bees that have been taught a lesson. At night, the yellow dandelion flowers, who are somewhat exhausted from twisting and turning, not to mention being heartily sick of flinging off boofy bees, close their flowers because there's no sunlight. The original solar panel. I've been out at night with the torch and have often seen struggling bees, caught in lion's teeth.

I had a hive of bees. I also built another box, bought the flat wax hexagons as foundations and captured a swarm. I sat nearby and talked to my bees, not in their flight path though. I'm not stupid. And shooed the rainbow bee-eaters away. Come honey harvest time, I applied a gentle smoke, pulled out the loaded frames and softly wiped the bees off with a soft brush that used to be in a theatre make-up room. I brought the frames up to the house, and with a hot knife, decapped the wax, popped them two at a time into a centrifuge and spun their honey to the bottom. Pure, rough honey. Bit of wax, crumbly bits and honeycomb, but pure, so pure that Pharaohs phoned me.

One hot morning I left the frames in the back room. Do them a bit later.

When I went back in, the three-thousand bees had snuck in through the open window attacked me. I ran into The Creek and stayed under for such a long time free divers contacted me for advice. I came out, lumpy, aching and a wee bit wiser.

Only the female bees sting. The males, called drones, have a grandfather but no father. They provide the genetic diversity and when he roots, he dies. You would hope it was spectacular sex. Be a bummer if you shot your load quickly, or she was an ugly queen. Until then the male bee drinks nectar and hangs around. Obviously related to pretty much most human males. And some drones don't even get to mate because if times are tough the girls will starve them then turf them out to die. Just as well human females don't get wind of this practice. Maybe the drones could smuggle hooker bees and wee bottles of nectar into the hives. In buzzes. Check out their boo-bees. Talk about the birds and bees. Every bee wins a prize, including diseases like hib. Medical records bee kept in the ark hives. There'd be increased crime which would lead to prohibition, then after that failed (again), import duties and higher taxes. There'd be nectar testing facilities at concerts, safe drinking rooms and watered-down nectar.
I'm not pollen your leg honey.

The dandelion leaves contain more minerals, vitamins, and goodness than all the lettuces in the world combined. The flowers and taproot are also edible. In a vegetable garden, we weed the rows, that is, we pull out the weeds to let the vegetables grow better. Maybe with the dandelions, we could vegetable the rows.

* * *

On the table.

Going up the behind the house
Be back tonight.
If I'm not,
Please look after the chooks, water the vegetables and orchard, and watch out for lizards that leap from high places,
And watch out for lions
Looking for a dentist.
And look out for cranky bees.

Behind the house the land rose steadily then it hurried in a race to the top of the ridge. What would it do when it got there? Brag how it beat the gentle slopes? Plant a flag? The first two-hundred slow yards or so captured a deep dark dense green light of vegetation, crowded but walkable, on moist leaf litter through nervy pademelons, white cedars, tamarinds, lilies, ginger, stinging trees, and even massive ironbarks. The next section rose fairly steeply and had no qualms about imprisoning light, so it could dry the ground and let its army through. Forest oaks thrived here, as did the grey gums, brush box trees and native grasses. The thin-trunked forest oaks had brown deeply fissured bark, really great to grip; the grey gums were lonely but healthy (like me, they enjoyed solitude and fantastic health) and the box trees looked like they needed a feed, unlike their healthier fat cousins in the wetter areas. The grasses looked spindly and perhaps undernourished, but this was not so. They ebbed and flowed with the tide, and said Come through.

Crossing the heads of gullies was easy but if you went thirty yards lower you had ravines, and steep crumbly rock steep-sided canyons. Which hid secretive magic birds.

Then at right-angles came an easy ridge, a soft full-tided kangaroo grassed entry to a new world, and without any fuss it took me to the back ridge, the main ridge that was a mile-long saddle between a large rock and a larger rock. A rock and a hard place got its name from here. In the western corner, wearing granite-coloured satin shorts was Rock number 1, and was called the Fort, shaped like a big dick, swollen, curved and dripping. In the eastern corner, wearing a Sherwood green onesie, was Rock number 2, and was called the border ranges.

The mile-long saddle was exposed and had hot stout grey gums packed full of koalas. There's no water up there, they said.
And they were bloodywell right.

* * *

'Excuse me, would you like to have sexual intercourse this morning?'

'God, I like it when you talk dirty. Sure would, what did you have in mind?'

'Perhaps you would care to remove your pants, lift up your skirt, sit on the table here, and bring your knees up so I can walk up in front and fuck you? I'm in charge, remember.'

'Well, kind sir, I would be very interested in partaking in your lustful in-charge submissive suggestions, but alas, I cannot.'

'Fuck Joan, why not? I thought we …'

'… because I don't have any pants on to remove.'

I took my stiff cock in my right hand and gently steered it to her soft pussy. I let the knob rub up and down, just the knob. It was a game, a game of who would crack first.

'For fuck's sake, put it in, will you?'

Close call.

I pushed slowly, sliding slippery tightly all the way in. A thrusty sliding engorged cock into its soft delicate pink cunt, that wanted, and got, more.

Joan. Smelt better than a clean soap smell, or a prostitute's perfume. Her body, her sweat, her salty hairy armpits, all smells heavier on her shaved pussy. A stronger, warm, hot, fishy smell. Moist, groany and slippery. Life, Earth, woman. Yet within the total sluttiness that was us, we still gave privacy. And were polite to one another. Within the cheekiness and ribald jokes, we were good.

But no, I don't want to marry you Joan.

* * *

Table note.

Going up the slope opposite
Then to New South Wales
Not sure why
I think I might hate them.
Be back in three days.
If I'm not, be a kind person no matter what.
The death adders will love you for it.

I tied the chooks' door back, gave them extra water and grain and kissed them all goodbye.

On day two, from the top of the plateau, I saw a slope that led down to New South Wales. I knew it led there because anything lower than Queensland must be New South Wales. If you don't live in Queensland, you're only camping. It was a long and winding road, an enclosed slope, and new to me. A new sloping spur encourages caution, but not fear. If you have fear, a new slope is not a place to be. Nor is life for that matter. Fear is only relative to insecurity, not adventure. I picked up an old logging trail, it wasn't that heavy, and followed it for three miles to a house surrounded by palm trees. A couple said, Hey, want to have some lunch? Lovely, lovely people. We swapped stories. I said, Come over one day.

The retrace home was up, up, and away, but because I knew the route I could relax a bit. Caution eased, fear conquered, insecurity under control and the adventure exciting. I went back up to the plateau, headed west, found and followed the rabbit-proof fence for a while – a strong wire-netting construction with powerful corner posts, and excellent stays. Either side was cleared for access and it made for an easy stroll. Green dry dangling moss and cloud rainforest changed to open eucalypt and led me to a valley. Across this valley over a creek not unlike mine, along a bit, then down the steep slope to home.

* * *

I needed some money, so I worked.

I helped shift irrigation pipes,
And with my bus licence, I drove backpackers around.

Irrigation pipes, aluminium, four-inch diameter, thirty-feet long. The sprinklers are proud by three-feet and are forty-feet apart. If the pipes were moved say twice a day, on a 50 acre paddock of lucerne, which belonged to Billy's father, Billy the genius, Billy the scholar, it would take approximately five days to water the crop. You uncouple one then pick it up in the middle and balance on the high wired cultivation to its mate who is waiting. Where have you been my silver stallion? You join them in holy pipamony, and their coupling is sealed with a piece of rubber. One can't be too careful these days.
'Okay, turn her on!' someone calls out.
There is a movement within the thirty-foot pipes and a few clunks as they gather their rubber rings together in a huddle a rugby team would die for, a slow squirt, then in no time, chick-a-chick, and then lots of spray. And not a few groans.

* * *

I said to Joan, when we were drowsy and gearing up for number three, 'I'm going away for a few days.'
'Sure. Where you going?'
'Going inland. I'll be driving a bus with travellers.'
'See you soon.' Then she straddled me and said, 'You'll miss me. And here's a reminder of what you'll be missing.'

* * *

To a table it might concern.

Taking some backpackers for a drive.
Be back in a week or so.
Chooks all good.
Say hi to Joan, Coffee Shop Girl, and Wendy who has moved into town.

Backpackers weren't called backpackers back then. They were just people. Mostly from overseas but not always. I drove us west to see a range, a white limestone sandstone artefacted range, which we did, we went northish to some Gemfields, to find sapphires and rubies, which we did. East to see wheat, a mountain range and the coast. Which we did.

I said, 'Hey, it's Christmas. Want to come back to The Creek? We'll share stuff, cook a turkey in the donkey and swim in The Creek. What do you reckon?'

Two Danes, four Pommies, three Spanish and one Kiwi said, Yes. We all went to a bush dance in the city first. The Kiwi and I danced. We danced the dance of a warm BBQ sizzle, the dance of hope, the dance of things to come. And we laughed and lost ourselves somewhere in a mist of lostness, a mist of slow lostness that was a light-headed dizzy. A light-headed love of the moment. We Stripped the Willow, Barn Danced, and when the slow waltz came on, she melded and melted and I whispered, 'Thanks Grandpa.'

Oh my God, she was so light, so leadable. It was like dancing with a blue triangle butterfly, and I've done that heaps of times when there were no available chairs. I said, 'You sweep across the floor so beautifully, you are soft and delicate. Please, who taught you to dance?'

She said, 'My grandpa.'

Please don't say that because now we are connected. We are joined by a grandfather, by the beauty of dance, and possibly by something else.

We did Secret Santa, and the world was good. The two Danes, the two tall blonde gorgeous Danes, spoke in their yor yar sing-y language. It stormed, a smashing storm and the Pommies had never seen such a show. They only knew mosquito piss. The Spanish made tapas while my dancing Kiwi and I swam naked in The Creek. And I looked. Later, around bedtime, she said, 'You were watching me down there. And I mean, down there.'

What was I supposed to do? Hey, you show your fanny, I look.

'I was. Come in and join me?'

'I have a girlfriend.'
'Maybe, but you haven't answered my question.'

* * *

Joe said he had an old friend who lived at his scrub block. This friend paid no rent nor was it required. 'He doesn't take up much space, doesn't eat much, and boy, does he smell nice!'

Now there was an interesting intro if ever I heard one. Joe said that he was a trusty friend, a bit old, but of sound mind and body.

His old friend was a 1957 Landrover, registration not needed, not even a considered option because of where he lived. This 4WD was in better condition than many of its legal relatives. When Joe would drive down the steep roughly made roads, with three or four corner posts, a roll of number eight fencing wire and a few ton of kikuyu runners in the tray (which he'd previously bull-dozed into furls), he'd put it in first gear low-range 4WD, then turn the ignition off. This meant that only the engine's compression moved us forward. When we got near to the bottom, he'd turn the ignition on and she would kick over and away we'd crawl.

Back at The Creek, I tried this in the Dodge. Never mind wearing the same laconic bush clothes and pretending to be Henry, never mind trying to copy Lena's earthy bush cooking, I was Joe, driving down a ridge with the motor turned off. But when I turned the ignition on there was a loud explosion. The muffler ended its life, sending shards of its metal into the petrol tank and the surrounding scrub.

Joe said, 'When we were little tackers, there was a bounty on crows. You'd catch them, cut their heads off then go and collect sixpence each. But they were hard to shoot, the cunning bastards. So I would shoot chillawongs and leave a bag of heads in the sun for a week. Mix a few crows in. Then dump the bag on the man's desk and say, 'Thirty crows.''

What Joe, and most locals, called chillawongs, I called currawongs. There's a bird, the channelled-billed cuckoo, that lays eggs in chillawong's nests. As Joe and I yarned under such a nest with two chillawong fledglings, a pair of channel-billed cuckoos flew in, picked the babies almost to death and tossed them at our feet.

Joe said, 'There's a shilling, right there.'

* * *

A long-time ago, a plane had crashed into a mountain a few valleys over from The Creek. The media had said, No, it didn't crash there, it had either crashed into the Hawksbury River not far above Sydney, had streaked at a test cricket match, and/or owed millions in taxes. But they were incorrect. The downdraft from a cyclone forced it into the side of a mountain. The plane had no radio. Five dead, three survivors. One went for help and died along a creek. Another fed another with berries while the maggots stopped the gangrene in his broken leg, the berry eater's leg. Joe said he knew where it was, but he said, 'Each time we packed the ponies to go and search, dad came up with news that the downed plane had been found in the Hawksbury. Or below Sydney, or the Blue Mountains, or at drinks in a cricket test match, so we'd unpack.'

Another local found it. I met his daughter and she told me stuff, even though she was a little kid at the time of the rescue. Stuff like, how locating the wreck had affected him. Joe was pretty much the first person contacted after the wreck was found. After helping raise the alarm, he went back to the wreck to lend a hand. Joe said, 'When we got to the crash site, the two pilots were ash in human form. When the wind blew, their ashes scattered all over us.'

I took a film crew up on the fiftieth anniversary of the crash. There was a Christian service. Not my cup of tea by a long shot, but it was solemn, low-key and appreciative of death, sacrifice and bravery. It honoured old-fashioned ideals of doing the right thing, helping when others need and honesty in all actions, all of which have been lost in Moscow, Beijing, Rome, Tehran, Riyadh and Canberra. I also saw the crash site from a helicopter. There was still a hole in the rainforest canopy after fifty years. It must have been terrifying. Like lunatic leaders and their dictatorial arrogance are to the people around the world. In particular, to our original mob.

* * *

Is one of my selfs so insecure that it must copy? And if so, who (more like, how many), and is this okay? Or is it that emulation is a high-level growth hormone, necessary for future self-development? A pituitary-gland of self-muscle? A steroid for unsure muscles? No, one of my selfs is not so insecure as to copy. All of them are. Or at least the main one is. Joe, Henry, Lena, Peter, grandpa, I took a little of each.

One morning Lena invited me down for lunch. I said, 'Hey, what's for lunch?'

Lena said, 'Dust sandwiches.'

I said, 'Well that's a relief. I thought we'd be having snake's bum on a biscuit again.'

She was a gentle person, a sweet gentle person, and a great cook. I copied her way of making simple meals. One evening I made a wallaby stew, perhaps a bit thin stew. So I steamed an orange sweet potato, mashed it, then mixed it through the stew to thicken it.

Life's reel keeps on playing, and it has a limited pause function and a seriously faulty rewind button, but life can default straight to a living end if you want. To be dead yet still breathing. I must do what I do and just maybe, maybe each night when I ask myself – which of course everyone does this – Have I been a good person today? My emotional brain would hopefully say, *Yes, you have. You're not a zombie. Yet.*

If it doesn't, it means I have been a fucken prick and I must ask my rational brain how I can make amends to whomever I had wronged. To right the wrong, to apologise in person, or write, or give back the thing I took. And promise it will never happen again.

Maybe I need to copy more heroes?

* * *

The need to be touched is a strong need, perhaps outdoing sex itself. Perhaps. The light touch, the full-on hug, the soft tickle, bodily contact, a reassuring touch that is safe. 'Hey, how was the bus trip?'

'Great. I enjoyed it more than I thought I would. But you were right …'

'Again?'

'… I did miss you.'

We lay side by side, spooned, legs over, an arm or two lazily flopped, like we did.

Joan said, 'If I get any hail damage on my car this summer, I'll contact you.'

'Why would you do that? I know shit about panel beating.'

'Maybe so, but I heard you do insurance work for free.'

If I ever need a detective, Joan is my first call.

'Hey, what do you do for work?'

'Who said I worked? I do stuff.'

'Glad that's cleared up.'

'I help people.'

'Your skin is so smooth.'

'Cause I'm a black chick?'

'Nooo! Hey, all the other black women I've been with …'

'You fib.'

'Oh yeah?'

'Yeah. If you had been with a black woman anywhere in south-east Queensland within the past twenty years, I would have known by now.'

I believed her.

'I'm a mixture. Born of oldish parents, mum a black woman, dad a whitefella.'

'Both still alive?'

'Yep. Sort of. What about you?'

'Hell yes, I'm still alive.'

'I'm going to slap you one day.'

'You will never do that because you're too nice. Must be your smooth skin influencing your moods. I never had long with my parents.'

'Really? You're not kidding me?'

'I never kid, kid. Or if I did kid, kid, I kid because I care. Grandpa did his best to raise me. Still is. That was supposed to be funny. And he won't tell me nothing.'

'Maybe you're a blackfella? Maybe you were stolen? And hey, I'm still going to slap you one day.'

* * *

Some nights, and even some days, I looked up and cried small slow-flowing tears of thankfulness because here I was, free, with choice as a base, and grateful for what I had. Where I was right now, and at this minute right now. When the moon made the black green turn light blue green, even a bit silver, so bright at night I went for a walk without anything to do. Do now plan later. After I had counted seven stars, I walked and was carried away by a moonlight shadow without a suitable warning whenever I saw him, to the top of a mountain, and it left me there and I couldn't find how to push through. I talked to the man in the moon. I said, 'Do you have a friend in Cheesus? Do you ever get sick of eating cheese?' The moon never answered; only smiled.

In the dark darkness I reached up and touched the stars. They liked being touched. 'Very few touch us. People are scared. They think they are so small, or insignificant.' When you touch stars, you never get burnt. 'It's all here, waiting. Could you please tell more people to touch us? And that fearing fear is no way to live?'

At night, without a torch, my eyes screamed. They said, 'What the fuck are you doing man? You can't see shit.'

I agreed, but kept going, because are not self-criticism and self-knowing stronger for being challenged? Is not a search for the real self a continual challenge and change? Before, during and after the search? During my moonlight walks, the walks when I walked silently, I was wary of, but not scared of the logs, ditches, rock, and branches. But I was respectful of the snakes. Snakes can be active at night, even on warm rainy nights, and not just the carpets looking for a chook, but browns, death adders and tigers. Possible to tread on one sure, but lots of things are possible. There are times when I wonder how I got to this point. Or maybe I could stay home and not live life?

Snakes are not slimy; they are shiny smooth. They have no ears like we know ears. They don't hear sounds like we hear sounds. They pick up good vibrations from the ground through their jaw, and use their forked-tongue to smell stuff. Snakes have broad shoulders, so they can carry huge weights; the weights of sin, Satan, wisdom, rebirth, healing, fertility, eternity, defending, medicine, the Zodiac, sexual desire and God. I say a snake is a snake, and I respected snakes not through fear, or any of the reasons for their strong shoulders, but for who they were.

* * *

Grandpa taught me how to play cribbage. It's a card game, with a board with wee drilled holes, and markers. When certain cards are turned up, you get points, so you'd advance your markers. 'Crib is a game of skill, not patience, so get with it. Learn the appropriate comments, and don't shuffle the tits off the queen.' Fifteen two, fifteen four, that's all there is there aint no more-fifteen two and the rest can screw-a five is cut, fever in the whorehouse, run girls run-that's a bad cut, no better than a screen door in a sub-a Jack is turned up, his nibs and take two. Crib has been described as a substitute for social discussion among those with limited intelligence. I'm not so sure. Though it did take me a while to learn the terminology. Grandpa would take me to a night out. Not to the pub, a game of footy, bridge, bingo, no, we went to play cribbage. One night at home, grandpa said, 'Marriage is a game of cards.' And he dealt me blank cards.

* * *

At the sawmill with Joe. He had said two brothers would be bringing us a couple of logs. Was it too hard to see that they were brothers? Oh, you mean, the identical blue Jackie Howe's, the muscled shoulders, the cut-off jeans with a hem, rolled up top show thighs that would not be out of place in a steel mill, a rugby league front row or in a weight-lifting competition? Or thighs that belonged to a long-distance runner, or a national butterfly champion? I could picture them, powering down the pool at night with the lights making the water seem a wriggly white and blue. They'd be so strong and so far ahead it wouldn't be a fair race. Give the others a chance, the media would say, let the others start ten seconds ahead. Or some shit. Their barrel chests so thick through from front to back, and stomachs so flat that you could set a vertical level on.

Okay, you win, no it wasn't hard to see that they were brothers. What a pair; not twins, but not far off. Slow, strong and easy going. Like me I guess. Hey, they said to Joe, We've brought you a couple of logs.

Jesus and Joseph, a couple of logs you say? How about a short history of south-east Queensland, how about every logger, every snigger and everyone who ever dreamed of bringing red cedar logs to a mill, was here, present at the inaugural opening of red cedar day.

These were real red cedar logs, too. I'm talking eighteen feet long with a nine feet girth. They towed the two massive logs in a trailer behind a green Massey Ferguson, which, I might say, was unregistered. Joe said that they would even take their sawdust home. Which they did after weighing it first.

Joe and I broke the logs down and they smelled ever so nice. When freshly milled, red cedar was a furry timber, red and soft and grainy, and sweet to the smell. You could toss it around like wafers. They wanted slabs done, huge 11 x 4 inch mothers that they could strip and store in their shed to sell later.

The next morning, to collect the remainder we had cut, the brothers brought in their father. He was eighty something, and while seemingly pretty fit, he was destined to die in six months. After the first stroke he called all the family around to say goodbye and to tell them he really did love them after all, and to thank them for being there for him when he needed them. A fair way to die I guess. You know, a bit of warning, Hey guys see you later, and then bang, you're gone. Anyway, for the minute he sat on the end of the bench like a bloody overseer that's watching and waiting. He wore short shorts, baggy and blue, and his balls hung out of the leg bit like a sack of spuds waiting to be tossed over your shoulder. Must be a great sight at a church fundraiser. Probably is a draw card for the old boilers.

'Come on' Florence, don't be a'wasting time now. We have to get down to the morning tea. Father will be waiting you know.'

'Yeah sure, Betty. You're in a rush 'cause you want to see the old fella's nuts hanging out. I know you.'

Just sittin' there, seemed to be waitin' just for you to make a slip up so he could come in and say, 'Righto sport you've done fuck-all today, pack your bags Sonny Jim.' I never knew what he wanted. Maybe to watch the tree his father planted get cut up into slabs? Maybe just to sit and enjoy his last few months? Sometimes he would rush in to help do something but he always seemed to be two seconds behind the action. Maybe even these old blokes needed confidence at something that was new?

* * *

Joan said, 'I have something to ask you.'

'I'm listening.' This type of conversation usually doesn't end well.

'You know how we're not going to be married?'

'Right.' No more sex.

'You know how we're not even going to live together?'

'Right.' Joining a nunnery.

'And I go out and socialise and get drunk and stuff.'

'Hell Joan, I had no idea …'

'Fuck off. And you're a hermit, right?'

'Right.' Sister Joan for sure, and no sex for me.

'Will you stop saying fucking *right*!'

'If you stop beating around the bush I will.' Wants to kill me in the face because I'm a whitefella and then reclaim her land.

'Shit … Damn!'

'Right.' Leaving me? Coming out of the closet?

'*Fuuck*! Okay, I'm ready now. Can we only fuck each other and no-one else? God, that was like pulling teeth.'

'Sure, it's a deal. Why, you been getting offers?'

'Yes, frigging hundreds. You?'

'Hell yeah. Lost count.'

This one ended well.

One morning my Joanee was different. I could see it in the air, in the thick fumes of confusion, and feel it in the silent soundwaves that surrounded us. Her big black eyes, not cranky, her big black eyes, quiet, unsure, sad. A longer than usual happy wraparound hug, burrowed her head into my chest like a chicken under a hen's wing. Her gripping fingers her quiet sobs, her quieter sorrow, vibrated. Talk to me, I said. She shook her buried head, Just hold me, she said.

Joy, elation, happiness, can be tempered by despair, yearning, insecurity, hurts, worries and doubts. Mine not hers. I never knew why then but now I do. But I was there and that was enough. She said so, too. Hey Joan, We'll never be young again, but I do know something. I believe in all of your young charms. You are cute, you are special, and you always will be and may we always have a strong love and stay close.

And yes, let's fuck no-one else.

* * *

Flooded gums (*Eucalyptus grandis*) were called eucalypts, because eucalypt is a Greek word meaning nice nuts and the grandis bit says they are large; a big tree with big balls. Flooded gums grow to be over 200 feet tall. In summer the flooded gums shed their brown bark. It's a strip tease, just a bit of white flesh slowly exposed each time. I know that's what it is because I've been to a real strip show. Which was much better than watching shedding bark. Thanks grandpa.

Bell miners love them. Flooded gums. Bell miners are naughty birds, not only for confusing motorists by tinkering with their mechanical anxieties, but they are leader-onerers. Judases all, one kiss and there he is. That one. One late afternoon, I came down through the forest and heard them, softly tink-tinking. I thought they were guiding me to safety, but no, they were secretly telling the soldiers where I was. I followed them, not thinking that they were luring me into a trap, these traitory pied-pipers of the flooded gum forest, these bush deceivers, these evil fairies.

It was ten minutes before dark when I saw the soldiers; an impenetrable wall of lantana, waiting to capture me. I could see the clear forest fifty yards away, so I went over the top. In my escape to avoid that identifying kiss, I damaged the shockies, got a whine in the diff and had to have a wheel alignment, but I got through.

The miners all crowded around me and laughed. I still have scars over 80% of my body. A week later I went back to the edge of the lantana and shot half a dozen bell miners.

Spangled drongoes build a hangy-down nest in flooded gums.
Flooded-gum hollows are used by parrots, possums and politicians.
Creatures that are furtive, secretive and sly during the daytime.
Possums, too, sometimes.
Thick sapwood, rose pink true wood for flooring and wall boards.
No good in the ground.
Which is weird because that's where the timber comes from.
Though it splits easily down the line,
Is dreadful as firewood.
It burns black,
Gives no heat.
'But wait mister,
That's your version of me.
I'm just a tree.
Look after me,
I don't grow on trees, you know.'
These trees are smart
They twig onto nuances,
And have been known to say, Leaf us alone.
They branch out in life,
Put down roots, send out shoots and are a sap for lame jokes.
'Wood you like to be a …
They log on to their favourite sites
They are really shady
Although, they say, 'We are knot.'
I saw you too, said the axeperson.

* * *

Are there too many selfs on the self-shelf?
How many different selfies can you take?
'Do you take this self to be your lawfully chosen self?'
'Not sure but I think I do, sometimes. Maybe.'

'Right. If anyone can show just cause why this, suppos-ed couple, cannot lawfully be joined let them speak now or forever hold their pieces.'
    I'll bet your other false selfs, just waiting there in the wings of rejection, in the church's wooden bench seats that are shit to sit on, holler out. 'No, wait! He promised me I was the one!'

'Huh! Stand well to the side, O polite one, I'm actually his real self.'

'You? You're a fucking slut. It's me he loves because I am kind and gentle.'

There's a sign in town near a row of sheds,

'Self-storage. Liars at this end, mean people to the back, two-faced bastards on the right, cruel cunts … wait, we have no room for you here. Go away.'

How many times do we avoid our real self in order to let it be the one? And if you do let the real self off its leash, in its controlled dog-park unleash, would you get shunned by society, arrested, or sent to the loony bin? What if we all went to the dog park at the same time? I had my real self with Joan. The one I had at that point anyway.

* * *

Hermits.
To live without the need to maintain some other fucker's idea of cleanliness or dress code
Sort of almost, was incredibly freeing.
I did wash,
Occasionally.
Though when I went to town, I did make an effort to be washed,
Though Joan had said, Jesus Tony, why do you wash so often?
Excuse me? And you called me a sick puppy after our previous smells discussion?
And me telling her about me smelling my sweaty balls.
Get a grip girl.
Dress.
This is a tricky one.
Did I dress nicely to go to town?
I did.
However,
Up in the mountains,
I wore them.
I preferred a knee-length dark blue number,
Small sleeves, buttons all the way down the front.
Large deep-yellow buttons,
That said lots.
And skirts.

Why didn't someone tell me how nice it was to wear skirts?
I've got a nice arse too.
I particularly adored a simple wrap-around.
Either red and black, or a soft ochre.
With patterns.
The freedom, the sensuality, the part-time crossing over,
Were liberating.
Were totally sexy.
Not to mention practical.
Squat to piss,
How sensible.
Once I shaved my legs,
Not my armpits though,
And thought,
Not bad,
Nice curves,
Bit wirey and muscley though.
But I also liked hairy
Too much I suspect.
It's hard when you don't know you've been had,
By yourself.

Hermits.
I was a part-time hermit.
With some overtime, the occasional penalty rates for public holidays and
Sundays and four weeks annual leave.
Because life gives me enough with which to consider my big questions.
That's it.
Live life.
Do shit.
Give.
And be kind.

* * *

Visual excitement in the loins is a stirring awakening, and occasionally a
release right then and there. (Depends on your age and how horny you are.)
It shrieks of uncontrolled lust that has nowhere to go but within an erotic
fantasy, one to keep you company for years. It is untouchable, literally, yet

so close that you can smell it. You may have had it when you saw your sister getting changed, or when you saw your neighbour taking off her shirt. That low belly stirring is friggin immense. I once watched through a window, a hooker getting changed and it was mesmerisingly erotic. And I had just been in there with her. Bad and naughty, but fucking beautifully stimulating. My cock turned into a rod. It went beyond horniness or immediate pleasure, and not because of what had just transpired, and it transcended into a what might be, according to my still-alive fantasies. Again, Joan hinted at a threesome, and I was getting more excited. Not only because of her fantasy, which I was warming to, but also because that I felt secure within her fantasy. And that she had said we would fuck no other as in, me girls her boys. Therefore, it was safe that I could listen, and her fantasy was pretty much now imbedded within me too. No idea what would really happen, but never mind.

My emotional brain had an idea. *Keep in mind Tony, that a desired happiness, particularly lust, finds it hard to wait.*

* * *

A cow and calf.
everyone should have them
when kids turn twenty-one
never mind the key to the door
a keg of beer
or a stripper,
just hand over a cow and calf.
Open, drink, kiss your fantasies okay,
but get a cow and calf;
maybe even a block of land with a tiny house as well
and a living wage, indexed
of course.
Social problems;
Nil.

The mum was a Guernsey, a cow with a long tan handsome face, a white blaze and a wet shiny nose. Her rough tongue could leap out and go straight up her nostril. It was a purple-coloured tentacle – in, out, never missing its cave. You don't ever want a cow to stick her tongue in your face.

I loved to lean on her and rub her shoulders. Not her flanks because that bloody fly-swishing tail could take your eye out. She had a smooth brown hide. I would brush her down too, singing as I did so. She didn't mind. She said, I love it when you do that.

Her calf had a Hereford father. An arranged marriage. Not so bad, she said. Had worse. Well excuse me, you little brown hussy. I chose special and complicated names for them – Cow and Calf. If I needed milk, I locked up Calf for the night. That she wasn't entirely in agreeance with this arrangement would be an understatement. She tried to kill me many times. Many times she succeeded. You fucken lock me up again and I'll headbutt you forever. How can you do that, I'm already dead. At daybreak I'd call, Cow, comeon it's time! And the circus would start. Roll up, Roll up, laydeez and gentlemen, come see the bearded lady, the tattooed man and the high-flying, the death-defying, the intensifying quantifying trapeze artists. Stay a while after the show and watch two clowns drink milk.

Calf would butt mum's udder to bring the milk down. We shared the tits. Amazing stuff milk. When I squirted her tits with a strong hard squirt, it made the milk go frothy. Calf and I would swap tits and there'd be white slobber everywhere. When she was done drinking, her eyes would roll back in ecstasy. I considered having a suck on a tit myself but was too scared I might get a kick in the head. And then it would be tricky explaining how I got this injury to the ambulance people. I was raking the yard, when the bloody cow kicked me. You sure? I swear …

I had no refrigeration, so I drank the milk warm. A bowl of milk and some steamed chokoes.

No wonder I'm so friggin old and healthy.

I built a small yard, as in cattle yard, to hold the cattles. Same size as a small bedroom. Round posts five foot out of the ground, rails 6 x 2 spotty gum wired on with a Queensland hitch. The gate was special. Special because it wasn't level; it wasn't plumb because the ground wasn't plumb. If you built a yard gate spirit-level straight horizontally on uneven ground, there's a big chance your bovines will walk underneath this gate. On the upright post (vertically spirit-levelled plumb, or, sighted by eye) that will be the hinge post you must use a moveable setsquare to set the gate. Put the side of the setsquare vertically on the vertical post and move the arm thing to be the angle you want the gate boards and then after you build the gate and hinge it, it will close following the lay of the land, and not be plumb wrong. And no animals will sneak under.

The gate was 6 x 1 spotted gum. A eucalypt that has yellowish timber, is no good in the ground (after it has been milled), the borers love its sapwood, but it is a strong timber with a bit of bounce. Perfect for a yard gate. Not greasy like tallowwood, just a dry, clean finish without being planed.

Double verticals each end, around five foot tall. In between these are bolted four cross timbers. Double bolted. An angle piece goes from the outside top to the inside bottom, and is also double bolted.

The lock is simple; a short piece of 6 x 1 slotted in between the upright and double angle, and it slots into a mortise in the non-hinged post.

When I look at that yard, pretty small by comparison to anything else related to dairies, cattle yards or high-rise, I feel so friggin proud. I built it like Peter taught me to do, and it's a good job, solid and true, and I did it.

Peter told me something amazing about sawn timber. He said if you leave sawn timber out in the weather, say a 6 x 1 piece of spotted gum, it will turn grey. Even a nice licheny light green grey, my two favourite colours. If you then scratch or saw the 6 x 1, it will return to its original colour, in this case a soft yellow. I sort of knew all that, so we're not up to amazing as yet. But then he said, If you strip newly sawn timber to dry it, it will shrink across the grain and possibly split down the grain. Still unamazing. Once it's dry (this could take up to two years, depending on the width, thickness, type of tree and whether or not you ate all your vegetables) and you build with it, or make something, the timber will remain true and stable. Unamazing number three. However, Peter said, If you get a piece of oldish grey dried sawn timber, and plane it all back to its original colour, the shrinking and possibly splitting starts all over again. Now that is incredibly amazing. Who said grey was a boring colour?

The Guernsey is a dairy breed and the Hereford is a beef breed. When you cross them, their calves grow stronger and fatter than if they had a same-species parenthood. And therefore, would get me more money at the market. But I did not sell this Calf. Because I loved her so. When she was ready, and you can tell, I mated her with a local Murray Grey bull, another beef breed.

When cows are in season, they go all funny. They lift their tail, discharge, moo, and look longingly at anyone nearby. Done it myself heaps of times. When an in-season cow moos, they open their mouth and softly breathe out an almost invisible sound which is deep and low and travels through the universe at a wavelength not yet recorded by geeks, nerds and other incredible people, and is only discernible to bulls. The bulls, and there's quite a few in the known universe, would salivate and their red pointy cocks would spring up and down and leak in anticipation. Done it myself heaps of times. Not for a cow though. Although, there were a few times …

Even artificial insemination straws get an erection when they hear the low moo. The local farmers were happy for me to walk my cow down to be serviced because it saved them the time and expense of repairs. Bulls who had received the Call have been known to flatten miles of fencing, sheds, and even whole towns have been razed.
Done it myself heaps of times.

I wonder what happens when you lose the lust? When you lose the desire to be raunchy, to want to fuck? Free up a lot of space in your brain and give you a lot more time to pursue hobbies I suppose. But what if you still had the lust, but couldn't fuck? Be a bastard hearing the moo, then going, Fuck, there's no point following the line.

we project lust
not only by lifting our tail, discharging, or mooing softly,
but by smiling, talking, singing, hugging,
or even just by looking
maybe even by looking when they don't know you're looking
and our lust is also love, the love that is also lust
and it moves through the air like a soft breeze in the scented springtime.
when you meet someone who has it
that lust and love, that poured gentle sweetness that is life itself,
that beauty that is not just beauty, a beauty that goes beyond prettiness or
hunkiness, that goes beyond tits, a stiff cock, a quivering pussy, a nice arse,
that is a pure kindness, a gentle niceness, a naivety, innocence,
and the real reason we breathe, the real reason we exalt in the universe,
is because of daily lust
you will fall in love with this person,
no matter who they may be
because true love that has no limits,
no prerequisites of whom you are allowed or not allowed to fall in love or
lust with.
and lust and its close relative eroticism
are as much thought and fantasy as they are deed

and eroticism also has its lifted swishy tail in the arms of love.
do you love?

* * *

'Hear you're dropping in vegetables and eggs in to the Homeless Support
Centre?'
    'Yes. How did you know that?'
    'A little birdy told me.'
    'That French singer, the Little Sparrow?'
    The morning with Joan was different,
    Yet a nice morning different
    A niceness that was real,
    A special real.
    She said, 'You're a good person.'
    'Thank you. You're not a bad person yourself. Guess you want to marry
me then?'
    She didn't say Fuck off,
    And we hugged for a long time
    A tenderness that fulfilled something deep in both of us.
    A love and a lust.
    And I drove home, singing songs I knew the words to.

* * *

Jenny the teacher had said, 'Why don't you want to be paid? You work really
hard with the kids. And they just *love* going on excursions with you.'
I shrugged and had no clear answer.

'Our excursion today kids, is to a sawmill. It is a place of high-pitched
whines, rough edges and strong smells. Then there's the saws and logs.
Haha. We will learn how weatherboards are made, these angled sloping
protectors of your houses, and how these little babies relate to 3D shapes,
sort of. So get your clipboards, water bottles and manners, and line up in roll
call order. Yes Billy, you may go to the toilet. Again.' There's always one.
What on earth will become of this kid.

'After that log has been debarked, wire brushed and scrubbed with
industrial-strength detergent, it is dragged onto the breaking down bench by
a motor towing a hook on the end of a wire rope. The log is then set up on

the breaking-down bench with wedges and the log's base, the larger end, is facing the saw. That saw, by the way, is large and fast and will cut you into two pieces should you stray, so keep behind me. Uh! Whose foot is that in front of mine? Come behind now. Flitches are then cut off, the leftover log reversed, bet you didn't know a log had reverse gear did you hey, and the next flitch is cut off. The flitches are pushed down that ramp, did you see how it slid so easily? Yes Billy?'

'I saw 'im sir, 'e put sump oil on the ramp!'

'Well done, Billy. Have next week off school.'

'But sir, next week is …'

'Now, we come to the big number two. Ha-ha. Saw I mean. It revolves at …'

'Ninety-miles an hour sir.'

'… Jesus, Billy. Aren't you on holidays yet? Here comes the start of our weatherboards. See that board? It is at least twenty-feet long and seven inches by three-quarters of an inch …'

'But sir, we work in metric now.'

'… I swear Billy … and this board is recut at an angle to produce not one, but two, glorious seven-inch weatherboards, each measuring one inch by one-quarter of an inch.'

'Sir, sir! It's an isosceles triangle!'

I had him. 'So, oh wise one, how many sides does a triangle have?'

'Three, sir.'

'Ah, correct Billy. And our weatherboard might indeed be a triangle, if it were a 2D shape, which it isn't, and had three sides, which it fucking doesn't. It has four, because the tapered end doesn't have a sharp point. Therefore, our 3D shape must be a …'

'A quadrilateral, sir,'

'Thank you, Mary. However, we may yet have to do more work on your geometry.'

'Sir, you swore.'

'Did not.'

'It's a rectangular prism!'

'Nope.'

'It's a non-Polyhedra!'

'Nope, sort of.'

'It's a polygon!'

'Oh, please! I'm dealing with pheasants.' Back of hand to forehead. 'Where have I gone wrong?'

Then Billy, wise incredible Billy, who is no doubt heading for a career in scientific reasoning or head of the United Nations, said, 'I know sir; looking from the end, it's a wedge. Just like the ones under the log on the breaking-down bench. And I think you meant peasants.'

'Billy, this is a further excellent example of your powers of observation. By the way, never question my choice of words. Anyway, have tomorrow off school ...'

'But, Sir ...'

'... And I would agree, except a wedge must have a sharp pointy end.'

* * *

Joan said, 'So, you now do school stuff as well as insurance work without being paid, and you donate vegetables to the local orphanage?

'Bugger off you.'

She hugged me.

'Yes, I do those things. I do need money, but there are times when I help others, well it seems to feel better than accepting money.'

I didn't mention that I saw a name on a brass plate at the orphanage, listing 'Joan Pascoe' as manager. She helps people alright.

And I wondered how long before she found out the freebies for the rich horsie kids? I loved working for the build-stable people and one day, one of the rich-bitches had come up, took my hand and said, 'Thank you. Thank you so much for helping my daughter.'

Joan hugged me better, and said a little nothing. But I do know what she really said. She actually said one of those nothings we want to hear every day: she said, softly whispering, 'I love you.'

Of course you don't want to marry me, you silly girl, but whenever I hold you close to my heart, I can hear your voice whispering that you love me.

I was feeling her warmth, her deep genuine love, even though Joan had said eight-thousand times *I don't want to marry you* I knew she meant the opposite, because when you say stuff you adamantly oppose, lots of times it means you really believe it. I was feeling our closeness, that deepness that went within the lust and came out the other side.

And I didn't mind it.

I had no idea about any of this, but I knew in the back of my mind, or even in the front, that we were special, a true-love special. And even within this newness, its uncertainty, I was feeling alright.

But, a good feeling may also have an opposite, but only if you are ready and willing to accept both. The good with the ungood, the marriage with the divorce, and the elation with the deflation.

'Hey,' she said one day, 'Dress me good?'

'As opposed to undressing? Be a change, but sure, I'd love to. First of all, where are you going?'

'Oh, let's say, to meet a new family member? Not a party, not formal, a casual new meeting, but a little cultured and European classy.'

'Okay, I've got this. Come over here.'

I made her stand straight and tall.

'Look at this beautiful young lady. She is so pretty.' I touched her face lightly and kissed her, softly. 'I'd go with red lippy, say, fire-engine red. See her black eyes, sparkling, honest and true. Her beauty is ethereal, her beauty crosses cultures, her beauty is stunning. It turns heads, both male and female. Her cropped coal-black glossy hair shows her slender neck. (As I softly stroked her neck) Pure grace. I think small sapphire earrings, subtle and powerful. *Could you please take your top off?* Thank you. Look at her shoulders, my goodness. Curved and shapely and deserving of being shown. Her back is divine, but let's only see a small section. This is not a time for an evening gown.' I took her bra off. 'Her breasts are too provocative, too full and pointy, way too strokable to be shown. A little cleavage with some lace maybe.' *Could you please take your skirt off? Pants too.* 'That, boys and girls, is a cute arse. Curvy perfection. Fuck me. Womanhood, a pure womanhood of the Gods. The dress must come down flat, not tight below her arse, otherwise we are into trash territory. Let it flow in loose delicate swayings of sexiness. My God, look at her flat tummy. Spunky or what. We are now into supreme fitness melded with the womanhood. The dress must be flat-tight for her tummy with an inverted thin-leather triangle to lead us to her mound, her stunning mound. And short, not too short, but above the knee enough to show her long slender shapely legs. And make us pant when we might get a glimpse of those firm thighs. Flat shoes or low heels? Not sure. By the way, the dress, the soft flowy dress, should be dark navy blue – with medium-sized yellow buttons – to highlight her caramel-smooth skin.'

All the while, Joan had her eyes closed, in what I thought was rapture and that any minute I would get lucky. But no, tears rolled down.
And I was confused.

* * *

Guinea fowl are independent, but too noisy. Loved their independence, but gave them away. Peacock, vicious bastard. Ate him, just like the circled snake. Quail, trod on them. Pigeons. Now we're talking. The ultimate in sustainability, almost. Almost maintenance free because they home. Leave the loft propped open bit of wheat, fresh water, and Robert's your father's brother. Squab pie and chokoes. No wonder I'm so old and healthy. I was given two pair of pigeons by a man in town called Mr Robert Good. A blue-bar cock and a mealy-pied hen, a blue-chequer cock and a white hen. Their multi-coloured offspring were named after their person-grandfather as follows:

No, Not, Very, Always, Often, Johnny Be, Extra, and You're fucking Kidding Me.

* * *

Joan.

We were still good. Raunchy as ever, but the air still tasted a bit tangy. I had done nothing and Joan had done nothing. It just was. Some wases are okay because they speak truth and induce a self-questioning and often an other questioning. Which may be a good thing if done nicely and leads to greater depth. But I wasn't sure about this was. *Hey, we need to talk* … so I ignored it, and my persistent rational brain.

* * *

One of the eight baby bantams, I named Jayden. He had a mullet accompanied by a mohawk. He also developed furry feet. Who the fuck were his parents? Punk rockers from Bilbo's Shire? A Royal spoonbill in nesting plumage father and a great crested grebe mother? Jayden was on the spectrum, fidgeted, and had social anxiety, he had Dyslexia, Dysgraphia and Dyscalculia, was listed as ADD, ADHD, OCD, and had eaten DDT. Off task every ten minutes. I gave him a small tennis ball to squeeze, but he threw it in the lantana. I hoped a snake would get him. But Jayden grew up didn't he.

He survived his teenage years of fast hens, an absent father and several pecks of magic mushrooms. He survived his false chickenhood memories of all the tries he thought he had scored. And became a father himself. Thank Christ Jayden didn't mate with a brush turkey.

The Creek would be like a fucking zombie movie in fast motion. I named his children, Drumstick, Soup, Meatloaf, Lovely Legs, and Croissant.

One morning, a stalking goanna spied Jayden's delicious children, who were zipping around with their mother a little way away. Just dicking around, running at each other and puffing their chests out. Just like men do when they play football. Just like men do all the fucking time. All idiots because they refuse to accept that their angry misogynistic arrogance shit is obsolete. Our Jayden, still carrying his diagnoses of mental health issues, hyperactivity and social ineptitude, not assigned nor accepted by himself, hurled himself at the goanna. Beak and feet first with no thought of self, his aggression a cross between a Pitbull, a hyena and a dumb-arsed rugby league player. The goanna hissed and puffed a fake defence, and galloped away.

Jayden 1, goanna 0.

Justified anger.

* * *

Town.

There were gossips. I could hear them at fifty paces.

'What does he do up there? A wash and a shave wouldn't hurt him. He doesn't dress very nicely for town, does he? Have you seen him with that aborigine? Disgusting.'

I had been back to the barber's whenever I thought my hair had grown an eighth of an inch. Which was every ten minutes. One must present well, one must. No point looking like a ruffian all the time. Georgie was fun. She stroked my head with both hands, swooshed them up above my ears to meet at the top of my current erection. She was sexy for sure, but maybe more sensuous in the way she moved and laughed. We spoke half-English-half-French and this added to the excitement, the stimulation of young lover dreaming, of a flirty what might happen here. Once I took a handout from under the gown and placed it on her arse.

She didn't move.

Town.

'Where's the frog?'

'You mean Georgie? You liked her?'

Don't you love it when people don't answer your question, and come back with their own question that is reeking with judgement? Reeking with oily smarmy inferential rhetorical cuntness. 'If you must know, she's gone back to New South Wales. You want the same haircut or what?'

'Yes thanks.' But for Christ's sake don't lean on me like she did.

Does the true self have an indemnity clause? A copout-independent clause-truth that understands nuances and kicks you in the arse when it thinks you are avoiding a dependent clause-truth?

'Yes, I liked her all right.'

* * *

If you see an eel in a freshwater creek or pond, consider this: this eel has swum back to this place, its parent's home base, from the Coral Sea, without a map or compass, as we know them. We're talking a three-year journey, from salt water to fresh water, travelling thousands of kilometres. Next time you see an eel, get down on your knees and honour greatness.

There was an eel I wanted to eat.

The Creek was full of eels. A writhing mass of seething slimy green-brown underwater snakes, a seagrass of tentacled-tails swirling in the sweeping current. They would poke about under rocks like honeyeaters probing into flowers, like little kids licking the bowl, like CEOs sucking up at a board meeting, like politicians before an election. The one eel I wanted to eat was over two metres long. He lived in the cold deep water under a rock shelf and I was determined to catch him as he was determined to not be catched. When you hook eels, they do the crocodile roll thing with extras, and if you haven't got a swivel down there near the hook, you will be spun in tight circles until you are encased in a cocoon of nylon. I have seen heaps of skeletons wrapped in nylon.

'Ah look. There's Fred. Didn't have a swivel, did he. Silly bastard. Serve him right.'

This big eel, my meal-to-be big eel, was cunning, and that is not anthropomorphic. This baby could trick better than a crow counting sticks and rifles, better than an insect masquerading as a spider, better than a conservative politician pretending to be caring and honest. I tossed in three or four bits of bait to get him active, and he rose like an awakened dragon and scooped them up. Over two metres, remember. The minute I put a hook in a piece, he swam up next to it, left it alone and grinned at me. I did notice that he needed some serious dental work. Not that I would mention this of course.

But I caught him didn't I.

One late afternoon, I crawled along on my belly to his hidey-hole. No luring, no tempting bait, I was going in for the juggler straight away. I can be cunning too, you slimy bastard. I lowered a piece of baited salami and he smacked it. And didn't he kick up a stink! He thrashed and roared, and I stood up and laughed at him, I gloated. I taunted. I said, 'Sucked in, buddy. You will be in my pot tonight.'

He rolled frenetically, he tossed and turned, he spat, yelled, and cussed; but I had him covered. On land he continued with the headstands, backflips, and tight tense circular curls.
I waited.

'You done?'

And when he stopped, when he settled; he changed. He was no longer cunning, he was no longer an adversary, but he was also no pleader. He accepted his fate, and lay there, waiting for me, the victor, to cut his throat.

As I watched this monster waiting for death, his not mine, (I had used a swivel), I wasn't worried that he would die from being out of water. They can be out of water for forty-eight hours. And travel overland. Apparently, they can get 50% of their oxygen through their skin.

You see them hitching on the highways.

'Yeah, slither in buddy, where you going?'

'Oh, just heading to the coast off New Caledonia to breed.'

I leant down, pinged out the hook and gently pushed him back into the water. Then got back up off my knees.

I like eels
Because they are a nice oily.
In and out of the water.
If you had one as a pet you could put it on a leash and take it for a swim.
I like it when brush turkeys get pissed on overripe bananas.
'No, you may not kill me just because I am a drunk turkey.
Let me go. Like you did that eel. Put me on a leash too.'
Nope, if I can catch you,
You are going to be mine tonight.
I used to like getting drunk.
I may need some sherry.
Soon.

* * *

Town.

Joan said, 'I'm going away soon.'

'As in, leaving town?'
'Yep.'
'How long for?'
'Not sure, not for long.'
'That's cleared that up then.'
'Got friends, over the border.'
'Okay then. Say hi for me. And I'll see you soon.'

What the fuck did she mean, Going over the border?

What the fuck did she mean, Got friends there? Silence separates, not distance. Light may travel in a straight line, life seldom does. On the way home, after Joan had said she was going away, the wind blew into the truck. But the window was closed. And I didn't know the words to my songs. Back at home, the hurtful winds started to pick up and even though the door was closed, I could feel the sneaky ice, the scathing screams and the hurtful hints. None of Joan's decisions, whereabouts or reasons were my business, none, none whatsoever, I knew that, I know that, but the wind still cut me in half and I bled fiercely.

I had never questioned Joan on who her friends were, what she did, where she went, or anything. Never. Nor did she me. Especially because we agreed to fuck no other. However, when you hear something like Hey, just going for a burn over the hill, get back to you soon-ish, it comes out as, or is perceived as, Yeah, you can come to the party if you want, or, This is gonna hurt, and whichever way the mop flops, whatever way the cookie crumbles, it comes loaded with an incoming pain for your heart, a pain that sticks out like dog's balls as it advances, reversing its protruding shining marbles of doubt into your insecurities. My rational brain screamed at me. *Fuuuck, you need to heed this warning, Mister. Things aint right.* Even though I just knew something wasn't right, I dismissed his message, I rejected the pain by telling myself I did not believe my gut feeling, or my rational brain because I wanted peace, I wanted love, I wanted girl, I wanted my life as it had been. I felt breathless, I felt a physical pain, a churning worried pain. Yet still, within my rejection of the what was, the rejection of myself, I knew I was wrong, because when you say stuff you don't believe lots of times, it means you really believe it. Especially when you say it to yourself. Especially when you try to lop off the worm's head. Maybe the nags had moved closer? Closer to being believed? Closer to my real self?

As quickly as I was slowly believing in owning up to myself, to listening to my rational brain, emotional brain kicked in. *Hey, excuse me, don't listen*

*to that fucking whinger, we have stuff that needs doing here. Like that hole
in the orchard fence, the chooks' water dish needs a good scrub and the old
Dodge needs a service. So let's get cracking.*

* * *

Avoidance is a god
is a god
that is a self-god but
a let's not face the truth god.
What did I expect?
A god who helps me avoid and deny?
Or did I expect, want, desire, need, a god who advises then helps me decide?
Would I listen to a god like that anyway?

Joan and me, our was wasn't right. Our tangy air tanged and I needed to
untang this tang. I had to wait for Joan to contact me because she had to be
the one to do the contacting. That's if she wanted to. Not only because I
didn't know where she was, but because it was she that had gone, not me.
Yet she was free. We were both free.
I knew that.
Fuck, I was hurting. And still, I didn't listen to my rational brain.

* * *

The brush turkeys ate a few things of mine, but we remained friends. I was
a good friend to share with, but I had a friendship cut-off point, and that was,
if I saw ten or more turkeys devastating my gardens, I would shoot one and
eat it. What friends are for. One day five turkeys picked and ate the corm of
one of my banana trees (or herb, as it is so classified), and the whole tree,
including an almost ripe bunch, fell like a giant in the rainforests of Borneo.
Or Brazil. Or South-east Queensland.

Turkeys have two escape strategies. One is running and dodging, and
they are swift and therefore not so easy to shoot. The other is that they will
fly up to a low branch. They think they are safe from predators there. Sucked
in I say. I ran at the mob, flapped and yelled, and they flushed up to a low
branch. While their red heads and some yellow wattles peered down at me,
a quick straw poll followed by a democratically accepted misuse of statistics
quickly deemed the numbers to have exceeded the cut-off point.
I put one in the spout.

Brush turkey males, those that survived, build a nest on the ground. If you could call a mound of leaves and compost as big as a car that. More like a friggin crocodile's than a bird's. The male turkey has a heat sensor inside his mouth to keep the inside of the mound at a little over ninety-degrees Fahrenheit. The chicks have no assistance after they hatch. They find their own ice-bath.

All by myself

Naturally.

Some days, like these, I couldn't be fucked plucking a bird, so I'd skin it. But then you'd have to keep the oven low, because with no skin, the bird would cook differently. Burn even, or dry out. Nothing worse than a dried-out turkey.

I did fix the hole in the orchard fence. I walked around and touched each fruit tree, some now with patches of lichen. I stopped at one avocado tree and smiled. I had planted it from a seed from a fruit from a tree I had collected from a few valleys over. This seed was from an avocado that was from a tree that had been planted in the 1930s. Just one tree which had come from a seed from a fruit from a tree in Fiji. From there to here is not such a long way.

* * *

Hidden in a rainforest over the border there is a small town, a town so small it doesn't even have a name, a small town loaded with grubby beautiful hippies, dope-smoking hippies who may have just got life's balance right, and in that small no-name town there is a girl. This girl is waiting for me. She is waiting for me to come down to sweep her away, to sweep her back to our little town so that we can be as we once were. I liked befores. They are way better than wases, maybes or willbes. I liked everything before, but I felt a small earthquake starting in my was stomach.

'Yes, he will come for me, he will always come for me, he will always be there for me. Today? Maybe not. Perhaps tomorrow, but he will come because friendship can be forever. Not to mention slutty sex.'

There is a knock on the door. But is it a real knock? Or is it just a hopeful knock?

I went over the border to that small town. I went chasing that girl. Isn't this what life is about? Fuck growing chokoes, wandering about in the rainforest and birdwatching.

Joan had travelled there to see some friends. Apparently. I had some dread about that apparently word but didn't know why. Didn't understand why I had a dread. One of those deep butterflies that fly in and out of your insecurities and although they may land softly they carry warnings. My rational brain yelled, *Fuuuck! When will you listen?*

'Come down, I need to see you.' She had written. Ha! Couldn't do without me for even a month could she? It's hard being so gorgeous let me tell you. We would soon be running naked. Joan, come back here, you little hussy. Let's rub oil over each other. Let's soak in a bath together. Let's lust together like we used to because we fucked no other.

'Hey my sweet. Jeez you look great in that dark blue dress.'

'Oh, let's say, to meet a new family member. Not a party, not formal, a casual new meeting, but a little cultured and European classy.'

Come see this beautiful black girl, this stunning woman. Look at her curves, her full, firm, bouncy breasts. Her black tight hair is maddening. Her red lippy is totally fuckable ... the soft flowy dress, the dark navy-blue dress – with big yellow buttons – to highlight her caramel-smooth skin.

She wrapped herself around me and gave me a soft wet kiss that made my blood heat up and my heart explode.

'Hey Mister, I'm with someone else. I'm sorry for us.'

'Oh, that's fine, really it is. We are free, we both know that. Good luck to you both and give him my regards,' a strange voice said.

'Will do, except he is a she.'

She was with another, as in, now living together. Not me, a new person; and I didn't care that it was a girl person. I had no nothing about it being a girl, only an acute achy disappointment that I had been ditched. Again. First time by my parents, this time by my Joan. I was gone, out, finished. And when it started to sink in that Joan had indeed left me, someone slammed me into a brick wall, and it hurt my head.
And my heart.

our love was started
middled and ended on lust
pure hot moist fuckable cock cunty lust
with no guilt only deep satisfaction and deeper pleasure
it did move a bit though

it did change a little within the hotbodies of just us two,
it moved yes
and became perhaps a dreamy
a dreamy thought of how the world might be
or should be,
of how love should might be,
a lust that became that love
became a true and deep love
yet while, or maybe because of, it stayed largely within its fucking.
maybe it lost a something because of its narrow field of vision,
it lost a something
and I don't know how to try and get this lost thing back
or even what it was really
or maybe it didn't lose a something?
or an anything?
maybe it gained a few things
and we didn't keep them
because we were too scared.
what the fuck would I know about love
not enough, that's for sure.
oh, the pain! The deep anguish pain
is not a victory but a handsaw of cruelty
cutting my arms off
cutting my head off
but I won't die until sunset
and now, this now of shit time coming my way on the new channel
this now of confused loss time
with no ads, no promotions no teasers
only a stay tuned till the next episode
of rabbit traps snapping my feet,
repeating the unravelling
the opening of life's jaws
I will not accept that it is over
because fuck me
it was so good;
and that's how I wanted and want it to stay
otherwise, existence is only a hopeful essence
of a started unfinished ended love.

At least she had told me to my face. No Dear John letter, no lies, no tricks, No, I need to spend more time with my family bullfuckingshit. Travel expenses would be nice though. Bit of petrol money and a cash advance to pay for my thermos and sandwiches would have been nice. Just kidding. Just kidding because love doesn't count money, but it sure as fucking hell does count feelings. Yet even within her honesty within her upfrontness, within the situation being as it was, I felt a lost, an empty lost. Then someone else slammed me into that fucking brick wall again. Would they ever leave me alone?

Fucking bullies.

I was a coughed-up furball of hurt, an owl's vomit, a rejected piece of unwanted bones and skin. And the hurt kicked in worse because I was now home and lonely, not just home alone. The rejection brought up insecurities that I had left half-asleep, those drowsy insecurities that tried to get me to wake up, but I had turned the alarm off and went back to sleep. But I wonder, are these almost-warnings, these nags that will not go away, are just that, insecurities? And not based on truth? *Or just maybe, they are truth? One day you will listen to me.* Or are they a part of the real true self that understands you? Maybe one day I'll stop asking questions? Or one day listen to my rational brain?

* * *

Solitude is great if you don't have heartache,
If you do, it's the tightening tummy turmoil time
Just like an impending conflict.
It's a doubt your-self time.
I was going nuts missing her.
My known world wobbled on its scattered degree axis.

* * *

Because brush-turkeys spend a lot of time on the ground, you would naturally think that they nest on the ground. And you would be correct. Have the day off. Satin bower-birds spend a lot of time on the ground too. But they don't nest on the ground. Back to work, you. Their stick nest is up in a tree or a vine. The male builds a bower on the ground which he decorates with all my blue pegs, blue toothbrushes and blue moods. But this bower is not a nest; it is a means of attracting the female for purposes of rooting. Same reason why blokes drive gurgly utes, strut on the dance floor or play rugby-league. A mature female satin bower bird is green and brown, and the mature male is a soft sheeny purple.

These birds were flogging my fruit, my white mulberries, persimmons and one stone fruit that had escaped my wrath. Gone, or picked at, and left to rot. You don't keep doing that to me with no consequences. Just ask the brush turkeys. The remaining ones that is. I shot a male, a deep purple male on his way to make smoke on the water. Don't steal my fruit, or listen to heavy metal while you smoke or there will be fire in the sky.

And I hung his deep purple body in a mulberry tree that had a few berries left to frighten his rellies. Yet, the others landed next to him and continued making music. And memories they may never forget.
Satin bower-birds, 1. Tony, 0.

* * *

I became angry with the world. And I needed something to base my anger on. How I skipped over real estate agents, bankers, politicians, to settle on the treatment of a bunch of dead logs, I'm buggered if I know.

In my way to find my chosen anger, I wasn't concentrating on anything else, and I tripped over. Barked my shins badly. The chooks all stopped scratching and turned around to stare. 'What are you looking at!'

There were huge sawed stumps with their dead white logs on the ground next to them. One-hundred and fifty feet of smashed tree, left to rot. Some in the open, some hidden in regrowth. I found out that these were brush box trees. The area was either cleared of so-called good trees, or clear-felled, either way, these trees were left to rot and not milled locally because the cut timber was spikey and hard to handle. And they dulled the saws. And could twist and get uneven when drying if it wasn't cut at the right time and not stripped properly. And because there were plenty of other trees, which were easier to slaughter. Fuck me you wasteful precious poxy cunts, was the timber that plentiful? Were you that greedy? What about only taking a few at a fucken time?

I was angry, fucking angry. 'Oh, but that's what we did then.' That is way too short-sighted for me and an excuse that was as bad as city folk wasting water because they have the cash to pay their fines, as bad as throwing vegetables away because they had a mark, and as bad as saying, 'Oh, everyone else does it, so I can too.' I know the government back in the day had said, 'You must clear so much scrub each year to retain your selected land.' Don't start me on anything to do with government. Any government.

While the shop's open, by-the-fucking-way, from whom did you select your land? Did they say, 'No worries brother, take my land and destroy it.'? Doubt it. And yet, and yet, within my filthy crankiness, my dark black anger, my rational brain whispered. *Hey, you, you work in a timber mill, and live on land that was stolen. So get a fucking grip.* Did anyone hear something? *Will you stop ignoring me!* Sawn brush box timber is a deep pinkish-red-brown colour and is excellent for bridge beams. Shit in the ground, just like flooded gum. It is also a fantastic floor and wall timber. You can see some in the Opera House in Sydney and in the new Parliament House in Canberra. Only the best for these people. I wondered if the entitled privileged cunts knew where it came from, and how it was milled.

When I took breath and mellowed, I thought, What if we logged selectively, including the remaining brush boxes? A few sawlogs here this year, a few sawlogs from the other slope next year. Say, one tree per five acres? What if we had local industries as well as sawn timber to sell? Like nurseries, forest regeneration, furniture making, charcoal from the offcuts, selling the sawdust to butchers and outdoor dunny people, and the offcuts to stove people? What if you had more control over who you sold sawn timber to and for how much? And cut out pricks who dictated what and how much and when?

'Oh dear, that piece of spotty gum has ten percent sapwood. It won't sell as easily.'

You want that stick of wood; you pay me top dollar. Or else get your own,
You snivelling fucken arsehole cunt.
Have I said yet that I don't like middlemen?
And that I'm cranky?

get your own unreality
your own tree
and your legal access to it
fell it without killing yourself
snig it to and onto the truck you don't have
drive it to the mill
you don't have
unload
without smashing the truck yourself or the neighbours
take the bark off

the tree not your shins dickhead
and good luck with that
use the wire rope hook and winch to drag it up the oiled-slides and onto the
bench
position it
correctly
or you may die
or someone ese may die because of your stupidity
but you knew that I suppose
because you're such a fucken smartarse
break it down without sawing yourself or someone else into chunks
push the flitch onto the oiled-ramps
then with some other poor sucker
cut the flitch into pieces
shift the metal pin to four inches
saw regather flip return to sender
shift the pin to two inches
saw stack
fucking easy
wasn't it?

Sawn timber should be ten times its current price. The skills needed to fell
trees, transport them, and then cut them into sawn timber, are fading into a
sunset of memory and faded sepia images. It's hard and dangerous work too.
And the trees themselves are becoming scarcer.

I milled some brush box logs with Joe. Had to wear gloves. It's a spikey
sucker. Planes up smooth though. Joe gulleted and sharpened the saws after every
session. What could I do to save forests except rant? What can one person do?

* * *

I was masturbating more, not erotically, but quickly and almost harshly. I
deserved better, and my cock deserved better. It became a necessity of pain
over a plethora of pleasure. What a waste of pleasure, of the pure enjoyment
of life? Where was my eroticism? Where was my lust? Where was my
friendship? Where was my laughter?
I missed her so much.

The me that blamed me made me kick things, and whinge, and I become negative and down on the world and I was a misery guts. Planes crashed, ships founded on rocks and the nights became lonely. The little things that usually went wrong every now and again were usually nothing to write home about, merely one-hundred-yard sprints, but they now became high hurdles over twenty-six miles, became excuses just so I could blame them, so that I could blame me, not as a failed sprinter, but as an exhausted unrequited unfinished marathon of miserygutness. Of a self that was based on pity. The piece of wood that split when it wasn't supposed to, the totally burnt roast pumpkin, the next snapped drill-bit.

They were all my fault, my loss without victory, my fixation, and I couldn't see that they came from somewhere else, a somewhere else of, Hey, I aint thinking straight, a somewhere else of, You need to snap out of it buddy, another somewhere else of, You need to talk to someone.

My rational brain tried to intervene again.

He said, *Wooo, hang on dude, you're okay. Let's look at this. You're okay, really. You have a home, a nice home, fresh food, cool water, some money (cough, cough), and your health isn't too bad. Well, your physical health anyway. Meet every challenge with justice, self-control and reason. You are too attached. Let it go.*

But I was having none of it. Those things were of no importance if my heart was broken, surely? Emotional brain understood. She said, *Stooop! Have none of his shit. Jesus Mary and Joseph! Too attached? You fucking emotionless piece of dirt! Our hearts are splintered our hearts are stabbed herewith and sunder our hearts are wounded bad! We are hurting man. This is no time for fucking lists! Ignore the cunt! Jesus fucking Christ, we need the anger we need to get it out we need to smash something! RB, get a life!*

RB-Got one thanks. And, unlike yours, it's a settled, measured and sane one. Screams were heard across the mountains.

Then I was angry about fossil fuels. The, Yes, we have accepted the unparalleled environmental guidelines, you know, the ones we won't follow. I still avoided the real estates, the bankers, the politicians. The air pollution, the oil spills. I had read an article that said, 'Did you know that in the seventies and even before, fossil fuel companies knew that there would be severe pollution and health risks? They knew, they schemed, they denied, and then they delayed. And that there were over twenty oil spills …?'

I was angry about dirty coal. Dirty coal for what? So we could have lights at night? Whoopee. A kettle? An air conditioner? What, are we that soft? And

I was angry mining waste and factory shit that was being dumped in waterways within government guidelines.

Fuck me. I was pissed off at our shortcomings, our inability to realise that what we are all doing is fucked. But in all this I was never cruel to my animals. Never. My anger let me know that it was me it wanted to hurt. But I still failed to see the things that you reject, you are.

The brain is powerful and knows when I'm down, when I'm weak, when I'm susceptible; and it strikes like a death-adder hiding under dead leaves. My immune system of the mind was fucked. And I let it be so. The choice of self-belief. The choice to be a victim. My rational brain had tried, and my emotional brain left me hanging because I was too strong, too not listening, and too not watching where I was going. I banged my leg on a post. And I didn't care.

* * *

Henry said, 'See you're limping.'
　'Correct.'
　'Get a tub of horse liniment.'
　'But Henry …'

'How may I help you?'
　'Couple of tubs of horse liniment thanks. My horses are playing up.'
　'Okay, make sure you read the label.'

For animal treatment only
A muscle and joint relieving gel.
There is a meat withholding period
Of two days,
For humans.
The rest of you make your own arrangements.

I rubbed it in, it eased my leg, but it didn't help my mind. Why did Henry suggest it? I suspect my self-lies and self-denials made my heart limp as well. A Dear John letter from me to me. *I'm leaving you now because you're avoiding me. You're not listening to what I'm really saying. I have listed reasons, I have …* Piss off rational brain, you have no fucking idea. The gel did take the leg pain away though. Took the physical but not the mental. Took the what was the representative outgoing from what was the continual original and avoided ingoing. But if I had to rinse and repeat like shampoo bottles used to yell, I suspect I would go broke buying horse liniment. Or when that ailment was cured, which one would be next because the underlying stuff was still there? Shoulders because I had lifted wrong? Ribs because I had leaned wrong? I needed a liniment for my mind.

Henry said, when I told him that the liniment had worked but I needed a different one, 'Most of us need a different liniment every now and again, because most of us are worriers, and our dreams are held back by the need for too much liniment. Dreams that you don't follow aren't dreams; they are just wishful thinking to be put aside because you don't believe in yourself because you worry too much. A pain that is not faced is a pain that keeps needing liniment. Avoidance builds up and causes bruises.' He paused for a bit, then stabbed me. 'Love hurts, does it not?'

If avoidance as a means of escape, as a healthy survival technique, works, how long does it work for? Or does it just sit back there, having a pot of tea, waiting? Waiting until you face yourself? I went to an imaginary psychiatrist, 'Could I please have some liniment for my troubled mind? I'm avoiding my pot of tea.'

She said, 'Sure you can. One must not get burnt by a recalcitrant pot of tea. Here you go. Make sure you read the label.'

For those not in control
Of anything.
For those who won't listen
To anyone.
This an imaginary crazy-mind relieving gel
With a withholding period
For as long as you choose.

When the small daily jobs were done, and the routines become meaningless because the heart was absent, when memories seem irrelevant and when being physical to burn the heartache doesn't work so well, then it all becomes shit. There cannot be any, Comeon, just get on with it, because that sort of advice-talk is also not helpful to a troubled soul. It is demeaning and dismissive and defecating. I did nothing and became so exhausted from doing nothing, all I could do was lay down, point, and mumble.

I was confused, reused and abused. My rational brain and emotional brain were fed up with my incoherent ravings, my indecisions, my playing the victim. They joined forces, which was a little unnerving, and recommended a different liniment:

Okay okay, it's okay to feel angry, melancholy, flat, and not in control. No problem. But you're going too far too long. And you know we love you, right? We're a big fan. But for fuck's sake, stop with the shit, will you? Your current reality is based on avoidance, big time. You're grasping at air. Grasp at our liniment instead. It will fix your dicky leg (a dubious, almost non-existent injury), and your dodgy mind (this one is definitely fucked). Here is the real liniment of life, created by your two favourite advisors. Get off your arse, go have an adventure, properly prepared for all contingencies, with a superb list of course. Go back to your routines, their repetition will give you confidence, move slowly, give love and kindness, then go and fuck someone. Once you do all this, you will never need liniment again.

* * *

A table note.

Going up the slope opposite
To save my soul,
I hope.
I have the right liniment this time so I should be apples.
Look after the troops if I don't come back,
Please.
And feed the eel
Or he'll come looking for you.

As requested, and required, I wrote down my liniment list:

One water bottle (full),
One non-functioning brain.

There's no water up there, they said. 'Each person will have to carry at least four litres per day.' What do you expect them to do? Fill a fucking Olympic Pool? Up the steep slope opposite the house, up past the false ridge, which sounds easy but it aint, through the lawyer cane, wild raspberries, the stinging trees, and onto the real top ridge. Up on the plateau, the magnificent plateau, then down the other side to a beautiful stream. There was water alright. Not a soak, not a spring, but a stream. Then up again to meet a trail, an old bushwalker's trail. When I joined this old trail, I met a tree.

'Hey Tony, how you doing? About time we met. Come here and stroke me.'

They all say that. A thorny yellowwood – with thorns on her trunk like roses' thorns, but way stronger and sharper. Thirty-feet tall, deep green shiny leaves.

'Hello to you my lovely. I will indeed stroke you, somewhat carefully, and we will meet again because I know where you live.'

When I did walk along the trail later, I stopped at the same tree, and said to the hikers who were with me, with their drained swimming pools, 'Hang on a tick, give me your empty water bottles and I'll get us some water. Don't lean on that tree while I'm gone. She's a friend of mine. I know her well and she loves me, but she may bite you.'

* * *

And yet, and yet, sometimes it helps to shine a torch into a dark corner. I listened to my new advisory team. Having both agree together was unheard of, because they hated each other. Wonder how long they'll last.

Go back to my routines, they said, nay, they implored, they insisted even. Bossy cunts. What are routines anyway? I had heaps but they got away from me. They became a hindrance, a job and not a love. Maybe if I combined the old move slowly with the routines, things might settle?

When you move slowly, you are in the moment, the moment of safety, awe, awareness, the moment of the universe going in. Going in ready to explode, if you're ready, going in to save the world, if you're ready. Routines give solace to the mind via the automatic, the known and loved automatic. I know that. Routines get each job done through a pattern, a repetitive structured pattern that gives security and a knowingness of not so much, Hey bitches, that's another job done, but a small blanket to suck the corner of that gives a comfort, a warmth and a secret satisfaction. The memories that form from these deep routines delve into rituals, and these memories become who we are. Making meaning rather than just doing, or at least as well as doing, gives a certain oomph, a particular lift.

I harkened to thou, yon advisors, and will now sallie and go forthwith to be involved in the pursuing of a delectable young woman with which to have my unseemingly hairy way.

RB-What did he just say?

EB-Stick around kid. You might learn something.

I went into town to pay a visit to the coffee shop girl loaded with kindness and lust in my loins. Even though I knew from before that we were the couple who would never have sex, I persisted with my quest. I took in a wallaby skin, a bag of bush lemons, and a dozen eggs. She's a practical girl this one; no fancy flowers, no perfumes for her, just solid workable earthy items.

Just a hand on a hand and a shoulder to cry on. Never mind the strong coffee. No words. No words needed. Touch speaks, touch speaks way more than words. Way deeper. Combine a touch, a look, and empathy becomes the moment. Her hand and eyes, said, I don't really know, and that's okay. But I understand. I get it. The coffee shop girl said, with her touch and her smile, I have plopped a lure in the deep pool of your soul, of maybe the deeper pool of your desires. I have given you a teaser, a half-smile lure that is waiting to be snapped up. What do you reckon mister?

But there was that same problem.

There is always a girl that you know that you can never root. Not talking about family, or the general female population, but a girl you get to know, who is super friendly, gorgeously stunning, and even a bit all over you, but there's no chemistry, no lust, and if it did ever move across, you would go, Oh Jesus, what is going on here? The coffee shop girl was pretty and cute, no doubt about that, and now, incredibly understanding without asking a thing. But there was a blockage, and it had nothing to do with me being with Joan back then. I knew coffee shop girl before Joan, and it still wasn't on. I knew this from before and it was still the same. It was weird, a sort of sisterly comforting warmth, and the weirdest of all was that, regardless of her touch and her fishing expeditions, she knew it too. Now that I think about it, I didn't really think she was teasing, not at all, just a testing of her feminine wiles from her to her via me. It was a togetherness of something yet nothing more, a joining of no joining, a friendship of neutrals.

And so, to you my two ardent supporters, as one this time which, I might add, made the Earth wobble a bit, I had listened and I had acted upon, I had done your bidding, your fucking list, your adventuring, the return to routines, your slowly thing, and the kindness giving, but alas I could not run a chook raffle, I was as useful as tits on a bull, couldn't get a root in a brothel, and stuff like that. But never mind, I might be all out of love but I'm not needing to stock up on liniment.

Thank you both.

EB-Woohoo, we did it. We got the old boy out of a rut, off the hook, and into gear. This is good shit this working together.

RB-It is indeed. Quite enjoyable. I must go and have a glass of Port and get my pipe. Clearly it was my advice on the safety list for when he goes up that dangerous cliff face that was the precursor, the initial, the beginning ...

EB-Oh fuck off, you dopey cunt. You see the list he made? A water bottle? For crying out loud! There's a lengthy list for you. It was me, moi, who indicated that kindness would help, not to mention my little cracker at the end, to go and fuck someone.

RB-Ha ha-well now, miss pretty perfect, miss psycho bitch, he didn't get a root, did he now? So I win, you stuck up little cow!

So nice to be back home.

I was starting to feel better, less quick to be cranky at myself and anyone, dead trees included; or anything else included. More settled, more accepting of this thing that was. It was over and there you go, meant more than it did before. An easing of something deep, the accepting of perhaps more than what was, but of my place within it.

I returned to the early morning structure. Jerked off, stoved off, coffee potted off, chooked off, cowed off, then onto the day to day off. Gathered wood, tended the vegetables, watched the sky. It comes after you face yourself, work hard yet slowly, and these replace the Poor Me. That one who can't talk properly because his mouth is full of self-pity. And it finally worked because freedom comes within and after discipline, and some time.

Time, yes,
Lends a hand in love and life,
Not too much, just enough
If you are ready.

Because life must be lived, is what life is. Life must be lived, yes, but by each person, and heaven knows what you bastards get up to. God, it's hard being so wise. Particularly after the event. Which is where wisdom comes from. From your afters, and others' afters. Where else? After experiences, after stuff happens, there's a big list available, with headings. 'Only choose from here if you've been jilted. Only choose from this pile if you've experienced death, denigrations, or denials. Not listening to Niggles? Fuck off, you should have listened ages ago. Bad luck.'

Actually, this list is available before life gets too far, but we choose to reject it. We think we are indestructible, not just physically, but emotionally. 'Please. If that happened to me, I wouldn't do that ...'

* * *

The soil is the result of the ending of lives, many lives killed by rivers, creeks, wind, sunshine and rain from a short time alive on the planet, compared to a human life span that is. A burial of volcanoes, trees, animals, and rocks in an environmentally sound coffin of natural materials (locally sourced, thank you very much), or cremated in a fiery inferno. Ashes available at a price to be stored in an urn or cast into the universe. Soil can be white, red, grey, yellow, brown, or black, a universal non-discriminatory friable see, smell, hear or touch, a race, penetrable and malleable. You could live in soil forever.

* * *

The early sunlight made the dark green leaves turn yellowy-green. It also made spiderwebs shine. I saw one strung between two trees. The gap was over twenty feet. When a breeze swayed this wire rope, it made the glint of sunlight move along like a piece of glass. If I hadn't been watching where I was walking, this tripwire would have taken my head off. Straight through the neck bone. I wondered how big the web maker was. I imagined a crouching hairy thing, up there watching me. Lurking in the leaves, legs bent in the spring stance.

* * *

Each evening, just on dusk, there was a hop with a limp on the roof. Then it would stop. Too loud for a lizard, not clunky solid enough to be a possum. Who might hop and limp? A one-legged wallaby? Maybe Captain Hook is up there. It was a brush turkey. I saw it and I left it to roost on my roof. Probably the drunk one that got away.

A black butterfly, blacker than night, with even more beautiful beauty within this darkness, had red blotches and a few blue blotches on each wing side, and larger white piano keys. The orchard swallowtail. Pay attention kids, here be symmetry. Bigger than an eagle. Bigger than an albatross. One flap, with wing tips touching high and low to force uplift of a metre, then she did it again. These butterflies have been to botany classes and can identify an orange tree even when it is hidden. These butterflies skirted around my citrus, this newly identified citrus, went up and down, testing the air, the sunlight, the wind, the colours and spectrums none of us can see, the up and down invisible colours and spectrums, the up and down black beauty magic. They choose a new tip, a soft, delicate new tip, and pop an egg, a tiny sphere, complete, and able to withstand 100-degree heat. Pay attention, kids, we're into 3D shapes now. With heat shields. Three caterpillars per citrus tree was acceptable, over that it was off to see Jayden for them. Rewards for the brave man. A life as a reward? Seems a bit sacrificially inappropriate, but too bad. Winds of change blow but sometimes we just close the window. And put on imaginary headphones, headphones that cancel the outside noise but cannot cancel the inside. Non-noise cancelling headphones.

Orange blossoms, any citrus blossoms for that matter are sweet, and have a sweet that carries memories, desires, and maybe fulfillment. 'Hey boss, you did it.'

The fullness, the earthiness, and the slated lust shall be mine. Should we not love, cook and drink wine, and live life while we can? Have I, am I? Are you?

* * *

Blue triangles.
Petite butterflies. I like French. I like butterflies. They say delicate, they say soft – the French and the butterflies. If one lands on your arm, you won't feel its legs when it lands, because the touch of life has no feel, no sound, it only has an energy. You mustn't see, but you must look. You must look, but not see. That's if you are ready for life, if you are looking at life, and not merely seeing life. That's if you are
Be thankful if one lands on you, be it French or not.

I knew some French people a long time ago. They told me things, language things and other things. About the war, snails, croissants, cafes, and some secrets. Be nice to see Georgie again and ask about her history, her thoughts on life, and does she have any secrets.

* * *

Some nights I didn't eat. I was hungry right enough, and my choice seemed a little insulting to those who did not have this choice and I am truly sorry if that's you. But I wanted to eat little to not overindulge, and to be lean. When you're hungry, really empty hungry, the first thing you eat explodes with a freshness, an energy giving freshness. And I wanted that feeling when I ate slowly that next first time. I carried a night of not eating to a new level, of absurdness even. I fasted for five days. Beyond absurd and bordering into craziness, obsession even. After two days, I lost hunger. I was dizzy but still thinking okay. I drank lots of herb tea, water, and pissed lots. Then on day three I had to physically stop my hands from reaching for their killing habits, for their murdering and eating of eels, wallabies, and turkeys. And stop these same greedy hands from picking wild greens, or whatever vegetables were close by. Day four was a bit blurry, day five was off the chart and I thought I was pooped empty until I ate my first meal of grated carrot and apple with a small squeeze of orange juice. A gigantic last poop removed itself and my tummy ached from its new emptiness. An emptiness I had never felt before. And I didn't mind it. I was clean and pure empty. A nothing drained empty. This nothing light became softer, clearer, and I saw and felt things I didn't usually see or feel. Like a clarity between a leaf and the blue sky, like the moons around Jupiter, like the electric energy from everything I touched. No miracles, only a new perspective. I floated on waves of aware waftiness. Maybe I won't have to eat ever again? Save a lot of time and money. And help save the planet.

* * *

No-one has told dragonflies about Bernoulli or Newton, I suspect the dragonflies wouldn't give a fuck anyway. They're like that, are dragonflies. Nothing worse than dismissive dragonflies. No wonder teachers are stressed. Leaving in droves. Each of their four wings has separate muscles. They seek help but then get more disillusioned and become real estate agents, or bankers. They are a jet, a glider, and a helicopter alone and together, but better, that's applicable for both. They can go forward, backward, they can hover, switch direction, and even reverse – even upside down – particularly when on playground duty, the dragonflies do all that with four independent wings. More money less stress less ratio less workload needed. They flap up and down, perhaps not in unison, perhaps not forwards to backwards. And that's only heading off to staff meetings, parent interviews or to start report cards. I watched them down at The Creek for hours, crying. The teachers, not me. More time to be with the family. Pursue hobbies. One came up around the house, landed on the clothesline and proceeded to walk along the wire. He carried a long blade of grass across his body and was reading a travel article about a waterfall along the north-eastern border that the USA has with Canada.

A vertical single-strand spider's web watched him. A shaft of light travelled along this strand, moving back and forward as the web bounced up and down in the breeze, as the web moved from side to side without a breeze. The clothesline did the same, but without the laser beam, and the dragonfly rode it. Does nature just do what it does, and it is our choice to be awed, to seek knowledge based on our insecurities to not only seek this knowledge, but to transform it into a mould of our choosing that is based on predetermined categories and narratives? Hey, says the dragonfly, you teachers need to travel more and do what you want.

The Swiss do watches, chocolates and have an interesting banking system; they also do science.

* * *

Trees.

Bush lemon trees were scattered around the banks. They had long spikes, longer than my thorny-yellowwood girl, but I refused to wear gloves. A high-risk extreme sport right there, seasonally adjusted with no kissing involved. The result was either marmalade, lemon curd or a thin slice or two in a jug of rainwater, served with love and multiple bandaged stab injuries. Tamarillos.

So much pectin the tap water thickened just thinking about it. A jam like grape jam. Better with the juice of a bush lemon thrown in. I took a few bottles of tamarillo jam into town to the coffee shop girl. She said, Oh thank you, you are soo nice!
I ran away. Sorry rational brain and emotional brain, I have let you down.
A-fucking-gain? Jesus, when will you listen to us?
So, we're all hunky dory now, are we?

* * *

palm tree rainforests
often next to a creek
or in or on one
are best seen in the rain,
like all rainforest of course.
palm trees say lazy

they say holiday
they say balmy heat
they say,
you don't need to take water where we grow
because we are water.
I wrapped some damper in some old newspaper,
and went for a rock hop
to find out where The Creek water came from,
such an easy thing to say
like I love you
at the top of a creek
anywhere really
up and up over scrambly boulders, logs and backyard cricket games
there is not one entry point
rivulets, creeklets, branchlets came in from many directions
and tried to disarm me, tried to confuse me
but I tricked them.
I followed one stream a further up and up
an up to beat all upness,
and got a huge surprise,
a surprise of
when there was no more mountain to climb
no more scrambly boulders, logs or football games
there was just air,
the water, the pure sweet spring water
was syphoning out of a hole
a hole that starts a living soft universe.

* * *

There were dingo footprints in the mud around the house. I had previously heard them howling. But this close? I wondered where they were in the dry times. Or in the grassed areas. Dingoes are killers. Dingoes don't bark, they howl. And on a windy rainy night it's a little Wuthering Heights up here. A little Hound of the Baskervilles. Pull the blankets tighter. As if that would stop a ravenous dingo. A real one, or a dingo of the mind.

* * *

The Creek

A new table note.

Going up the slope opposite
Then I'll keep going
To see a big waterfall.
Back in two days.
The chooks and pigeons have extra feed and water
Cow, Calf and children
Are okay.
Me too, thanks.

I walked up the plateau, to the water, then up to my spikey girlfriend. Gave her a kiss, and went west. When you kiss your true love, you never get spiked. Find a rock that looks different. Walk slowly, because when you go slowly, when you look slowly, things appear. When you move with the flow of the day and accept life, all will be good. A doctor told me that. Turn left at the rock that looks different, head south down the steep rocky rainforest slope. Find a creek and follow to where it meets another, head east, rock hop for a bit, then there's your waterfall, a strong cascade into a deep pool that is a cold as a glacier and cascades at its edges that are veils over a bride's face. Reverse.

* * *

Henry said, ''Spose I'll have to get Fergus put down.'
    'Wait, what fucken shit are you talking? Is he crook? Scrub tick get him? Jesus Henry! What's going on?'
    'Me and Lena are moving to town pretty soon. Remember our little town trip? The one where you tried to kill me? I had an appointment with a jail warden, and now we have a place in jail, commonly known as God's waiting room, or an old peoples' home. And Ferg wouldn't handle town. You know I'm right.'
    Fergus, the little poofter, would root anything with a pulse and not be too concerned about gender, or permission. And he would rummage in bins, front yards and get lost and get shot at and get caught by council.
    'Bloody hell Henry, can I look after him?'
    'Sure. Okay.'
Sometimes you don't know you've been had so expertly.

When two men go out to fight, only one returns. And I only know one way to return; and that's by winning. You're going down old dog.

'Tell you what, I'll toss this ball, and if you catch it on the full you get a point. Right? But if you miss, I get two points. Fair?'

Fergus put his paws on his hips, tapped his front foot and gave me a withering look, one that is a staple diet for all females over the age of three, or old dogs over ten, and said, 'A rule that gives an advantage to the one who makes it is indeed not fair. After you change your rule, let me know the stakes and I'm in.'

'Alright, alright. Give you the one-bounce one-hand catch rule. Jeez, you're tough. Best of three and if you win, you get to come inside. That's right, got your attention now haven't I?'

'And if you win?'

'You have to bring me a brush turkey.'

'Done. And, it'll be a point apiece thanks.'

Things I have to do.

'You ready?' As I threw the first ball, Fergus took off like lightning. He propped, spun, jumped and looked. But I threw it so high NASA enquired about the unidentified flying object hurtling above South-east Queensland. When it landed, it bounced sideways into some long grass. Fergus attacked it and brought it back.

'Thank you. That would be one for me. Pick me a nice young turkey thanks.'

'It aint over yet bitch.'

After I wiped the slobber off, I underarmed a dolly. Fergus leapt and his front paws bent softly as he flew through the air in slow motion and snapped the ball safely. 'Ha! Got it!'

He dropped the ball at my feet and his excited look was pure joy. His tail wagging mowed the lawn and his tongue drooped bently and watered the newly-mown lawn. However noble I may sound, that I am not. I like to win, I like to crush, to annihilate.

Later that evening, Fergus waltzed in like he owned the joint. He didn't smile, but he did smirk like a smug treasurer did when he had spent a nation's surplus on bribes for the rich, and he dragged in a bone that would not have been out of place in a Jurassic Museum, and he sat in front of the lounge and made a mess.

* * *

Henry rode up. I was planting rainforest trees on a slope. Sweaty mud dirt on my forehead, arms and legs. He stopped and leaned forward on his horse.

He leaned forward on his crossed arms and elbows like you see cowboys do in westerns, the reins all loose. His horse, that fucking old baldy mare, put her head down and nibbled on something. With a bit of luck, it'd be crofton weed and she would die a slow and painful death. Fergus wagged and trotted over for a pat.

'What you doin'?'

'Chopping wood.'

'Those two gullies you did are coming on well. Particularly with the ginger, the cordylines, the river oaks, the tamarinds, the koda, the batswing coral, the tuckeroo, the crow's ash, lime and the white beech. And I saw pigeons in one of your white cedars.'

'Well, good afternoon and hitch the fucking wagons. I thank you for your botanical scholarship, but could you please repeat all that, preferably in English? Slowly would be good.'

Henry blinked and said, 'We're leaving on Monday. Lena is doing crumbed lamb chops tonight.'

Two statements, just two statements, both loaded with friendship, love, and a ton of pain.

* * *

My guts were churning because Henry and Lena were leaving. Not leaving me, but leaving me. They were such a strong part of my life here. I felt all lonely, all isolated, and I felt like retreating to a cave. Me, a hermit? A true hermit? Fuck off. I needed people now. To be around human company for their energy. And Joan company for her love. Avoidance can be good, but only for a while. Running away only a temporary option. I felt strange, a bit strange echo, but still settled. I'm the normal one, and I spend a lot of time convincing myself of the fact.

* * *

Shared food and shared talk. Henry said, 'Up on the plateau, if you keep going south sort of, there's another section where no-one goes. It's full of prehistoric beasts, trees with moss on the wrong side and deep crevasses.'

'Sounds exciting Henry.'

'It's a crazy place, a place that plays with your mind. I know it well. Take the old dog. He'll enjoy it.'

'You can't leave The Creek. I need you both.'

Henry said nothing, but Lena looked straight into my eyes and didn't need to say anything.

* * *

A long table note.

Going up the slope opposite
To explore a lost plateau that old Henry told me about
To make sure I'm still sane,
A reinforcement of pain
Delivered via a place of extinct creatures, furry bits and deep fear,
Anyway, back in around four days, or so,
The chooks, pigeons and peacock (though he is lately deceased), have food and water,
Cow, Calf and children will not need milking,
Watch out for the dingoes and
Please tend to the platypus and drunk brush turkeys.
The old red dog is with me.

I went up to the thorny yellowwood, said, Hi my darling. She tried to grab me in a playful grab. Don't you just love those? A foreplay with extras for sure, but I don't like pain with my pleasure. I like my pain afterwards. I kept going south, straight through the tall mythical ethereal sub-tropical rainforest with massive trees, with shade and filtered sunlight, with giant butterflies, with fluttering fairies, and with dreams of how the world is and might yet still be. Maybe I should let the sixties go. The trees pirouetted, the strings played, and the little birdies tweeted. Then east onto a wide grassy plateau. The short trees at the edges, had crusty lichen, and stringy green moss hanging toward the west. Had lots of old man's beards of snot. Were so stunted and beaten were almost bonsaied. I had no map no compass because there was no point. You don't need a guide when you're in Heaven. I looked at the grey mist descending, smelt the remaining air that thought it was still daylight, and kept going south.

On Earth, south never ends. You may run into seas, oceans, cities, gullies, rocky outcrops, several countries and even creeks that all go the wrong way, but south it is until it curves and becomes north. Hope I didn't get that far. The sky is better than a map, because landforms, like some schoolkids, politicians and bosses, don't obey rules. I walked down onto a dark shadowy saddle, overlain with leaning grass, mysterious animal tracks and screaming laughter, and was stumped. Fergus looked up at me and said, 'Where the fuck are we?'

I said, 'Dude, where's the faith?'

'We're screwed aren't we?'

My confusion said, Turn back. My bush instinct said, We need to keep going south, swing east then go north down the first ridge you see. My heart said, I am badass and epic. But they were all wrong, because I was really lost.

I said, 'Okay Ferg, screwed it is. Let's make camp.'

Being lost merely means that at that moment you're not sure where you are in relation to the start, the end point or anywhere else on the planet. It sounds simple, like logic over emotion, which was never my strong suite, because I wasn't a believer, and never will be because my emotion tends to cloud over, to rule over, to be correct over, any semblance of pragmatism. *I know.* And in that moment when doubt trickles in like that cold sweat of fear you get when you realise that fuck, this is not so good, I took stock. In the swirly fogs of grey confusion and the encroaching dark, I took stock. No wait, I didn't take stock, my rational brain did.

Sit down, make yourself comfortable and shut the fuck up. Do not, under any circumstance listen to that other brain woman. She will have you running around in the dark, and you will trip over and hurt yourself. You are indeed lost, but you are not injured, you have water and food, so put the tarp up and light a fire and settle. Tomorrow is another day. No wait, that's dumb. Anyway, you and that mutt are alright. Is old EB still around? Seems to be a bit quiet here.

Thank you rational brain, but take it easy on the name calling of my best mate, alright? Not to mention giving lip to my lovely. I am sure the company of a small fire has saved many before me. I brewed a pot of sweet tea. This was real solitude. My previous solitudes had exit signs that are always illuminated even if there's a blackout, with half-time breaks to eat the oranges that had been cut into quarters, bank holidays and union picnics, all escape hatches of security. This one was different. It was eerie. The doubt multiplied into miniature buckets and poured water on my calming fire. Solitude plus loneliness plus fear plus heavy rain were not a great mix. One small accident could mean the end. And no one would know. What happens when you die? I don't mean some painful shit death, like falling off a cliff, or having to vote conservative, I mean, is it peaceful? Will memories flood in, will friends tell me they did really love me, will I see that white light thing? What if I died in my sleep? How would I know I was dead? Would everything just go all blank?

I curled up in the grass and cuddled the old dog.

I whimpered in my dreams and chased bitches. My dream brain searched, but realised he too was lost, and he asked for help. And the old red dog answered. He talked to me, but by not talking to me. It was a typical cryptic dream abstraction, a drawing in of memory, actions, hopes, worries and what was pertinently real.

A wayfarer was walking in a market, looking for the stall that had bantams for sale. He saw one, in the distance, but the quicker he ran towards it, it seemed to move further away. He dived, and flapped his arms like a bird flying in slow motion. His arms ached, and he became desperate. He sensed people chasing him, and he flapped harder. Why the fuck couldn't he just go faster?

To give someone support and confidence when they are confused is a noble thing. To listen without condemnation is approaching divinity. To talk to someone in a dream is epic. Thank you dream brain, thank you old red dog Fergus.

I didn't die in my sleep. Mind you, I woke with a confused head to a clear sky. We did two more full days and ended up swerving west which did not seem right. On the fourth day, I was on a large rock in a clearing way up high. The mountains to the south and west were so numerous and ongoing they looked like green and blue whipped cream made into peaks. I saw a spur heading north towards a creek. Fergus trotted off toward this spur like he had been here before. He looked back at me without saying anything, but I knew. I named this, Red Dog Spur, and followed him down.

We walked, skidded, crawled and fell almost five-thousand feet down this steep slope until we made it to a creek.

RB-Ha! I knew we'd do it. We just had to be tough, that's all. I'm the man, I'm the man ...

At home that night, (we arrived just after two a.m.), I worked out we had walked over twenty miles on that last day of being lost.

But the funny thing was, even though my legs were muscle sore and

cramping, I did something similar two days later.
Must tell Henry.

* * *

We are all fighting for what's lost but it's not enough. To be strong also comes with a chance, a cost, and often a loneliness. You might think you're strong, but you don't how strong you are until you need to be strong. Attributes, with or without the training, are hidden until they are needed. And this is fair enough. You wouldn't want to know stuff that you didn't need to know or weren't ready for. But the strength gets stronger. Slowly. A fight worth fighting for.

* * *

Henry and Lena had moved into town to a nursing home. They said, 'It is for the better because our health is declining.' This wasn't really that evident, but I guess the years of battling had hurt, and they had no-one to look after them back in the bush. But was moving to town, to an expensive unit the size of a postage stamp the way to go for two independent bushies? It was a shit arrangement, and deep down I think they knew it. No choice? I wondered what I'd do in the same situation.

RB-I can let you know some costings, room dimensions, health benefits, explain the Terms and Conditions ...

EB-Strike me lucky you are a piece of work. How would your financial data, your listed untested untried bullshit ever relate to a human being? Particularly to one whom we know doesn't exactly like jails, wardens or shitboxes?

We sat in the gardens, in a quiet space in a sort of arbored-off area. Fergus sat beside Henry, his head in Henry's lap. It wasn't a puppy-dog floppy wet-tongued keenness to be stroked, this was pure bliss, a peace that says, We have done stuff together and we don't have to do all the just getting to know you shit. We can just be in the same space and say nothing.
Lena said the food was appalling. 'It's mush, mash, pulp. And white bread, ugh. Can you bring us in something decent to eat?'
Me cook for Lena? 'Of course I will.' No pressure.
Henry said, 'So, I hear you went for a walk?'
Fergus looked at me and grinned.

'Well, yes we did. We went where you said. Sort of. It was as you said, full of decisions, crazy things and life. Extraordinary place, thank you.'

When I left, I didn't call Fergus. I let him decide. He stood up, shook himself like dogs do when they are shaking off water, and followed me. As we got to the gate, he looked back at Henry.

I smuggled in roast brush turkey, chunky baked pumpkin and steamed chokoes. Lena hugged me thanks. She said, 'I'm so hungry I could eat a hollow log full of bullants. How did you keep it hot?'

'I double-wrapped it in foil and put it under the bonnet next to the engine block.'

Henry said, 'That second white cedar you planted, it had no berries because you trimmed its lower branches to grow tall and be ready for the mill.'

'And did you see how far away I planted it from the other?'

'Yes, I did. They don't like each other.'

'Henry.'

'Yes Tony.'

'You didn't tell me you were a botanist.'

'You never asked me.'

'Henry, are you a brain surgeon, a pilot, or an Olympian?'

* * *

Fergus wasn't allowed inside (except when he won bets). He knew that. He lay on a mat at the door, his paws out in front, his head across them, watching. Everything. Even with his eyes closed, he watched. If I did a normal thing, like tend to the stove, he'd stay still, his ears still too. If I did something different, his ears would prick, and one eye would open. 'And, what the hell do you think you are doing?' Then he'd see everything was okay, close the eye and appear to nod off. His ears never slept, just like ours.

Ears never sleep. They must get tired though. Probably take sleeping pills when you're not looking. While you're asleep, you can still hear outside noises, however faint or loud. Because I had been here so long, the sounds were constant and even a little predictable. This was a good thing because familiarity breeds security and the night noises didn't wake me up. A grunt, a yelp or a churr kept me safe.

One night I heard a different noise, one rainy December night. Just a light *bang* on corrugated iron somewhere in another universe. A not-right different noise. Down with the lantern, sleepily recalling pleasant dreams and stubbing my toe at the same time. The chooks were lined along their perch as they do. They don't sleep in cosy nests; they sleep on a perch. In the middle of the bunch of sleepy hens was a ten-foot carpet snake, his tail coiled around the perch a few times, the rest of him was hanging down wrapping one of the chooks in a death squeeze. I put them both in a wheat bag for removal the next day.

Carpet snakes sneak up on chooks, as snakes are wont to do, (Except for death adders who don't move. They think they own the frigging joint.) They lunge and grab on with a bite designed to shock, which it does. The snake curls around the chook and crushes its body into jelly and eats this jelly, whole, without ice-cream or custard or sweetened rice-pudding.

I've been bitten and I was shocked. It stings more than hurts and the pressure on my arm from this bitey ten-foot carpet snake's crush stopped the blood flow and my hand went numb and threatened to fall off. When carpet snakes coil, around your arm for example, they thread their tail back through the last couple of coils in a half-hitch of security. Carpet snakes probably go sailing on their rostered day off, and drive trucks on weekends, after they have tied the load with rope. A real snake wouldn't use those clickety-clack strap things. Me neither. If I ever use those, may as well cut my balls off. But they're still there because I haven't used any and I still used a long-shanked screwdriver instead of the Phillips or an Allen key.

Sometimes I'd cuddle the chooks to sleep – minus the company of a carpet snake, and still possessing both hands and both balls. They would rub the side of their face onto mine then step up onto my forearms and sort of huddle together. At first I thought they were trying to get away, but I soon realised chooks like being cuddled. Maybe they have sensors in their feet and can taste what they walk on. Like flies. Or maybe, the soles of their little feet claws can feel body warmth. Or maybe my arms were easier to grip than a piece of wood.

I knew when the point of lay hens were about to lay, not only because I crossed off days on my chook calendar, not only because their pink small combs were filling out darker red, but because they let the rooster mate with them. If a rooster had attempted to hop on (approximately every ten minutes) before she was ready, she would either belt him, or run away. I named my girls Adele, Agnes, Amie, Babette, Clementine, Delphine, Fleur, Gertrude and Giselle. The boys were Grunt and Engine Room.

Sounds of silence. As you walk under trees, you might stop, because you know something isn't right. You don't know what it is, but you know it's a something. You feel like you are being watched, followed maybe. You slowly turn around, like a close up in a thriller where the camera, i.e., your eyes, are right in the character's face, and as she turns, her eyes will widen in terror … and you see … nothing. No-one is following you. But the ants are still crawling up your arms, and now they are going down your back. Jesus! What is going on here? You rub and squirm, and if you don't look up you wouldn't see the powerful owl, half asleep, as he watches you. Silent sounds, sounds that come through the air and picked up by a sense that is rarely understood. But it's a real sense and when you've been in the bush for a while, you'd better listen well.

* * *

If I had a visitor, Fergus would inch his way inside. It was beautiful to see his stealth. He will no doubt be hired by the defence force soon I'd say. Inch by inch, until he was beside the lounge. I watched from the corner of my eye, too scared to make eye contact because I loved him. On those times, I let him stay.

Sometimes he slept outside on some dry grass. He would make a nest like a swan's. He'd stand on his tippy toes like a ballerina on point, arch his back and walk in tight circles until it was right, fold his tail and slump down in his nest. I never made eye contact when he did that because I loved him. Watching someone's personal stuff can be invasive. Acknowledging a vulnerability can sometimes be belittling and create mistrust.

Fergus would also lay in the dust. He liked the dust. The dust was near where the chooks played because they liked the dust too. A dustathon. The roosters would cluck warnings to the girls, but they ignored this unnecessary bravado. They said, You're full of shit, That dog is a nice person. Leave him be.

Jayden liked Fergus and would walk up close. No fear for sure. Hey, if you've smashed a dinosaur, sidling up to a dusty old dog is a picnic, but I suspect it was curiosity anyway. At first, when he got too close, Fergus would growl, real low. Just letting you know, Jayden old son, you're fucking crowding me. Then after a few more times, Fergus would say nothing, and Jayden would stand on his back, like a wee bird on a hippopotamus's back.

* * *

Hey anyone, another table note.

Going up to the cock rock at the southern end of the back saddle.
Be back tonight.
Hopefully.
Dog with.

It was a nice steep, even within the crumbly rock, an easy stepable steep, with a bit of grass, a bit of stunted root. On top, on top of the tall, isolated grey phallic rock the views were for and of forever. And forever is a long way away let me tell you. I have been there (took a while) and it is full of doubters and full of shysters. The doubters are in the background, looking downwards, too scared to face their insecurities. The shysters, in front with their ducktails, their oiled black ducktails, talk of love, of promises they'll never keep and their Would bes.

Coming back, Fergus and I were weary, feeling small. Tears were in our eyes, which is when you have to be more careful than at the start, which, although seems strangely more important than safety employed earlier on, was true. Because when tears are in your eyes and you have no-one to dry them, tired people and dogs slip. I had taken a leather pouch for Fergus to drink from. I stopped, turned to check on him, to give him a drink. He was head down, foot sore, just concentrating on his steps, panting a little maybe, not aware of his surroundings. Courtesy of an idiot who overheated him. Thanks for letting me know about this Henry. Coming through the trees behind him was a stealth bomber, with its wheels lowered, and it meant business. I raced in, waving my arms, 'No you don't you bastard! Go and catch yourself a fucking wallaby!' And the eagle swerved away.

* * *

There was a rainforest. It had the usual storeys with the canopy uniform in its height. One day a tree was heard to say, 'I want to be different. Why can't I be different? I want to grow taller than the canopy.'

All the other trees said, 'Oh no, don't do that. The storms will break your branches. Your branches will splinter and then smash down on us. You may even be totally destroyed. Do the right thing and follow us, and relax before we all get a nosebleed.'

The tree didn't listen. It grew tall and mighty and free.

The summer storms came and smashed its protruding branches, and hurt other trees.

The trees scoffed. 'We told you not to do that. Now look at what you've done. Your broken branches, your stupid actions, have hurt us. Why couldn't you just be like everybody else. Shame on you.'

The once taller tree hung its head. 'I didn't mean for anyone else to be hurt. I just wanted to break free of the sameness, the doing what I'm told I must do. I wanted to be my own self with freedom. I am sorry. Will someone help me fix this?'

The spirit of the rainforest waited but all the rainforest trees looked away.

So she sent a plain bird, a brown ordinary bird, to help the tree who dared be different, who needed help. This bird patched up the broken branches, rubbed nature's ointment onto the breaks, and spent time reassuring the broken tree that he had done the right thing. She said, 'It's okay, trying to be different, trying to search for the real you. At least you had a go. I want to be different too, but I don't know how. All the other rainforest birds are so pretty. The orange and black bower birds, the rainbow-coloured pittas, the green and red pigeons, they are all so beautiful. And me? I'm just a drab old brown thing. I want to be pretty too.'

The tall tree listened and thanked the compassionate brown bird.

And the rainforest spirit listened.

And said to the now repaired tree, 'Yes, your actions hurt others. But you have a kind heart and you are sorry. You can grow higher, but only a little bit higher, and you will be different, but still a part of the rainforest.'

And said to the brown bird, 'Dear brown bird, when I asked you to help, you did so. You worked hard and showed great courage. Next year when the red leaves of that rainforest tree get ready to fall, next year when the berries turn blue, I will join them, and they will change your colour. And I would like to give you a pretty voice. It will be a pure whistle, as pure as soft rain in a rainforest.'

The patched-up rainforest tree is now a blue-quandong, and grows to be one hundred feet tall.

It spreads its wings to fly over the canopy, but is still a part of the canopy. Its roots are giant anacondas swimming on the surface of a river; its roots are curved saltwater crocodile tails, are brontosaurus tails, powerful and thick. It has largish green berries that turn bright blue. It has leaves that die and turn bright lipstick red.

The brown bird is now the rosella, a handsome bird with a flat tail, a crimson body, blue wings and blue cheeks. Every now and again it looks up to the sky, and makes a fluid tinkly whistle.

* * *

I didn't need much money, but I worked hard to get it.

I guided walks in the rainforest. Five people, no more.

One bloke, bit of weight on, said, 'I've got health issues. Will you still let me come on a walk?' I said of course you can come, but if you don't mind, try not to die on me.

He had a watch which measured his heart rate or something. On day two, he was in strife. We stopped near the Hang on, I'll get us some water tree, and I said, Hi, old friend. And gave her a hug, a deep, long slow hug. Real hugs, like true love, are never prickly. Got us some fresh water. We shared his pack around.

As we walked on, slowly, which is best anyway regardless of any health issue, there was a distant rumble. I said, 'Mate, was that your heart?'

The rumbles got closer; the walkers got nervouser. 'Will we be safe?'

'Maybe. If we stop, we're going to get wet and we might get flattened by a branch, or a tree. If we keep walking, we're going to get wet and we might get flattened by a branch, or a tree.

We trudged, got smashed by the storm, and the heavy heavy raindrops became waterfalls. Lots of light and dark noise, and not a few whimperings. Then, a slow cracking sound in slow motion, a grinding creaking cracking bending sound. Feeling a bit nervous myself. There was no-where to run and hide. A massive canopy tree came smashing down parallel to us, and kerthumped into the ground thirty feet away. There were branches, sticks, leaves and an assortment of injured animals struggling around. The walkers looked a tad pale. I said, 'Hmm,' and changed my undies. The storm blew through and we did photos all round. Ninety feet to the first branch.

I said, 'We're all going to die one day. This is not our day. Let's go.' A crimson rosella flew past.

The dicky heart man had said he wouldn't last real long and wanted to experience what was left of his life and the bush because he just never made time for things. And had said sorry to people he'd hurt. And had said sorry to himself. He sent me a bottle of sparkly with a handwritten note, 'Just in case I never said thanks.'

* * *

One chilly morning I stepped outside and saw Fergus asleep in his grass nest, whimpering and dreaming, just like lost bushwalkers do. And next to him was Jayden, snuggled in, his head resting against Ferg's shoulder.

You just don't know.

I had tried to communicate with Fergus as he slept. Nothing happened. Even though he could talk to me as I slept, I couldn't him. I suspect Jayden could though. Jayden's children didn't inherit his mohawk or mullet. They produced butch spikeys, ponies and man buns. God only knows what their offspring would look like. Maybe their grandpa will be there for them too? My grandpa was there for me, even in his own cantankerous bullying way, he was there for me. It wasn't his job to raise a grandkid, I know that, but he stepped up and I owed him, I knew that. One day, I said, Hey bitch, thanks. Okay I didn't exactly say it like that. I said, I really appreciate what you've done for me. He just grunted. But it was a good grunt. A grunt is a grunt, but you can tell a good grunt from a shit grunt.

* * *

Wonga pigeons don't walk, they strut, and call, woop woop woop, for a week without a breath.

Catbirds. My goodness, you wouldn't want to be out of your tree and hear one of these chaps.

'Wait, there's a cat just up there. I swear. And a crying child too. Quick, get help!'

* * *

Sexual desire is a lusty linear line of Earthly beauty that starts somewhere at an age you choose (one that is hopefully legal), and keeps going along its crazy journey until it changes or stops. And I wondered, when it does stop, which it must, are you relieved that it's all over? Or maybe just disappointed? Or a bit of both? Is performance a true indicator, a sign of this changing, or stopping of lust? I'll get back to you.

Desire can reach heaven, or that other place, it may waver or falter, but in one form or another, it keeps going until it changes. Desire and lust are all healthy, natural and wholesomely fulfilling. They are sexy, they are the Wow factor in the everyday, they are what keeps me thinking, I'm a hero, I am worthy, I am spunky. Yet occasionally within the overbearing stud-delusionalness, there is a flop, a Whoops, even a disaster, or maybe even some soft laughter? Regardless, if you are with the one, it is deeply satisfying. If you are safe within the lust, it is a beautiful thing.
Like my first time with Joan.

Before Joan, my drought time was nearly two years, and I had been in dire need of rain. This sex moisture thirst affects all working parts. My confidence hadn't had a wet season for a while either. Just dry storms, false hopes and falser forecasts. And the occasional wet dream, and while they count, they are not the same as a real dream cum true. When Joan and I first lay down, I began to shiver and shake and I wasn't breathing normally. The urgency, the wanting, oh my heaven, I was lusting after this girl so much I just wanted to put it in. She pressed herself to me; slowly and softly. I pulled her shirt up and felt her warmth and smoothness. She had no bra and her breasts were full, pointy and bursting with excitement. She gasped at my touch and I felt my face go flushed. I felt the pleasure coming up through my body and my explosion of short-lived lust made me drowsy; and then I fell asleep.

I felt embarrassed, like I mean embarrassed, but Joan didn't laugh at my early-to-arrive petit mort. She said, 'Hey mister, I'll make it up to you by coming quicker more times than you.'
And she did. Heaps of times.

We were all good, me and you
Are we still? A little bit?
The hurt sticks in down lower than a low cello chord, like a pumpkin seed
in a craw, like a perpetual ache
That no horse liniment will ever cure.
But what a girl.

One time, it had been three weeks since we met. When Joan let me in, she had guests who were sort of about to go. Nice people, really polite people, but bugger off will you. Joan and I were edgy animals on a hot tin roof. When they left, fuck me, it was a beautiful rush of smashing urgency. Never mind being a slut, fucking hell, it was Get your gear off bitch. Crockery was swept away; chairs were turned over and tables were hurled out the window. God it was good. I think quickie is the term that should be applicable, but I suspect there's a better version. Like, 'You touch me down there and I will squirt all over you. I will not consider you or your desires, right now, mine are way more important.'
It was kind of breathlessly cute, an exhausting revitalising dual lust.

One time, we lay. Just lay. And talked about anything and nothing. The urgency wasn't there, it was a subdued relaxed sexiness. The talk was interspersed with the odd soft touch, the occasional brush of arm, a short gasp. And the stroking was quietly electric, like a follow up storm. The tenderness came through before the lust. A different, deep sex.

* * *

Whenever I would see someone near The Creek, they would often say, 'Wo, that rich smell. That's lantana, right? Or a wallaby?'

Wrong, sorry.

That rich green smell is not lantana, is not a wallaby. It is a native shrub that has a ventriloqual smell. I have been challenged on this by more than a few locals, way more botanists and several prime ministers, but they are all wrong. You can get close, you can crush a leaf, but no, you will smell nothing. Turn your back, Wham. Hey, where are you?

It's a soft warm aromatic rainforest smell. Not spicy, not sweet but Earthier, more fur-ie than leaf-ie. It waits till you're not looking, then when it deems you are far enough away, (and not tricking), it releases that forest vegetation smell. A shrub that defies the listed lists and experiences of the colonials, current academic knowledge and certainly anything that comes out of Canberra.

It is the green kamarla.

* * *

Wendy called in. 'Well,' she said, as she handed over a wee baby, 'This was sort of your fault.'

'Was I asleep?'

She grinned. 'Just kidding. Although …'

I cuddled her baby and thought, Wendy, you are naughty. I felt the love from her gratitude she had for me for just being there from way back there on the rock where we started. Not to mention the result of her changes. My fault for sure.

'What a cutie!'

She hugged in with her baby and the three of us went soft with something better than all of us, a small place in the universe, a togetherness of love that says, I think we may have helped each other.

* * *

Trees.
Red kamarla. Same family as the aforesaid independent member for The Creek.
Yet it doesn't send its scent.
It has red berries that dye
Lots of cloth and satin from the Philippines to The Creek.
Booyong.
And what a name.
It means, I will grow to 45m.
The taller ones have buttresses,
But they are not real buttresses,
They are washing machine agitators,
Quite large machines I'd say,
They are whale flukes
About to smash the ocean of leaves.
They are sweeping, curved, dinosaur tails.

Erythrina vespertilio, the red bat, commonly called a Batswing Coral, is Australia's equivalent to the hardwood balsa. Up to 30m, will grow in drier places, leaves are wee mouse bats flying away from the tree but restrained by thin cords, like you might see kites being held by little kids at the showground where they had just this minute been ripped off by the call, 'Roll up, roll up! Every child gets a prize! No chicken will be left abandoned beside the road!'
Flowers are red
Your hand is red too,
Because you grabbed a corky bark branch
That had short spiny spines;
And you didn't have a fucking clue.
Tulipwood
Dense shiny green leaves, orange seed pods, back seeds. An umbrella-shaped tree grows to around 10 metres. Nice white blotchy trunk. You can see these in towns and cities. Ask them if they'd like a lift to the rainforest to see their rellies.
Other vegetation things.
Orchids
Are nuts. They hang on and grow. Take up trunk/rock space without depleting the host. Mind you, getting water off or out of a rock, not to

mention indirectly from the air is a challenge either way. Orchid species are many and varied, like a lot of our vegetation, I guess. Robust or delicate, sweet or neutral, all are outstanding. Let's keep them.

Walking stick palms.

Nice hard stem up to five feet. Drooping nature, bright red berries.

Cordylines.

A type of palm lily that grows to nine foot tall. They can branch off the main stem. They like semi-shade. The feel of a rainforest right there.

Ferns.

I love ferns. Shady and wet with droplets of beauty. They have delicate fronds and they have intimate and secret discussions with fairies and other wee people; this is what ferns do. I've heard them. It is a whisper. Did you expect yelling? Ferns never yell. They can also communicate without noise. Try that in your weekend off. Ferns are also the link between the storeys, the conduit between Earth, Heaven and the Afterlife. Some say you can access all three at any time if you believe. The Styx of the forest, the fleurs of the forest. They have no enemies because they don't do revenge, hatred or deceit and everyone loves them; they are kind, they are peaceful, they share, and they don't steal from others, their land, culture or memories. Even the Darling River country says, Oh, how I wish we had some soft ferns out here! They are green even in the full shade, which takes a lot of concentration, and underneath the fronds are brown spore spots. Ferns have a droopy hangingness that says, Yep, look don't touch. I accept you as you are and I expect you to return the sentiment. Should be more of them.

Mosses.

Mosses need shade and water. Lots of both. No-one knows anything about mosses. They are enigmatic. To us humans only; they don't think so.

Fungi

Eat dead leaf litter. And don't need light. How cool is that? And will eat your leftovers. Wouldn't get a look in at my place. There'd be a fight. No-one understands lichens, mosses and fungi except a mountain man I met once. He is a mathematician, a naturalist and a linguist. And as tough as nails. His fitness, strength and endurance were to be admired.

Ginger

Has multiple stems up to six feet that bend. They love the shade, with maybe a bit of sun. They get bright blue berries that are chewable (then spitable), though the underground bit is totally edible. Like bulrush except not as tender. Nothing worse than not being as tender as a bulrush. Ask Moses.

Lomandra.
A dense thick (four-feet-ish) rush that will grow in fast moving water, in the
dry, under cover, in pots and even in real estate offices. Can't be perfect. I
have seen wee green tree frogs hiding along the stems, their little legs all
folded as they sleepily crouched. One must never disturb a sleeping frog.
Native grape.
Bitter, acrid, and nothing like domestic table grapes. A gorgeous, lush nicely
invasive vine though. Will take over civilisations within three wet seasons.
Watch out.
Cockspur.
Because the thorn thing is like a spur on a cock
A rooster, colourful and proud
Who roots for power and pleasure,
Viper fang thorn hooks
That wait for butcher bird's prey
To be hung.
They use trees to lean on and scramble upwards rampantly,
Higher than Jack's beanstalk.
Cockspurs are protective of seedlings and small brown birds.
I like cockspurs.

* * *

I was breathing again, slowly,
But I could see the forest again
And all things green again.
In town, I flirted with the coffee shop girl,
I was cheeky and had spunk again.
Might even wear a dress into town one day,
To excite, justify and feed the gossips.
Or should I wear one because it was my true self?
Doubt it.
I'm not that brave.

* * *

The colour of raw meat. Eels are white. Spongy but nice. Except for the ones
you let go.

   Brush turkeys deep blue-red. Sawn into quarters with my grandfather's handsaw. The oil and grease stop it rusting. The saw too. And you must cook the turkey correctly (i.e., over approx. three weeks). Otherwise, throw it out and eat the cast-iron camp oven. And the non-rusted saw.

Wallabies. Red.

Pigeons. Pink. Snakes. Pink.

Bandicoot. White.

Water dragons. White.

Wood ducks. Black. Oops, wrong geography.

Chokoes. White.

Tony's brain. Green.

* * *

Town.

I could see the hazy mountains, and I could see black and green clouds heading towards my Creek. Rolling in along those hazy mountains, and I knew it would be tricky getting home, because if it had stormed, The Creek would rise. I walked the last two miles because the road was a moving mud slide. Along the way The Creek was brown swirling and bellowing. How would I cross the crossing? It was nearly dark as I approached my crossing, the crossing that would decide my fate, but three feet before the crossing was where the storm had started, and The Creek was as I had left it that morning.

And the world was getting better.

Town.

I saw Joan. 'Well, hi to you young lady, who is back from over the border. Hey, want to spend the night with me? Or do you have a girlfriend?' How cool was that? She looked at me. A tilted head, hand on hip, tits poking forward, a little tarty even. Me, not her. Just a casual remark to an old acquaintance. My thumping cock didn't think so.

'No, and thank you for your kind offer, you gorgeous man. My word, you are lookin' pretty spunky in that long flowy red number. But I would like to go to your house up The Creek, if that's okay?'

'Right.' My default response disguised a somewhat confused and rejected hurtful heart. If Joan came out to The Creek, she would surely be humping my bones in around ten seconds, hopefully. Jesus, so why would she say No, to the night together, yet still want to visit?

'I cannot spend the night with you because, as you know, I do have a girlfriend. But I would like to come up to your place – with my girl. That be okay?' And she looked into my eyes.

Hang on a tick, did she really expect me to be okay to her visiting with her girlfriend? While I did what? Listened through the wall and jerked off? No, I'll be right, don't worry about me.

'Sure. That would be great. Look forward to meeting her,' someone said.

Weird, unsure, annoyed and scared. Used. And a little Poor Me, creeping in again.

They came out and the world did not end. It didn't even wobble on its axis, reconsider its 24-hour revolution or waver in its 365-day orbit. Not even close. Actually, I think it recalibrated, reorganised and restabilised.

Joan was not my girl, anymore. I knew that. And the prejudices and judgements that had made me choose to be emotionally blind, the anger and jealousy that had made me choose fear, the confusion and doubt that made me choose unsettled, and the non-listening to my niggles, were all cancelled by two beautiful women.

Joan's girl was Georgie, the French barber.
Fuck me.
Hole-ly shit.
Wow.
Wow again.
Fuck me again.
I was not offended, hurt or angry, not that Joan had left me for a girl, and not that it was my favourite barber.
No-where near any of those,
But I sure as hell was surprised,
But only another little bit,
But not totally another little bit,
Because I had partially listened to what my deep rational brain had said and continued to say,
What I had sort-of agreed with but had denied and not acknowledged.
To myself, which was, that Georgie was the girl.

Avoidance of the inner voice is not always a good look. *Hey! It never is a good look.* It can help, but only after a swift acknowledgement of what your self was really trying to tell you. You know I'm right about this. Bet you've done it.

Two beautiful women, my two beautiful women. *In your dreams mate.* Life, give it to me why don't you? Test me, ask me if I am worthy of you. Give me pain, give me suffering, give me raw emotion, give me shit, but you know what life? You can fuck off, because I'm doing good. I am spinning out on beauty, on love, not rejection or pain.

I liked Georgie. She wasn't a black woman like Joan, but she sure was dark. A swarthy Mediterranean woman with an Aboriginal woman. And a white fella tripping over his dripping tongue. Slipping over his table tipping newspaper clipping that had on repeat, 'Sorry, I have a girlfriend.'

Wish I did have a girlfriend, like right now. Or even two girlfriends.
Georgie, slightly younger than Joan, was lean and slim. Short tight hair. Small pert tits. Boyish curves. And armpit hair.
Jesus, let me out of here.
Hope she leans all over me again. Please Dear God, let me smell her sweat. Georgie had tatts. Like, I mean tatts. None of your, Mum, in a heart, or, I luv Mary, these were colourful delicate artworks, featuring the faith and freedom of butterflies, her legs cluttered with the divine beauty of birds (including a cockerel) and the maturity and confidence of roses across her back. She was wild, she was sweet. Genuine and humble, and I thought, Georgie, you're alright.
Excellent choice, Joan.

Yet, we all laughed, and I had no regrets.
No, 'What we had before …'
No, 'Why did you ditch me …'
Couldn't believe it.
It's hard being so mature
Let me tell you.
I hugged them both.
Had a squeeze of Georgie's arse too. Again.
Georgie said, 'Thees valley 'as got emoshons that are souns end enershzee.'
To anyone who had been here, this was not new. But what she said next sure as hell was.
'And theese souns and enershzees are feminin'. See zat mountane? Well that ees 'er 'ead.' Then she kept pointing along the mountains heading west. 'Then 'er shoulder, 'er breasts, 'er flat tummy, 'er gorjis mound and zere are 'er long legs.'

When she pointed these out, I was amazed. Totally mouth-open amazed. 'Yes, my God, you're right. How did you know that and I did not know that?'

'Becos I am more intellijon' and better lookin' per'aps?'

That was pretty good. And so true. 'Hang on a tick, is there a male? I mean, some women like males you know. Or at least, they used to.'

Georgie ignored my stunning wit, my pointed lonely sarcasm of I am a victim none of this is my fault, and pointed her head to the west. And there was the Fort, the tall hard stiff phallic rock.

'Hmm, jus' maybe, zum ov zees wimmin, zey steel like ze cock, n'est-ce-pas?'

Joan said, 'Hey Pritch, come over here with us?'

'Sure. Are we going to do some cooking together perhaps?' Kidding me. I could smell the heat, see the heat and feel the vibrations of heat, like you would see wafting off a tar road in the summer.

The girls had their tops off. Their backs were curvy muscular but not masculine, a fit muscular, a sculptured strong curvy feminine firm muscular. I stroked their backs, their shoulders, and anything else I could reach. We shared hot wet kisses. Erect breasts screamed to be touched, or kissed. Softly.

I slowly slid my hands down both pants. Soft slippery moist flesh. Erotic groans escaped from their pants. My cock almost burst in its hardness, its tight-as-a-drum stiffness, as they stroked and played. Then I spurted; stayed stiff, and fucked them both hard.

I'm ready God.

Giving. The male giving, maybe even thinking he controls these submissions, taking them, then receiving them. Why would he be so fucking vain? It was an honour, given and received with great honour. Strong independent females, horny I might add, letting their lust be shared with me.

Then a three-way warm cuddle. Arms lolling, legs hanging over, just like me and Joan used to do.

And we slept.

God, you there? I'm still ready.

Just before they left to go back over the border, Joan came over and hugged me.

'I'm sorry.'

'Hey, it's alright, it's really alright. Georgie's so nice, I love her, but you and me, hey, we're still good. We both know that, no matter what. Besides, it's nice when fantasies come true, n'est-ce pas?'

She lay her head on my chest, nodded, and said, 'Just hold me.'

Then she looked me straight in the eyes, which I didn't mind because she had such black stunning mesmerising eyes, and said, 'Hey mister, you find out where you come from yet? Which mob? No? You were born in a good place and looked after well; I know that. I also know you have confusion about your parents. And I know there are times you hurt and want belonging and perhaps a forgiveness, or even a deeper acceptance. Maybe something's missing, I don't know. But you know what, you are a spiritual person and you absolutely have a right to feel connected to this land. And to belong to it. And hey, maybe you'll find out stuff about your parents pretty soon?'

What did she know, and how did she know what she knew? Those were always my eternal questions for Joan. My God, she knew things before they happened that girl.

They left, but I was feeling good. A little surprising to me perhaps, but I had no pain, no hurt, and no missingness. I felt good, really good. When done is done, then done is done, and we had done. And the memories of love will tide me over I'm sure. I gave my heart and it's still there. And I was ready for life. Horny though. And I did wonder whose mound it was over there that Georgie had pointed out.

But I felt a sort of relief, a relief borne of lust for sure, but also of love, and even a little, might I add, of male cockiness.

And I was at peace at my Creek and almost totally with myself. Yes sir, things were coming together with this search for the real self. I was almost there; I could sense it.

And even though the race had started; there was just one more hurdle.

RB-A hurdle you say? Yes, you have made a start but never mind a hurdle, how about a fucking mountain to climb? Mate, you are full of shit. And your girl left you for another girl. How does that make you feel? Jesus, you must be a good root.

Don't you just love it when your rational brain starts a conversation? A rational brain that should be excluded from all conversations regarding love, a rational brain that should be banished to another country. Yeah, thanks for that, cunt, but by the way, Joan never said I was a bad root, so take a hike. Nor will Georgie for that matter – the opposite I suspect. So fuck off.

RB-But Tony, aside from your apparently extraordinary masculine attributes, isn't this Creek, the one that is now a happy place, the same Creek as before that was pissing you off? The one I did my best to talk you out of even moving to?

Thank you for your consideration in this matter, you fucken dickhead. But, no it's not. Sure, the trees, the birds, the rocks are the same, the mountains, the green, the sparkling creek; but, no, it is not the same Creek, because The Creek knows. The Creek knows that when you are all good within yourself, then it reveals its true self, not the one that married someone else in that busy crowded off-leash dog park. And then you can also reveal your true inner self because you are a part of another, another way more powerful real self. More than a part, maybe even a belonging. You can be open and vulnerable to yourself in such a state of mind, in such a place. And it will answer your plea.

Revealing a truth to yourself when you are in such an accepting physical place like The Creek, can be raw and confronting in a self-delusional about-time-you-owned-up sort of way, and can make you want to duck your head, because you are not just exposing yourself to yourself (which your self-eyes already knew about, but decided not to open them), but you are acknowledging this truth out loud, so to speak. And once you do that, once you admit this thing to yourself, in thought or voice, courtesy of the rational brain, in such a peaceful place like The Creek, which has accepted you, and after you had stroked two beautiful women, you are liberated, but fucked at the same time, because then you have to deal with it. No more avoiding, no more denying, no more hiding behind extra maintenance jobs or angry bullshit, because she's all out in the open, in the air of honesty, in the sunlight of disinfected truth.

Like I did not do when I knew that Joan was going away and would leave me. I avoided this truth because I was scared of losing her, but also because I had a fear of truth. Fear of a truth about my self, because this fear is greater than truth, greater than a daily acknowledgement. A fear about fear. Yet, how does one acknowledge to oneself a fault, a deficiency, a hidden truth? One that you already know about but have avoided? I knew I had a whopper coming, and I was scared, really scared. More scared than ever. Do you just say, Hey, can you come over? Got something to tell you? What if such an exposure had a helping hand? A non-judgemental helping hand that guided you towards the light? A mentor perhaps?

Fuuck, just when I thought I was getting my shit together, I was going nuts.
RB-Will you listen to me this time?

Before they left, Georgie and I had sat quietly, and had spoken in French, and there had been a beautiful connection, through language for sure, but also through caring for the planet and being able to help.

Georgie had said, 'Eef we stop 'earing the rivèrrs end zee forests cryin', zen we stop carin' for ourselves an' each otha'. An' should ve not care for zose less fortunat'? Zose who need somevun to lissen? We are all 'ear togeffer, yet one pearson can make a deefference an' bring zee change. *Parfois le son d'une seule voix.* Becoz, zometimes zee soun' of vun voice … a voice that leeves its beleefs, she gets lou' soflee.'

I liked her one person talk. That excited me to keep caring for the world. But I also knew that with Georgie, there was more, and I knew deep down, there was a lot more. And I had secretly hoped for another lot more. A lusting again for sure, but I wanted an acknowledgement of something that was whacking me in the face, because I couldn't do it by myself – because I was scared.
I needed Georgie to help me.

I practised what I would say to Georgie, 'I have stuff to tell. Can you help me?'
Soon as I looked at her, about to unload my heart, she said, 'M'sieur, I know. I alreadee know vot you are about to zay.'
Fuck me. Forget the free haircuts and the pert tits, this girl was related to Joan's mob for sure. She knew, just like that, she knew.
'You do?'
'Oui, je sais. You are hurtin' yes? You 'ave treecked yourself. Somewhere, somehow. Je ne sais pas où, but it ees somevere. C'est vraiment, oui?'
I am going home. This girl may not know specifics, but she had nailed me. I could still run, you know. *Sit down, shut up, put your seat belt on, and fucking get on with it.* Shoosh you.
'Yes, I have tricked, I have lied, and I have not been nice to others. But I am too scared to tell you anymore.'
'C'est d'accord, c'est la vie, vee all do thiz, from dime to dime. It ees no big deel?'
She wasn't being dismissive, not at all, she was giving me a chance, a chance to really be true, without condemnation, blame or judgement. A chance borne of some pretty high-level intuition. Georgie would be a listener, a true listener. This was my call, my turn to stand up. By the way, Georgie, you married, or what? Oh, that's right. I nearly forgot; you already have a girlfrien'. So I told her. I told Georgie my deepest secret, my lowest

moment of deceit, my exposure laid bare, right there, on the verandah at The Creek. I finally did it. Thank you Creek, you have answered my plea. *Hey, what abou' me?* Fuck off, rational brain, I'm currently busy. Thank you Georgie. An ouch from me to me via The Creek and via Georgie, who was just being there (although she had read me like a well-worn novel).

'Ok zen, eet ees a beeg deal. But now that you 'ave said eet, eet makes eet a vee bit better, nes't-ce pas? Un peu, peut-être? Aussi, you 'ave broken dreams as well? Ha! Suck it oop and shoin de club m'sieur. Vith your treek and untruth to yourself, you are vunn of us all, yet like us, vous êtes special. You fink you don't feet? Oui! You do not feet, becos you do not want to fuckin' feet! Vous est moi, I fink we are the same, n'est-ce-pas? You and I are a vun pearso'. We must always be vun pearso'.'

I get that. I get the getting loud softly thing that Georgie had talked about. I get the one-person thing. It's like, Shut the fuck up and do stuff, stop complaining, help fix things the best way you can. And stop lying to yourself. Can't believe I had owned up to my lie. Even though she nicked my girlfriend, the bit about her and I always being a one person was intriguing, n'est-ce-pas?

Hurdle jumped over. I think.

Thanks Georgie, for helping me, you're a doll. Look after my girl. Hope you were taking.

RB-A jumped over hurdle? Hmm, who you kidding? I'd say you knocked the hurdle over on the way through. Maybe this race needs a rerun?

* * *

Could I ever reject society altogether? And be an Old Harry? Eat corn, drink sherry, have pet snakes and not wear leather? No, I couldn't do that, because although I don't mind corn, I don't drink, and I'm not rapt in death adders as pets. And, I absolutely love leather, especially stuff by the coffee shop girl. More to the point, I couldn't be a Harry because I am a fake, a hypocritical imposter fake person, a fucking liar who should shut the fuck up. I condemned society, because its system didn't care for individual people or the planet. Yet as I ranted against its greed, I was conflicted, because even though I hated its destructive forces, its wastes, its false real estates, its forced consumerism and advertising aimed at the heart of insecurity, I was confused, because I knew I sometimes didn't care, and I had moments of greed too, I had waste, I needed medicine, fuel, you name it. I was exactly the same as those I condemned.

'My name's Tony,

I like mining, cotton irrigation, fossil fuels, medical research, polluting waterways, and the consumer society.'

'Jesus, you poor bastard. How long have you had this problem?'

'Oh, since I was about seven.'

'And you've never had help?'

'Well, I did try to join Hypocrites Anonymous a while back, but they wouldn't have me.'

'Quickly everyone, stand and hold hands. Let us welcome Tony into Imposters Anonymous.'

'But hang on, don't those words … never mind.'

* * *

Two scientists were in The Creek, in waist-high wellies like fly fishermen. The boss was Julie, the offsider from before. Her offsider was Billy the Kid. Billy the True, Billy the Wise.

'Hi Julie. What you doing?'

'Oh, hi Tony, just checking the water quality. It all seems okay. This is my offsider Billy.'

'Nice to meet you Billy. Do I know you from somewhere?'

'Hi sir, and no, you don't know me from somewhere. Only from a specific place.'

He hasn't changed. 'Would you both like to come up for some tea and biscuits?'

Julie said, 'Sure, that would be nice.' She leant towards Billy, Billy the Philosopher, Billy the Seemingly Innocent, and whispered, 'He eats animals. I wonder what species of protected wildlife he has slaughtered this time.'

Billy the Never Silent, said to Julie the boss, 'Even money it's a wallaby.'

I forgot I had a brush turkey hanging upside down, dead, not bled or plucked.

Julie said, 'Goodness me, what is that!'

Billy wasted no time. 'I know what it is Miss. It is a bad debt, a memory of sweet swallows that have come home for the summer, and it is a beautiful memory of a teacher I once knew who inspired me to dream.'

'Billy.'

'Yes sir.'

'You were right, you were always right.'

'But that's a brush turkey.'

'Indeed it is, but the biscuits were cooked in wallaby grease. Have tomorrow off.'

'But sir, it's … anyway, as I was saying Miss, beauty is not always the pursuit of the glorious, of the pretty blue triangles that aren't really so. It is often the residue of life's numbered reasoning, the chase of the already decided, and the formula of the what is and the what is left.'

My word, RB and EB said together, *who is that one?*

* * *

The Creek had its fair share of daytime humidity, but at night there was always a creek breeze, like being next to the ocean. Hot air doesn't rise, they got it all wrong. It's the other way around. Cold air sinks. And therefore, pushes the heat and humidity up onto the trees to help make rain clouds. The air hummed with its humidity, and it also beamed along with a fecundity, a fecundity of confidence.

I felt a lightness, an unloaded emptied baggage. And I felt weird, a strange weird, a lightness weird, almost a warm weird.

I think I love you Georgie.

RB kicked in. *Hold on a minute you. Yes Georgie listened to you, and accepted what you said, and it needed to be said that's for sure. About time you listened to me. Georgie has given you something as a base to rebuild, because you built on a lie, and the foundations of that lie weren't dug deep enough. But love? I don't know.*

EB. Hold your horses buddy. Taking a bit of credit for prompting the emotional unloading, along with the dodgy analogy, might get you a couple of brownie points, but what-the-fuck would you know about love? Stick to being a niggle will you? And leave the loving to me, and him. Hope she wasn't taking. We want that fertile thing happening.

Maybe the unloading of the bad stuff had left a vacuum and it would take a while for truth to leak in, like a dry river trickling after rain. But did I just love Georgie because she was the one who heard my secret? A sort of relief love, a sympathy love, a love of convenience? Perhaps if I'd have unloaded to a tree the same love would have happened. How unfair is that? Georgie was certainly empathetic and quite witty. Cute arse too.

But the warm weird stayed and I had to choose to be free and stay with it, or stay trapped within the solitude of a cracked mind. Solitude's cracks can be the start of disaster, or not. Because cracks can also let daylight in. That's if you were inside the cracked solitude thing, and it was daytime. If it was night, you'd be pretty much fucked. If solitude is done with a troubled heart, fuck me, look out. Or a troubled heart encroaches into an existing solitude, look out worse. Or if an old dog dies, look out again. One evening he said, 'Play me some mountain music.' And he tilted his head upwards to the orange sky and he howled. Lonely and alone are not the same. Nowhere near it. Lonely is a killer no matter where you are, alone or not. Alone by itself can be wondrous and exhilarating. Or maybe solitude only works if you're alone? Not alone as in alone by yourself alone, I mean not in a relationship alone. If you are in love, then time away from your loved one can be secure, uplifting, or it can be agony. If you are secure, if you are uplifted, there can be no agony, if you are rejected it hurts, it bites. Solitude can be then undesirable and destructive, depressive and dangerous. All choices I know. A little bit of pain, a possible inevitable pain is okay if it's quick, because this is what life can do, but a chosen pain is a waste of time, of life. Suffering for salvation? Fuck me again. Salvation from what or whom for Christ's Sake? Someone else's shit? Get off your arse. Suffering is not only personal; the fucker is optional. The old dog died. But if solitude and living simply, with limited use of resources is the ideal, I'm in. Sign me up. Growing stuff, eating wild stuff, strong physical work, deep in nature, deeper sleeps, simplicity and giving kindness and love to those you do come across. I must do this, but when and how? He was stiff and dead in his nest, Jayden standing next to his body, guarding him. Oh Jesus. I wept for two days. Inside the cracked thing at night, in The Creek breeze coming through the window, open this time, and letting me to return to choko vines, Iced Vo-Vos and watching Grandpa take out his false teeth and dunk his biscuit into his cup of tea.

Yet I still chose freedom. I wanted life, and I wanted life with all that it had.

* * *

During my next visit to the old folk's home, Henry said something strange, sort of random, but really nice. And even though I was busting to tell him the bad news about Fergus, I listened. Half-heartedly, almost not-focussingly rudely, but I listened.

He said, 'You are an inspiration.'

'What? Really?' Tony is now awake.

'No, I made it up. You do a lot to help others, you do what you say, and you are a person who changes things. And you are rebuilding the rainforest.'

There was a pause, a warm, slow pause that gave me time to let my head to resume its normal size and for the blood to flow back around the rest of my body.

Then Henry looked up at me and said, 'He's dead isn't he?'

Fuck me, how would he know that? 'Yes Henry, Fergus died. I'm so sorry Henry, I really am.'

Henry's response has stayed with me forever, 'We should have stayed and died in the bush. Like the old dog.'
And we both wept.

'He saved me up on the plateau when we were lost.'

'Not surprised. He talk to you?'

'Hell yes. You too?'

'Bastard never shut up.'

Then Henry again said something strange, even more random, but somehow right.

He said, 'You want a sherry?

I said, 'Yes thanks.' And looked around to see who had said that. But didn't wonder why. It was delicate and smooth, and it spun me out, nicely.

Henry died the next day.

When I went in to see Henry and Lena, and found out that Henry had died, I was devastated. Lena, who was always quiet, lovely, respectful, staid almost, held my hand, and said, 'Here, Henry said you were to have these.' It was a photo of a skinny young fella, an athlete, having a medal put over his head, and a letter. And she looked into the distance of her memories with Henry.

'You were accepted you know. Straight away. You didn't need seven years. Don't beat yourself up so much, you're a good man. Peter told me that you were a genuine fellow, and that he liked you being in his family. To get what you love, you must be patient with what you have. Watch out for the death adders. They may seem friendly, but they're not. Was I a surgeon, a pilot, an Olympian? Yeah, I did some of that stuff in my early days I guess. And I'm sorry about the baldy mare episode, but you did well. And thank you for the wheel brace lesson. That was the best pay back I've seen for a while. I deserved it too. Look after Lena for me.

Your old bush mate, Henry.'

* * *

One morning Fergus had bounded up to me as I was going to feed the chooks, and he said, 'Woof.' A normal dog saying Woof, may not be news, but for starters Fergus wasn't normal. Secondly, Fergus rarely made a noise, except for the occasional low growl when early on, a certain rooster came too close. He was telling me something, something joyous, something pretty special. He then grinned, whined and wagged his tail. I looked up and saw Henry riding up the hill on the baldy mare.

Lena said that Henry had died on his back with a framed photo of Fergus on his chest.

* * *

I whacked a cockroach. He flipped onto his back, wriggling his legs and pooping everywhere, as you probably do when you've been swatted. He lay underneath a low cupboard and I couldn't get to him until the next morning. Then, still on his scuttly back, his wife (a cuntroach) was next to him and she was trying to help him up like you might see a human wife trying to lift her bedridden hubby up in an old folk's home, so he could slurp his soup.

Death cannot be avoided, unlike taxes and gravity and solitude, and I felt ashamed for what I had done. She looked into his eyes (all 8,000 of them), then up at me and said, 'Death is coming.'

Lena died.

When do you say goodbye? That final goodbye. Do you say goodbye, like really early just in case? Or do you wait until someone is deadly sick? Or so old, you know their time is near? Or do you avoid such moments? It's as much a fear of death, your death, your mortality, as a fear of acknowledging it in front of the possible dying one. Lena died not long after Henry. She had been lonely without him for sure, but she seemed well. A sudden death, a coincidence; I'm not so sure.

Joe the sawmill legend died. Peter the bush carpenter died. For Christ's sake, turn off the fucking light, it's attracting them. I'm sorry little cockroach, I had no idea what I had done. Am I stupid, uncaring, or merely inattentive? Possibly all three. Joe had a creek crossing named after him, Peter did too. Henry had a new species of tomato named after him. A species that could withstand colder weather. And yet, and yet, even though we may get old and feeble, and diseased, if you don't do it yourself, death chooses when to arrive. Not all heroes wear capes. Some are clothed in sawdust; some carry a setsquare, some cut lantana, some cook homely meals, but sooner or later they all die. When good people die, stars go brighter. This time, they lit up the day sky too.

* * *

Grandpa had said on one of his visits, 'Have you been looking after that handsaw?'

'Yes I have. It's such a beautiful tool. Where did you buy it from?'

'I didn't. I stole it. I gave it to you to get rid of the evidence.'

'You what!' That the one who taught me to do the right thing, to always be true and honest, would not only steal, would implicate me as well?

'Hey, relax Your Highness, he was a prick. And it's okay to steal from pricks. That one is in my memory easy because of the shit stuff he did. It's the other bad stuff I did that I choose to ignore.'

'What bad stuff? What do you mean?'

'I can't remember.'

Hang on a minute; here's my grandpa, my saviour for all sorts of reasons, not only morally judging people in order to justify knocking off stuff from them, but telling me now he's done other bad shit? And choosing not to remember it? Where does this end? Fuck, I was confused. Never mind that I dared to think even less of Grandpa, which I now did, what about the notion of not being honest with those who, in our eyes, have been morally corrupt for starters. Do we need to check out everyone before we deal with them? If so, apart from the obvious criminally recorded stuff, where would we get this info? Hand out a questionnaire?

'Have you ever had naughty thoughts about someone else's missus?'

'Have you ever stolen fruit?'

'Run a red light and not fessed up?'

There'd be no commerce, no international trade and certainly, no politicians. Ever.

Maybe grandpa never said he was perfect?

Maybe it was me who thought he was, who eventually thought he was. And I wondered, was I?

Grandpa was still kicking, more than ancient but still alive. Just. I sat by The Creek and thought about him. About how he helped me when it probably wasn't his job. And I was ungrateful while I lived my lie. How do I say thank you properly? Maybe he was the mentor I searched for but I overlooked him not because he was mean but because basically I was a shithead.

He said, *occasionally listen.* I was okay with this one. He said, *You are not indispensable but you are irreplaceable.* That is sort of nicely put. I think. He said, *Give to others.* I had done a little of this one. And when I had, I liked the feeling. Point taken, more coming. He said, *Lie occasionally.* Chip off the old block, me. *Sleep well.* I've got that one covered. *Always be kind.* More needed. *Dance well and be a gentleman.* Yep, just ask that Kiwi girl. *If you are true to yourself, you will be so when you are alone, as you will be with others.* This has caused me fucking pain for many years and I avoided the why. Me with me I'm sort of good, except for one thing which I did my best to evade, avoid and avert, but when I am out with others, or talking to others, I default to a desire to please the situation. Am I true to myself when I do this?

* * *

Do we have to leave something? If so, what do we leave? An art piece, a Booker, a diplomatic coup, a handsaw? Or just something simple, like, 'He was a nice bloke.'? Why leave anything anyway? Way too selfish an aim? Are people who desire to leave something just conceited cunts who strive to upend their current insecurities? Attention seeking at its worst? To please whom anyway? Someone you don't love? Who never liked you anyway? Someone you don't even know? Or could we just be, just live and be kind, and see what happens? If you don't get what you desire in this lifetime, then you won't see the next section.

Sometimes I wondered what I leave behind. Not after I may or may not die, I mean for each person that I spoke to now. When Joan had said, *'I suppose you're alright. You're a bit rough around the head but you'll do. Not a bad root. And you treat me nice.'* I felt so proud, a leave behind now proudness. Maybe we only need one person to listen? To give appreciation, and maybe love? So we can be a one person to another as well as to ourself because of that other? A from without other?

Live by example of what you desire. I'm a slow learner, but I'm listening grandpa.

* * *

I like letters. Mostly. Sometimes. Grandpa wrote. 'I had a letter the other day. He wants me to get ready, and he wants a reply. But I said not yet. Told him to fuck off.'

* * *

I sawed blue quandong seeds with a hacksaw to aid their germination, I potted white cedars, silky oaks, forest oaks, tulipwoods and cheese trees, I regenerated gullies and forests because they had been flogged and to make up for my timber usage, because the beauty of the forest, new or old will promote love. I planted red cedars, in full sun and away from each other. They would need some management to be future saw logs, but this I can do.

I saved two belts of local rainforest though blatant tactics, and a few lies; thanks grandpa for the tips. 'Look at these rare birds! If you leave the forest, it will benefit you financially in the future.' And help to keep ecosystems a bit more secure, you greedy cunts. I'm going to hell anyway because I judge harshly, lie and swear heaps, so what the fuck. I grew more vegetables and fruit, all 100% made in Australia, with all local ingredients, organic and sustainable. The turkeys, grubs, bower birds, king parrots, wallabies, and eels (overland, remember), left me enough.

I bought second-hand clothes and books and memories. Others' worn and loved clothes, others' stories they had finished with so I may learn from, because they had lived, others' stories to help me feel good via their memories. But also, second-hand to also to ease my guilt of self-righteousness. Because when you preach you become one or more of the pricks from those capital cities in Russia, China, Italy, Iran, Saudi Arabia and Australia. And self-righteousness and those pricks are finished. Hopefully. Hopefully soon, and with ease.

I used others' stories so I may live now, to be better, and to look forward to learning and living and maybe giving back somehow.

* * *

I like letters. They give warmth, association, information, and at times, shit news. Grandpa was found dead with a pack of cards in his hand. This did not surprise me. That he was dead, or the cards thing. He had probably been stacking it. Now, I'm not the world's most intelligent guy, but I pushed away the truth that was about to be exposed; or would it remain hidden with the old boy's death? Even with Georgie's love and understanding, I somehow knew it was getting close to the time of the final facing up. To myself, my truth, and maybe eventually get closer to my real self?

The letter had arrived. Well, darlin', everywhere I look I see your eyes, and I used to like letters, but I still love ya, but now I'm not so sure. In a dark-brown voice she said, I will send you champagne. Now, I'm not dumb but then again, I just may well be. Well, gullible, anyway. Can I sit on your lap anyway? Fuck, go for it honey. I like letters. Little envelopes, some business-like, some rough-hewn but cute, all stamped with an historical sweetness they may appear to have, yet their inside sheets of paper, all crisply folded, they can bring connection, or even confusion, a heart known to none, solitary company, crowded houses, fear, bravery, avoidance, their words like those silent raindrops, without wings they teach me to fly beyond the sky, ancient melodies, all written to a simple man craving for love, but they can also smash you back to Earth. Thanks Ground Control.

'We regret to inform you that your grandfather has died. Our thoughts are with you on your loss, well, that's after the rugby is over and we chill the charders. Arrangements have been made to shaft you, and anyone remotely connected to the family. We promise to do our best to play on your emotions, force you to buy a headstone, and screw you even further soon as we can. We sincerely hope you want a huge, marble headstone. Didn't you really love your grandfather? That's a shame. Peace and Love, W. L. Cockhead and Sons, Funeral Directors.

Invoice enclosed. Hurry up and pay or the old boy rots above ground.'

I tossed it into the bin. Inside this letter, this, We are really sorry for your loss letter, this, I don't really give a fuck letter, this, We are pretending to be Solemn letter, was another letter, dated a few days before the old boy had died. And this one wasn't a letter; it was a fucking ticking time-bomb, a hand-grenade with the pin out, a tripwire that had been tripped. And it blew me to pieces.

'Hey you, You had two great parents who loved you. Okay, they may have drunk too much, which is probably why you chose not to drink. They gambled excessively, and died way too early, but they did their best. I don't know why you invented those stories about having no parents. And you did not go into an orphanage, you did not end up on the street … I took you on to help out, and you caused me so much fucking grief … but mostly you were a good one. Yes okay you were a good boy. I guess. You worked hard and I may have been mean to you, but you totally pissed me off with your made-up stories, your fucking fictions. Remember, we aren't what we are, we are what we hide. Maybe I won't post this … Look after that fucking saw. Used boiled linseed oil on the handle too. Raw oil dries sticky. I may not know where our mob came from, but remember, what you fear, you create, and kindness can't be demanded or asked for, only given.'

Except for the linseed oil bit, that was pretty much what I had told Georgie. With the letter was a small black and white photo. It was of a young couple, all posed and smiling, with a little kid, shading his eyes from what was about to happen.

* * *

The chooks were squawking loudly. All of them. This wasn't a goshawk call out, maybe a snake. Whatever it was, it was pretty close. I raced down and saw a feral cat in the garden, stalking the chooks, my chooks. One gets possessive at times, defensive, or even offensive. I hate feral cats worse than I hate politicians, real estate agents, bankers, funeral directors, and truth. I think. Bit of a toss-up really. There was no time to get the rifle, so I raced over and grabbed him. I grabbed with both hands, like you would when opportunity knocks, both hands on his shoulders so he couldn't claw me. Nothing worse than being slashed to pieces by a cat. This was a great move. One of my best. The fucker turned his head a full one-eighty and sank his fangs into my hand. Nothing worse.

In the doctor's waiting room, where I waited, because that's what you do in a waiting room, as I waited for a tetanus shot, a few stitches and some advice why not to grab a feral cat, I read an article about the Darling River. 'It's an ancient river system …', yeah, yeah, but the lead photo tore me open. Just a typical Darling photo, nothing special. Grey high banks, grey curving river, huge ancient red gums, nothing spectacular, just a typical Darling scene. Meant nothing to me. Don't care really.

* * *

Green to grey, and
Almost the last table note.
Gone fishing in the old river for a bit.
Chooks being looked after elsewhere.
Don't wait up for me.

Sometimes in life you get a swift kick in the arse. And at the time, it may seem a bit unfair, this size ten, but once you get over the throbbing bumcheeks and the hurt pride, you probably know you deserved it. When my kick came in the form of grandpa's letter, I certainly deserved it. My response was to run away. My rational brain said, *Woo, hang on a minute. What you're about to do is rubbish. Take a deep breath. Even though you shouldn't have come to The Creek in the first place, we need to stay and sort some stuff out.* But my emotional brain said, *Fuuck you, we are out of here baby. Let's go!*

It was time. Time to go green to grey. Here, at last, back on my Darling River. Saw my original note, still on the riverbank. I replied:

Going to a new place-yes I did.
Bit scared-still scared, mightily so.
Might stay for a while-stayed a long while.
Might come back-I did and here I am.
Not sure-am now. I think.

And to you I whom left after our many years together, I am really sorry. I'm really unsure why I'm leaving. I don't know what I'm doing basically. One day I may eventually come back over the red dirt dust to you. To you, who are always spiritual and beautiful. If I did return, would you have me back? Or would you say, 'No, I have a girlfriend.'

* * *

The doctor had looked at my puncture wounds and swollen hand. I said, 'Tiger shark.' I made a wire trap. Put out tinned fish for a week before I set it. Before I caught the cat, I caught a fox, an echidna and an eel. One morning I saw the cat, hissing and snarling in the cage. I said, Hi, remember me? He did, though I couldn't quite understand his words of greeting. A captured animal doesn't cry; it bites. I filled half a 44 with water and the cat went for a swim.

* * *

I had given away the pigeons, or what was left of them. The local goshawks had take-away so often there weren't many left. I parked the Dodge facing downhill, ready for a roll start. You never know. I unhooked the battery terminals, drained the radiator and wound the windows down a wee bit for feathery visitors. I took the cow and calf to the neighbour's and said thank you for the services, the girls are now yours, but the chooks, chooks are different. One can't just discard chooks without care. I had asked the coffee shop girl if she would look after them. She said, 'Yes please, I would love to look after your chooks.' Then she added, 'We will wait for you.'

I had bundled them into cardboard boxes and while they went fairly quietly, they looked at me. Nothing worse than being looked at by chooks who have exposed your gutless deed. Jayden was not impressed. Coffee shop girl's last comment did not go unnoticed. How was she so sure that I would return?

* * *

I had lied. And I had done it on purpose. And I only acknowledged this because it had been exposed. By me to Georgie, and thank God for this first edition, this original signed copy, and then from grandpa's letter, which, I might add, no-one else saw, needs to see or will see, but it was now time, now my time, to acknowledge all this to me from me.

Otherwise, there would always be a wee niggle there forever.

RB-And we know how they work out, don't we? All this shit will pass if you face it. Embrace reality.

EB-Sure, but whose? Not yours, you piece of cowpoo. A hopeful reality is our dream state, a breathless excitement of life, especially when we are being vulnerable. Shame you don't know what compassion is, cowpoo head.

I had told Georgie everything. Unloaded the sandbags off my shoulders off my brain off my heart. My God, she was so understanding, so beautiful. Never dismissive or judgemental, no, she just listened, Oh yeah, even though you have done wrong, you have told someone, me, and you are facing it m'sieur. What about Joan's earlier comments? '*I also know you have confusion about your parents. And I know there are times you hurt and want belonging and perhaps a forgiveness, or even a deeper acceptance. Maybe something's missing, I don't know ... And hey, maybe you'll find out stuff about your parents pretty soon?*'

It was like she had an idea of what was going on, and that everything was about to be resolved somehow. Maybe she knew grandpa? Maybe we're related?

The men in my life, Joe, Peter, Henry and grandpa, were real men who guided me, who were there for me, who tolerated me more like it, were all gone. Could I learn anything? Like, maybe it was my turn to be a real man?

What is a real man anyway? Is he so just because he and others identify him as a masculine person? Who is perhaps a bit hairier than other genders (but not always)? Who has a block and tackle? And different doses of hormones? On one of his visits to The Creek, Grandpa had said, 'A real man is strong yet weak, safe but vulnerable, forceful yet gentle, gives till it hurts, has dreams then does them, is lustful but respectful.'

No worries pop. Then after lunch …

'He smiles lots, shows empathy, is a listener, speaks out, accepts himself, is at peace, is honourable, and changes if necessary.'

'Jesus Grandpa, why didn't you talk like this, like fucking years ago?'

'I did.'

I used a Phillips screwdriver. Does that count? Not an Allen key though. I can only do so much. I used one of those strap tie-down things, but fuck me, give me a rope any day, give me a double truckie's knot and I'll show you tight, I'll show you how to tie a load that won't go anywhere. Trying to be man is a hard gig. What is a man? An action hero? Defence forces, contact sports, or the little weedy guy from down the road who says No more! and faces the bully? I realised that the attributes are not specifically related to being a man; unless you count having a cock as important. Is this list not applicable to females too, with or without the cock? Indeed, to all humans, regardless of gender? To all living creatures even? To the planet? Beyond?

Grandpa had said, 'Be kind, be considerate, be advisory, but only if requested, and then in a non-threatening, non-dismissive manner.'

Thanks grandpa.

He had also said, 'Giving to others is so a part of our true selves, and it doesn't involve a thing or even doing a thing, it's just about you being there for someone else.'

When I thought of the men I admired and loved and respected, I realised that they had all given me way more than a saw, a sawmill job, paid carpentry for payment, or company in the bush with an old red dog. They had given me their time and their love. They had given me of themselves. They had been there for me.

Real man wish list; sorted.

Could I do the same? Could I be a real man, or even a mentor? If I wanted to be there for someone, who would it be, and how would I do it?

* * *

There was a white-faced heron. He lived in a nest in a red gum beside an old river. His mother said, 'When it's your time to leave the nest, the one you continually shit in, you must stay along the river. Don't go across the dry flood plains.'

'Why not mummy, I say mummy, why not?'

'Because I said so, that's why not.'

That answer has never worked, and it never will. Kids want their questions answered, kids want truth.

'Because there are dangers. Because there are no other white-faced herons for you to marry. Because I will beat the crap out of you if you try. Because I am a control freak, and I don't have a life.'

The first day he leapt off the nest, the white-faced heron immediately headed toward the open flood plains. Dumbarse. Got caught in a storm didn't he. Blown around like a sheet of dirty newspaper. He was smashed into some reeds and lay there, dazed, disoriented, and dishevelled. He looked up to see a large bird standing over him. The bird was not unlike him. Long neck, long legs and a long pointy beak. She said, 'I am a white-necked heron and I live here. Who are you and why are you here?'

'Well, that is an interesting story. I am a white-faced heron and I live along the old river.'

'That's a long way away.'

'Yes, it is. My mother told me not to fly across the plains. And I did and now I'm lost.'

'That's strange. My mother told me not to fly across the plains too. What is it with mothers?

Maybe you could make a home here?'

They became firm friends then after a bit went on dates. They watched documentaries about different species of people and hung onto feet and kissed and stuff.

In no time at all, they were married, had built a nest and had an egg.

Young birds are like that.

'I was wondering,' said the white-faced heron, 'what our baby will look like.'

'You're not suggesting …? Wait, I get what you mean. Because we aren't exactly the same, our baby might look like either one of us?'

'No, but that'll do for now.'

At first, their baby looked like both parents. Long neck, long gangly legs and a long pointy beak.

'Look,' said the white-faced heron, 'she has my white face.'

'Look,' said the white-necked heron, 'she has my white neck.'

But her body pin feathers weren't light grey, they weren't dark grey.
They were white.

The new heron was completely white.

Her parents said to her, 'Because we are from two different places, you can either live here in the swamp, or go across the flood plains to the old river.'

She said, stretching her pure white wings, 'I'll live in both.'

If we are left to be free, we can make choices.

* * *

I do like it out here, the floods and droughts, the fish and pure white egrets, the river gums and a milky tea river. And I had truly missed these. It was an ache of longing, but I also suspect it was an ache of missing these as an excuse for wanting to run away. Running away not to the river, but from me because I wasn't yet deeply settled within me. Would I revert to an old self out here? A one that I thought I had already sorted way back then before I got to The Creek? Or would I be true to me no matter where I was, or had been? And if I wasn't true now, then which self in the unleashed dog-park would I revert to in order to be true? I wouldn't be the run around like an idiot one, more like the one who casually sniffs bums, pisses on everything and roots whomever is available, reachable, or I was able to service.

I do like it out here, even though I'm unsettled. The grey clay, the brown birds, the drab brown pretty birds, the hot heat and the hot red sand. The small towns, the wool sheds, the boat trips, the fish, the little campfires. The avoidance. There comes a time in life, and thank fucking Christ there aint many of these, to front up, to face stuff, to be this real man. But, thank fucking goodness, this was not one of those times. I am so going to enjoy this, or else. I was now exalting in the red dirt, the fishing, the black soil and the smell of an old western river.

And the avoidance.

I lasted a month.

Is this what life does when you're not enjoying yourself? Disillusionment compounded by stupidity? Inaction, or an action bounded by fear and justified by insecurity? Maybe I should not have left the Darling in the first place? But that's dumb, so fucking dumb, because where do you stop with that sort of futuristic hindsight rubbish, that poor-me shit? You do what you do when you decide to do. Or maybe I should have come back to the Darling earlier because this was my real place and I missed it terribly? Ouch. Come back earlier because I was unhappy at The Creek, and with my memories of Joan? Ouch again. Poor-me shit still. Settle. Or had come back before I met Joan? My goodness, this is getting sad. Or that Henry's death had affected me more than I realised? Or grandpa's? Or mine that's coming? My allocation of ouches had run out. You're only allowed two. Out of ouches I may be, but I suspect maybe it's more like being bereft of fucking brains, because it didn't take me long to realise that these thoughts were a pile of shit, and a harsh reminder that to produce negatives from love, from a true love, is more shittier, and to focus on negatives is even more shitterer, because all it does is produce more shit and as you slide down the sewerage of despair, the hand-holds get further apart.

* * *

Is it that after a time away from your love, you forget certain things that had been boring, and maybe a bit annoying? The things, that when the dust settled, like the sex that slowed down, and the realities of a living-together relationship really kicked in, tempted you to have doubts? And therefore, in this absence, this longing time, you only focused on the smooth times, the glory? Those intimate nothingnesses, that in reality built a closeness, developed and sustained a deeper bond within the mundane, the everyday? Or do you maintain the love no matter what? Was now the time to realise that life is made up of boring, those mundanes, those annoyances, as well as an enlightened joining of hearts?

* * *

Where do I want to settle, like forever? As in, is there a final place in which one chooses to settle? Apart from being laid out so the animals can have a feed that is. Which did I love more? The Darling or The Creek? But I knew; deep down I knew, because as soon as you ask yourself this sort of question, you already know the answer. Because the asking is merely a reinforcing of an avoidance of a known niggle that is waiting in the background to be asked to come forward. All you have to do is acknowledge it, and Wham, there she is. And when you do give acknowledgement, it's such a relief. And the answer, the already-known answer, was not a, Fuck, where am I, but a, Fuck, what am I doing here? It's nice when you do listen sunshine!

197

Then it became a rush. A, Come on, we're late for the train! I wanted to go back to The Creek. My true home, and hopefully to finish finding my true self.

And I left a new note on the riverbank.

I'm going home. Won't be back.

* * *

Grey to green and
Answering my own table note,
The last one.

Gone fishing in the old river for a bit. I did indeed catch fish
Chooks being looked after elsewhere. I'll pick them up directly.
Don't wait up for me. You can go to sleep now. I'm home.

Does one have to go away in order to come back? Not only in a literal sense, like going to town and back home, or to an old river and back to a rainforest creek, but like, after you lose something, you go, Fuck, wish I had that back. Or is there a short-cut of appreciation, so that you don't have to go to that away place? Or must we always go and return in order to better understand the original regardless? Maybe life has no shortcuts, and you have to do it all in order to understand the all? Or are the literals so joined to the realities, that we miss the fucking point anyway? Jesus, I need a drink. A slow learner I may be, but I had an idea on how to understand it all, how I could be helped to sort out life and finally understand my true self.

Inspiration and ways to sort out life can come from many places: time spent with a mentor, self-help books, or even from being close to your God, or through meditation, but I chose the Original Method, the One Way, the True Path to Enlightenment.
I grabbed a bottle of Sherry and sat in Old Harry's cave.

* * *

There was a time where Gods and men lived side by side …
    RB-Hope they showered occasionally.
    … there were no wars, only joy …
    EB-How old is Joy? She married?
    … but the king let the weeds grow …

RB-So that's where that bloody lantana came from. What an inconsiderate leader.

… and dissent raised its head.

RB-Well, chop it off his royal highness and everything will be back to normal.

EB-You are so fucking thick. It was the women who had had enough shit from the privileged entitled misogynist males who dissented. You are so literal, so unable to see anything beyond straightforwardness. You, old mate, you need to change, you need to look at life differently.

* * *

I sat and drank. Solitude in a cave with a bottle of Sherry, to find the Noble Truth, a Commitment to Wisdom, a Pure State of Awareness. Secure the back door, hide the jewellery, and lock up your daughters because I'm coming. I looked around. There was an old unhinged wooden slat door, which I could fix later, the floors were dusty dirt, no 4 x 1 hardwood boards needed or necessary, there were dried corn husks and empty Sherry bottles strewn about, and they were all circled by discarded memories of a forgotten war. Old Harry had suffered greatly because of his time in the First World War. There was talk of an horrific head injury, of a disillusionment, of a desperate need to reject society. He went to his cave, let his hair and beard grow long, and became a vegan. No leather belts even. He grew corn and ground it to make meal. Grey boulders, white-tinged lichen, and glossy green leaves surrounded my desperation to find meaning, to bring it all together. The things that I had thought important, like my likes and dislikes, the search for a true self, seemed to fade into a fog of self-indulgence, into a mist of confusion. It was now time to sort it all out; to find my true self.

I sat and drank, and I muttered. In my Supreme State of Being, my Transformative Peacefulness, I mumbled, 'I have come back to you my gorgeous Creek, *my fucking oath you have, you crawler*, to you, who are always spiritual and beautiful, back from the grey Darling, back to you, my green mountains and my Creek. I know I left you and I am so sorry *Really? I think you are a two-faced fucking liar, just like the ones you hate, the consumers, the angry men, the polluters, the real estate agents …*, but I sort-of-deep-down knew I would come back from over the red dirt dust, to you. *Well, that's a bit pre-planned, a little, you wanted her to just wait like a dutiful little missus while you galivanted and had a good time elsewhere.*

Will you have me back? Or will you say, 'No, I have a girlfriend.' *Whether The Creek has a girlfriend or not is irrelevant to you, you piece of grovelling obsequious shit.* But there was no girlfriend, no rejection slip for me, only forgiveness and open arms. Acceptance from a loved one is a beautiful thing that gives humility, and can help to create change in the acceptee. *For heaven's sake, you make me feel sick.*

I was shocked. The tirade from my rational brain was so out of character, not to mention pretty harsh. Never mind pure white doves and pretty nymph maidens waiting to welcome me home, never mind a soft landing, this was a trainwreck, a crumbling away of untruth, and a brutal reckoning. I sat and drank, but I stopped muttering and spoke coherently, sensibly, and relatively loudly.

Yeah, fuck off you, rational brain. I thought you were supposed to be impartial, you know, just making lists and shit? Just quietly, I never liked you. And anyway, who died and made you fucking king?

RB-Nobody had to die. It's an innate gift, a natural progression within the order of the universe. And you may note that I have taken advice from that other one, and changed my approach to life. And I realise that, though you've never liked me, I have tried to help.

Kidding me, right?

RB-No. For starters, I tried to talk you out of moving here, then I tried to reason with you when you first met Joan, I intervened when you got that letter from your grandpa and implored you to stay and sort yourself out, but as usual, you ignored me, and listened to her, that evil emotional brain slut, and then you totally fucked up by running away. At least you listened to me when I said return to The Creek. Previous to that, with Georgie ...

'... Yeah, yeah, settle. Leave Georgie out of it. Anyway, who needs reminders of your stupid advice, your boring data, your detail on finances, your fucking dot-points of icy death. Please. And hey, take it easy on the criticism of my beautiful, my treasure, will you? She's particularly sensitive.'

RB-Not to mention fucking impetuous, compulsive, scatterbrained, and totally a drama queen. Whereas I, your new king, am conscientious, articulate and gorgeous. Anything I missed?

EB-Yes, you piece of shit, there is. You are a fucking backward ape, evolution halted when it saw you, and you still drag your knuckles as you attempt to walk upright. Hi everyone, remember me?

Hi emotional brain, how you doing? And why the fuck is rational brain being such a cunt?

EB- And a good afternoon to you my Lord. I am indeed well, thank you for asking. I am your queen, and I thought you'd forgotten about me there for a minute. And I don't think, despite his outrageous insults, his bull-fucking-shit self-praise, that rational brain is not being a cunt on purpose. He may have a point. And he certainly changed his approach to life somewhat. Maybe we all need to talk?

Now I have a king and a queen who don't like each other and who seem to have their roles mixed up. Rational brain was being judgemental, and emotional brain was fucking about with reasoning. Have they been talking behind my back? Confusion often hits me, but when it's my own, from me to me, it becomes even more confusing, a confusion of confusions. 'Come again? A threesome you say? As you know, I don't mind those.'

RB-God save us. There's more to life than raunchy sex you know.

EB-Doubt it son. Anyway, I have an idea. How about we put up a white flag, a small concession, a willingness to talk sensibly so we can sort this fucking mess out?

Jesus, I don't believe you two. Anyway, what mess? And what is this, a look at life from both sides now?

RB-Yep, it sure is. Actually, three sides if you're in. No, not one of those, you degenerate. And you are a mess, just have a look at yourself, will you? Fucking indiscriminately, drinking again, not facing up to your own shit. Shall I continue? No, didn't think so. So, let's get to it. Let's work out a baseline to bring us all together, to acknowledge out differences, our strengths, our similarities, and then we can try to live in peace. We could even make a Mind Map, a Venn diagram, a ...

Stop! They are the most revolting suggestions I have ever heard. Yet, somehow, something feels right. I think I agree with you, RB.

This was nuts. Me and two brains, in a cave, drinking Sherry, sorting out life. We've had our arguments before, but this will either be the end of the world as I know it, (that new one I found when I was quite young – courtesy of a hooker), or heaven. And did I just acknowledge my rational brain?

RB-Yes you did, and praise the Lord. As for you, you salacious slut, I taught him how to build a house basically. How to measure and saw, the legal requirements, how to exist up here. Shit like that.

EB-Oh for heaven's sake. Yes, you may have helped with how much netting for the orchard, which type of fruit tree ... blah, blah, blah. Fuck me, I am dealing with a fucking retard. Where's your imagination, your excitement, your enthusiasm, your beauty for the planet?

RB-Hang on a tick, didn't you just say, like a few minutes ago, that we need to make peace with each other? How's that going? Anyway, your irrelevant notions of life, your leading him down a destructive road, is a road that never ends. It was moi, who made him tell Georgie about his big lie, his big clusterfuck fiction. And, can I just remind you, you fuckwit who avoids what is there right in front of you, you bastion of unbridled unthinking unwisdom and fucking stupidity, it was you who kept him busy with unnecessary shit when I tried to enlighten him about Joan leaving?

EB-You fucking arrogant cockhead! They were all important jobs, so fuck off.
RB-Bull-fucking-shit.

EB-You, you objective right-wing arsehole! You may have helped with some pragmatic shit, but I, good old me, gave him pleasure that was lacking in your cold, steely, insensitive unfeeling righteous white-male privileged, entitled cuntness. Don't bring a knife to the gunfight because I am going to take you down!

I began to see a pattern, a pattern of me ignoring a truth that sticks out like a sore thumb, that had been pointed out to me, yes, and a truth of the way I lived life. Both may need a bit of attention.

RB-Game on mole. You, you live in the boonies, that's why you're so illogical and fucking crazy. You are unsound, laced with moral depravity and the gates of hell are swinging open as we speak. Anyway, I did the outside bathroom, the rows of vegetables, which rainforest tree to plant in which gully, where the eels come from! You want more?

EB-For fuck's sake! You are such a hillbilly. You are an inbred. I bet you root sheep, and things. You think you're smart, but you, you are living proof that man comes from amoebas. If you had your way, we wouldn't have even met Joan, let alone fucked her silly.

RB-And just think of the pain that would have been avoided eh?
EB-You mean a life that would have been avoided, don't you?
Wow, that was below the belt. I blocked them out for a while.

Time to face time to honest time to admit. My parents, the ones I rejected, they did their best. I know that. It was me who had claimed to be an outcast, an orphan for Christ's sake, such was my deceit. Claimed to be something I wasn't. Why wasn't that one first to be cleared up in the initial search for the real self? *RB-Tried to tell you …* Shoosh you! And grandpa the cunt. God only knows how he put up with me. It was he who steered me, steered me with patience. He was still one of those though. The Darling, my old river.

Did I really love you? Infatuation? Wash my mouth out, sorry. The Creek. Jesus. Yes, here I am. Again. All that I had done here, the building, the vegetables, the orchard, the bushwalks, the town trips, the work, maybe, just maybe, all this was added to the real self? Or maybe it *was* the real self regardless? Henry saying that I was accepted, and thanks for not telling me earlier, you old bastard. You and your fucking seven-year shit. Peter, just watching Peter was enough to guarantee everlasting inner peace, my gorgeous Joan, my lusty girl, who did love me I know that. And Georgie. What of Georgie? Was she another of those reminders that my rational brain had prompted me to realise, but that I had ignored? Like when Joan and I had a feeling in the atmosphere we couldn't understand but pushed aside anyway? Like when I drove back from town after Joan had said, Yeah, going away for a bit? And I knew, but decided not to know by not acknowledging it out loud? I hate you rational brain. But if I did, which I did, and quite often he knew shit, but if I did and I ignored him yet again, what was I ignoring this time? That I now loved Georgie better than Joan? Holy Fuck. I need a drink.

RB and EB-Hey, we're back!

I love Georgie.

RB-Oh, for crying out loud!

EB-You beauty! Let's go find her and fuck her again!

RB-Wait! Wish you fucking people would listen to me occasionally. You do not love Georgie, you only love what she said, what she meant, what she awakened in you.

EB-Maybe so, you fucking dead rhinoceros, but she was a smoking hot babe!

Georgie, apart from indeed being a smoking hot babe, had certainly awakened deeper meanings. She had said, We must all care for the planet, and we must all listen to others and care for them. And that one person can make a difference. And this will give hope. This is what a true self does.

Hey RB? You were sort of right about Georgie. Not entirely, but enough for me to say thank you.

RB-That's nice. That Georgie girl, well, I suppose she was a bit sexy.

EB-And I guess that apart from her pert tits and cute arse, she did have some incredible insights.

RB-Wow, I didn't realise, EB, that you could be so ... rational. Not to mention nice.

EB-Flattery will get you places mister. Be careful.

They hugged, and EB had a quick feel of RB's arse-*Ooo*, he swooned, *I don't mind that.*

Dream Brain kicked *in-Hey you pair, you woke me up! I've been listening to your shit, and it is fucking disgusting, now cut it out!*

RB and EB-Hey, we've seen what you get up to some nights, so don't you call us disgusting. You fucking pervert!

Searching for inner stuff is valid work, doesn't pay much mind you, but maybe it is a part of the going away and coming back of life, of living life your own way as best you can? Maybe I had it all, as in right now? And therefore, I could stop looking for my true self because it was here, right now? Thank goodness for both brains (with a cameo from the third), a cave and a bottle of Sherry. Maybe, along with The Creek, and its building, its bushwalks, its solitude, maybe these people, these beautiful people, and what happened, regardless of what happened, as in me owning up to a lie, were part of the life I had wanted, had chosen, and was now realising were powerful in me being me? In forming and letting me to be my true me? God it's hard being sensible.

I took pride in what I had done with the house. The stumps, the studs, the floor, the bench … and those saw cuts! The solidness, the slowness, and the no shortcuts. I gave recognition of gratitude of what I had and who had helped get here. I had meaning, a purpose, which was to regenerate the cleared areas. I could live simply, no more kero for the lanterns because I would use lamps using olive oil, a cheap form of lighting I had seen coffee shop girl use, but I thought at this stage I would keep the old truck, my faithful Dodge, but most of all I had an acceptance of me, me with my faults, my hypocrisy, my lies and the fiction and the shit I told to feel secure and important, but no more, I was now me, my true self.

I may not be an Old Harry, and live in a cave full time with a pair of death adders as pets, but I can still visit and sit still and learn from him. I decided to not kill any more animals to eat. All wallabies and lizards and brush turkeys could rest easy. I was done. I was still a beginner at all this, I know that. A learner of being able to accept all there has been and all there is, a learner of life, and a beginner of when to search and when not to search. I still wanted to fuck the man, but this wasn't as strong now. Defiance I was good with, so maybe occasionally the man would get one less grain of wheat a week.

RB-Well, you may not have listened attentively from time to time, but you my friend are getting there. Getting to a place of quiet, a place of no matter what has gone down, you will be okay. Fuck I feel good.
EB-Me too. And well said old chap.

This is what I call real inner peace. Everyone, even with different approaches to life, at least accepting the other. A breath, a deep breath, in, and out. An exaltation of love for the planet. My true self was here, right now. I tossed the empty Sherry bottle in the dust next to its relatives, and as I staggered out of the cave, I high-stepped over a pair of locals, hidden in the leaf-litter. They slispered, 'Sssee you sssoon.' And wriggled their tails farewell. I said, 'Next time, move you bastards, or I'll tread on you.'

'Yess,' they slispered together, 'you do that and you'll get the same treatment as my grandpa did to Old Harry.'

'Well, not all grandpas are snakes in the grass you know.'

I saw Harry's corn grinder laying in the dirt. I picked it up and placed it near the crooked slat wooden door. I walked down to The Creek, stripped off and slowly submerged. The deep pool came over me and I opened my eyes so I could look in and see my face, my wavy riverweed hair and my rising bubbles, but all I saw was a giant eel grinning at me. You're safe old eel. All of us are safe.

* * *

Chop fresh beans and an onion, finely,
Cook in olive oil,
Mix this lot in a bowl with 1 egg and some Old Harry-type ground corn meal.
Dust with wholemeal flour,
And roll into small balls.
Turn the heat up lots (as in, move the pot)
And drop these balls in deep hot oil.

Some decisions had been made alright – a promise from me to make an effort to understand all of me. And I vowed to make The Creek my last permanent address. I like letters. Write me one; it'll find me.

The Dodge was facing downhill ready for that rolling start. I had left the windows down a little so the swallows could fly in and nest. Which they had done and were still doing. They flew around and squeaked at me, 'You're here again? Jesus. Great grandma said you went away. What's going on?' It's nice to see you too. Listen here you little squawky bastards, if you want to stay alive, clean up all that fucking mess (the wee babies looked over the edge of their mud-pellet nests and started crying), and either follow me into town or sit down and shut the fuck up. I wire brushed the battery terminals and reconnected the leads, filled the radiator and topped up the oil. I then disconnected the fuel pump and cranked her over a few times to get the oil up through the cylinders. I reconnected everything, and I swear I heard a purr, and hopped in. Rolling down a hill in second is a better way to jump start. Joe had told me this, but I couldn't remember why. A bit of blue smoke, a few shudders and we were away. The old girl wriggled her bonnet flaps and twinkled, 'Oh thank you so much! I knew you'd be back. Let's go to town baby!'

'So nice you're back from that old dirty river. We waited for you.'

Guilt or nothing, even a halfway point that sits between heaven and hell, take your pick. I felt uneasy, not because I had returned so quickly, not because of her genuine care towards me, the looking after the chooks for free, and probably the whole universe for that matter, but from her disgraceful description of my Darling River. No-one says that about my river and gets away with it. No more joy for you, coffee shop girl. Comeon girls and boys, let's get out of here.

I loved my chooks, particularly one, now pretty old and disoriented – my crazy Jayden. My fuckwit-feathered Jayden with the golden heart. When I picked the chooks up from the coffee shop girl, he pooped himself then looked around to see who had done it. He hopped up onto my shoulder and crowed loudly to the world. Back at home, he decided to sleep on my pillow. One morning he crowed loudly at around three. I said, Listen son, you fucken keep that up and you are going in a hamburger. He crowed some more. Wouldn't have it any other way.

When I was in town, buying supplies and collecting the chooks from my now third-favourite girl, I visited the old folks' home. The nurse, the lovely friendly nurse, who remembered me from when I had called in on Henry and Lena, said, 'Hey you, how you doing?'

I asked if I could possibly call in on my town days, and just hang out with some oldies. Nothing special, just maybe to be there for someone else. The nurse, the beautiful, ever-caring nurse, said, 'Oh please, that would be so nice!'

I said, 'But I don't have any skills, you know, any anything really. Just to maybe sit and listen?'

'Oh please, none of that other stuff matters. To give is just to give. If you can sit with them, that would be so special. Some of them will remember you. Oh, thank you. By the way, we're looking for a part-time groundsman and someone to tend to Henry's rainforest garden. What do you reckon?' And she hugged me.

'We must all listen to others and care for them. And this will give hope. We must leave behind love. This is what a one person can do, this is what a true self does.'

* * *

A pot of tea, a meal left on the doorstep, a listen about nothing, a talk about a nothing. It's not an avoidance of the reason for sadness, but an acknowledgement of a friend who will be there for you. A friend who will listen. Wendy said, 'Hey, come on in.' She linked our arms. 'Let me show you around.' I wasn't sure about coming in to a real estate office. The walls shuddered, a few house photos fell to the floor and smoke came off the For Sale signs. The office alarm shrilled, 'Warning Warning, Intruder!'

She showed me her advertising, and though I winced a bit at first, I relaxed. Here was no pressure for a prospective buyer, just a photo with a listed price, and details like how many rooms, the size of the block, and what the repayments might be. And a friendly sign, *Would you like to go for a look*? No tricks.

'Not bad. Are you making a crust?'

'No, but I don't care. Well, I get by, and the people that come in are so sweet and this gives me hope that things will pick up.' She leaned into me. 'I guess freedom can come with a price. Thank you for saving me. Me and bub.'

She walked to the front of the shop, turned the Closed sign to face outside, and locked the door.

* * *

When Joan and Georgie were about to leave The Creek, Joan had said, Just hold me, put your head on my heart.

I held her softly, I held her with a deep love, and I said, 'Whatever happens tomorrow, does not matter because we've had today. Maybe one day we'll have another tomorrow …?'

'Shut the fuck up and hold me tighter, will you? I feel bad, I feel like I don't fit.'

'… because a heart that is broken, is a heart that has been truly loved. A true heart. I read that somewhere.'

'You are full of shit, and you just made that up. But it's beautiful. Truly beautiful. I love you. And I am so sorry.'

'Anyway, I think you fit nicely when you're snugged into me.'

Remembering Joan's love gave me strength and I wanted to yell rather loudly. And I did. I screamed and roared. The eel rolled a fake death roll when he saw me, the brush turkeys ran in circles, and the wallabies thumped the ground in happiness. Then I hummed, not so much a chant but a repetition of soft sound. For quite a while. Everything still felt strange, really strange, but God, I felt good.

Because avoidance and denial can never better or equal a transcendence of the spirit, and that's what I had now; a settling of soaring voices, a forty-part choral masterpiece, an infusion of undwelling pain, a sobbing of deep weeping that is a happiness of heaven. This current euphoric state of mind, with its advances in spark, spirit and spunk, didn't make the past disappear, far from it, but it made one small step forward within the landing of daily life, and its mental stability, appreciation and growth, and it kept that daily life in perspective with its predecessor and its possible postdecessor. A giant step, an acknowledged step, from me to me, which made such a difference in the time of personal becoming of personal normalness of the true self.

If I acknowledge and accept, the what is with its uncertainties, it becomes an ownership, which, borne of toil, and time, can then at least help me try to deal with the uncertainty. And the worship of life that will come from within the pain will give an inner strength and solidness of character to ground these emotions. If I choose not to acknowledge and accept, the pain breeds, breeds faster than a pair of rabbits, and we've all seen how that ends. Not deceiving myself would help, too. I wanted the actual, the now, the now within reality, the subconscious, past experiences, dreams, hopes, aspirations, a power from within and a more than a little from without, a sharing, a kindness, a generosity, a consideration without judgement.

Simple man really.

* * *

I like letters. They bring good news, bad news, exciting news, and sometimes they bring the self home.

'M'sier, You are now fre' from ze thing that 'eld you. Our plase of connecshon eez come from ze shame oui, an' ze shame admitted eez not a veakness, eet iz a luv, non? An' ze luv, she never dies, n'est-ce pas?

A très bientôt.'

* * *

I needed money so I worked at the old folks' home. I'm a bit slower these days, but an honest effort is enough. The old folks' home was a pleasant place to work and the pay, while being low, was enough to get me by for the few things I needed. Contentment is a pair of dirty hands.

One morning in the garden, I overheard two oldies on the verandah. One old fella asked his mate, 'When's that hermit fella coming in next?'

'Fuck me Brian, give me a break. You just asked that.'

Our Brian lashed his wheelchaired-foot out towards the other bloke's leg that was crawling with thin light purple spiders and surrounded by dark purple bike-tubes. The nurse came in, 'Boys, boys! Stop that! He comes in same day each fortnight, and today is his day, you know that. It's his special town day, just to see you grumpy old bastards. Buggered if I know why.'

'Hey miss, that was unfair.'

'It's me he comes to see, not you, you old cunt.'

'Boys, boys! Settle! He'll be in when he finishes in the garden. I'm sure he'll spend time with both of you.'

As I sat with the grumpy ones, one of them asked me about my family. 'Oh yes,' I said, 'I had two loving parents. And a grandfather who helped me a lot.'

I had to go and polish my halo.

In various stages of decrepitation, both physical and mental, they existed in the old folks' home. Some of them looked awful. Not their wrinkles or lack of mobility, but their sourpuss fucking whingeing. Occasionally a few would be happy with their lot, make the most of their what was. One old duck was a black woman, who looked at me sideways.

'You, tall one. You knew Joan didn't you.'

'Yes, I did know Joan.'

'She's my girl.'

Oh come off it love, you are way too old for that. But hang on, didn't Joan say something about having old parents? The black lady said, 'When I was admitted, Joan was so upset she could hardly talk for days. I used to go out with Peter you know. He was such a beautiful soul.'

Peter? You went out with Peter the carpenter? Is this what Henry meant in his letter when he said that Peter liked me in his family? Slow, I'm slow. I could see Peter caring for this woman. Peter was so solid in his old school way, his own independent thermos and sandwich for morning tea way, his own metal setsquare and pencil muttering way, he wouldn't give a fuck about what people said in town, because he was above them, so far above them in his beauty, his peaceful beauty. Sometimes you just don't know.

'He was indeed a beautiful soul. Did you say Joan was your girl?'

'Yes, mine and Peter's. And you must have been a lousy fuck for her to leave you for a woman.' And she cackled, a loud deep cackle, but it was a nice cackle. I think.

'Thanks for that little gem. Maybe she'll come back to me one day?'

'Doubt it son. You're fucking history.'

I think I love coming in here.

The oldies talked about their lives. The hardship and the isolation. They all had a love for the bush, their families and for life. They all did their best.

'We could have done a few things differently you know. That block, way up the end of The Creek near the plateau? Well, it was a sin to clear-fell it. Those massive brush boxes … we wasted them … everything is fucked now. We must all restart the whole system. Reclaim the bush away from greed.'

And he looked towards the sky, a little teary.

Sometimes you just don't know.

Some of them knew Joe, Peter and Henry. Henry especially, because he had been an inmate for a bit. And they told me stories that at times seemed obvious bullshit, exaggerated bullshit, but some rocked me.

'Joe was in New-Guinea during the war you know.'

I did know that. Boys, tell me something I don't know.

'He drove a dozer.'

I'm still in.

'Yeah, he pushed all them Jap bodies into a pile and burnt them.'

Fuck me, Joe, I had no idea you did that.

I can see him now, pushing the lantana into a pile so I could have an orchard. And I wept.

'You alright mate?'
I hate coming in here.

'Peter ran a dairy.'
Girls, comeon, tell me something I don't know.
'Yeah, for a while there, just to help his brother out, he ran two.'
What? You are kidding me. Two dairies at the one time? Fuck, that is superhuman.
I felt honoured. Sometimes you just don't know.
Is it too late to say thank you to some people? Even to a bloke who was the dad of my girl?

Henry, they said, Oh yes, he was a battler. Comeon chaps, I want more.
'Well, Henry and Lena used to grow tomatoes.'
I already knew this. Wasting my time here.
'They grafted, cross-pollinated and bred a new variety that could cope on a ridge in the winter. He was awarded a medal you know, off some agricultural mob. Henry told them to fuck off.'
'Boys! Stop that swearing!'
'And you should have seen Henry run! He was as fast as a greyhound chasing a possum.
Heaps of medals, too.'
I probed, 'Soo, did Henry ever offer advice to people who were, like down a bit? You know, help and stuff?'
They laughed. 'Did he what! Got his second community award for doing just that. One time, he even got some idiot to use horse liniment for his depression! Har har!'
I hate coming in here.

An old quiet man, just sitting there, dribbling. So quiet I thought he'd lost all his marbles as well as the drawstring bag, piped up and said, 'If we don't cherish our heritage, our personal histories and our landscapes, then we have nothing to live for, nothing to go forward with. We need to know our cultures, our past deeds, good and bad, and what a place means to us if we want to find out who we truly are as a person.'
Hope comes from different places. Angels come in different forms.
I love coming in here.

They slow down and reflect, with aches and pains enough to share. Some, but not all, had the inner peace that said, I'm ready. Some threw regrets at the wall, a wall that didn't listen, a wall that didn't even give a rebound or a fucking echo because their regrets were too late. Reflections and regrets had caused anguish over lost times with family because of the tough bush work that took them away, and they said sorry, loudly, but only to themselves, like the heart-attack bushwalker who gives expensive Champagne as a thank you present, because no-one was left to hear them or come to visit them. The smell of death was here, but it was dulled, and occasionally extinguished, by an overall gentleness of life, of sorrow, but also of a deep love. I hate coming in here. Not because my turn will come to be old, but because I'm not as peaceful and kind as them. Reflection needed no rules for these people, and they needed no rules for reflection – backwards or forwards. They said, I own this shit, these times I've had, and I don't need to brag, about things I never did or things that never were. Even within any insecurities we might perceive, let us acknowledge their grace. Let us give beauty to these oldies. Their hearts are at home.

I still love coming in here.

These old people taught me so much beauty without directly meaning to teach it to me. One of the blokes had said, 'If you choose to live only in your memories, then you're already dead.'

The nurse, the ever-patient nurse, the ever-accepting nurse, had said, 'Pfff! Have you ever heard such a thing?'

No, I hadn't, but I got it. Because if memories delve into nostalgia, they tend to tell porkies. Well, I thought I got it, until another old fella said, 'What if that's all I got left?'

Ho-ly shit, now that is sad, but in a nice way sad. Memories are stabilisers, rectifiers in a truthful way regardless of their flaws. Defying death by living in the past. Why not? Memory is identity, draw it together from different spider webs, pack your port sensibly, because memories don't fade, they become brighter. The nurse, the overworked but caring nurse, said, 'Thank you for coming in. These old bastards look up to you. You mean so much to them. And to me.' And she kissed me on the cheek.

* * *

I like letters. Little envelopes stamped with an abstract beauty, but their inside sheets of paper, all crisply folded, can bring a heart known to some or none, their words like silent raindrops may indeed fall, and without wings they may teach me to fly beyond the sky. They also can bring me back to Earth. The Darling River wrote me a letter. 'Hey you, your soul is here, and will always remain here, whether you are here or not, we both know that. Anyway, you old bastard, you okay? You weren't real settled last time you were here.'

Thank you for your kind sentiments, old river. I am really well. And no, I wasn't at ease and I am sorry because you deserve better. And yes, my soul is out there with you. But that's okay, because I don't need it anymore. It's safe with you. Yours to keep.

I like letters. Regardless of bad news, good news, or in between news, they are always exciting and often full of kindness. The Creek wrote me a letter. 'Dear Tony, Your soul may be out there in the grey country yes, but your love is here, waiting. And with your time coming soon, will you know how to let go?'

I hear you, my Creek. And you are correct, my soul is out on the old river, but my love is here. It is with you because you let me be me. And it is with a girl, and I loved this girl, still do, this girl who stole my heart. She's still got it too. It was easy dancing with her, but then she changed partners. I don't think she meant to, because I know it hurt her too. I accepted her love, your love too. Still do. She's still waiting you say? Not so sure about that, but I sure hope so. And about the letting go thing. No, I don't know how to let go. No idea how to. I will take each day as it comes, even with the disappointments and pain and joy, and I will never limp to the finish line. I will die in the bush, just like the old red dog did. Just like old Henry said he should have.

* * *

Time is an old winding grey river, time is a fast clear creek next to a rainforest that never runs dry, time is your life as it flows downstream, no matter which waterway of life you choose.

* * *

'You see that old bloke who called in to check out the Darling River paintings?'

'Long beard, scruffy, bit vague?'

'Yep, that is him. Grandma told me stories. She said that every month he used to come in to the gallery to look at a painting of the Darling River, but then he didn't come in for ages. Grandma says he lives by himself next to the rainforest. And he has been seen, sitting in a cave, muttering as if there are others next to him.'

'In a cave?

'Yes, with a weird looking stuffed bantam on his shoulder. And apparently, he talks to a pair of death adders.

'Why would you do that?'

'And she heard that he won't wear leather and doesn't kill any living things. He drinks sherry, grinds corn, gets light from olive oil lamps, has an old hand saw mounted on his kitchen wall, and wanders about the mountains in a dress planting trees.'

* * *

I was in a better place. An older, better place. Me, not the place. Although, place is as vital as an age, no matter how old it is. Even with vagueness kicking in, I was ready.

EB-At last, another whorehouse coming up. Thank God!

RB-Noo, he merely means he's more settled, you fool. Ready for the end I'd say.

EB-Put your money where your big fucking mouth is buddy. And you watch your insults.

After the gallery, I had one more visit before I left Brisbane.

They were standing on the corner, wearing believably short tight skirts, and my heart was thumping, because I knew that I was going to have hot sex. The desire was still strong, but I wasn't so sure about the doing of the anticipated hot sex thing.

I walked up to a long black woman in a cool red skirt, a tiny tiny, tight red stretchy skirt, a light-black woman, I'm guessing mid-thirties, short thick black hair, flat shoes, stockings, firm thighs, and a low-cut blouse that lifted her breasts, and I asked her how much.

'You got fifty dollars old man?'

She closed the door, sat opposite me and slowly opened her legs. *Must be able to drive an old codger wild.* Stockings, no pants and a shaved pussy; I stared as if it were my first time. Thank goodness the world can still change me.

She said, 'You haven't done this for a while.'

Some people are just so insightful. 'No, and I'm not sure how I'll go here. Don't 'spose you speak French?'

'No. Do I look French?'

'Well yes, you do.'

We undressed and stood together, and I stroked her slowly. Her skin was the colour of light honey, untouched virgin honey, made from the nectar of Goddesses, from the beauty of all females. I kissed her red-lippy mouth, her soft inviting mouth and I ran my hands through her hair and down her neck. Who knows how this will end up? It sure was nice so far. I relaxed and stopped worrying about not getting a stiff cock. The lust was strong, and the pleasure of her gorgeous body was stronger. She laid on her back and closed her eyes and I continued stroking. She said, 'Ooh, this is so nice. You may continue.' Sure will honey, because I've already paid to see the show. Thanks grandpa. I've worked it out; it's the smoothness and the curves. I'm still a slow learner. She raised both arms above her head as I ran my hands from her fingers along her upturned arms and down her smooth body. It's also the thighs and the mound. Slow remember. Thank you for beautiful woman, thank you for the lust I have known and shared.

I asked, 'Could you please hop on top of me?'

I lay down and she straddled me, and slid her slippery pussy lips up and down on my bendy stiff cock. I liked what she was doing, and so did she. It felt really nice, but somehow weird. I was so horny, so wanting to bend her over and fuck her, but my cock wouldn't go fully hard. Hard enough maybe to do the job, but not the same. Memories here I come.

RB-How crass. You what, went with a hooker? Another one? Please. What is wrong with you? Apart from your low, or even non-existent morals, you have negated all that we, and I mean we, had talked about, and, I might add, agreed upon re focussing on the truth, goodness, and beauty.

EB-Oh for fuck's sake dude. For starters, go easy on the girls. One day, you ... no, wait, you'd never even think like that, I forgot. Your judgement calls are way out of your pay bracket, so just stick with numbers and shit. And, by the way, you owe me. Told you so. I was right. Again.

'Not many choose me, but you did. Why?'

I paused a bit. 'Because you are beautiful?'

'Thank you, but I'm guessing the way you've been caressing me, and your soft French words, I must remind you of someone.'

Yes. Sorry, I ...'

'Hey, we all have our reasons to be here.'

She kissed me and I left. Got dressed first though.

* * *

'I'm waiting for you
I want you to carry me home
Home to your place, our place
Where you smile in my heart.'

* * *

'Hey. Anyone home?'
　'Hi.'
'Can I spend the night with you?'
'Sure. I don't have a girlfriend. Come in.'

* * *

You know you can never truly be free of your likes and dislikes, of your awful hypocrisy, but with pride in what you have achieved and with this new understanding of your true self, you can keep going with everything that seemed possible. A hope for this true self, and even the giving of hope to others without telling them. Hey, if old Henry says you were wonderful, who's to argue? Life is a glorious adventure, one that still has choices, things that are exciting, simple, even mundane. And maybe memories that were done living life can be a nourishment?

You are in a time of light, of joy, of passion (and please, can we go back to that little hooker?), and in a time of beautiful peace. And I was a bit harsh on old rational brain back there in the cave with my rant. I know now that we must help each other, and I'm okay with that, as I know you are too. Tu ne regrette rien. Regret nothing my sweet, as long as we all agree that reason will never vanquish imagination and that I am the fucking boss. See you soon bitch. And give my love to that girl, the one we both love.

Acknowledgements

To Evonne Fisher. For your tolerance of my unrelenting dodgy jokes, my disappearances to rivers, and my disappearances to write. Thank you my sweet.

IndieMosh Publishing. Professionalism and kindness. And answering my endless questions. Thank you Jenny.

Rory Freemantle. Holy smoke you are amazing. Your editing and proof-reading were extraordinary. I am so grateful for all you've done for me. My shout.

Peter Harris. Thank you for your incredible skills and compassion and understanding and everything you do for me. I loved your cover.

Ally Mosher. For helping with the techs of the cover, and care and friendship and beautiful emails.

Trees. In particular, rainforest trees. It's no good just having a list of species, you have to know how to identify them. I started with, A key to the common families of trees and shrubs using vegetative characters, by J. B. Williams and G. J. Harden, Department of Botany, University of New England, Armidale, New South Wales, 1979. Next was, How to identify plants. Same mob. 1984. Then came, Fruits. A guide to some common and unusual fruits found in rainforests. 1979. Same again. Rainforest climbing plants. 1984. Guess who. Then came, Rainforest trees and shrubs, again by Williams and Harden. 1979. This field guide uses leaf features to identify rainforest trees and shrubs in New South Wales and South-eastern Queensland. These were my references, along with quite a few locals.

Birds. I started early, with field guides from Cayley, went to Slater, to Morcombe, then Menkhorst. And back again. Plus, of course, with Alan K. Morris, the man.

Dandelions. Now there's a plant. 'Ten Things You Might Not Know About Dandelions', by Anita Sanchez, is beautifully written and full of love for the plant. Thank you Anita for permission.

Peter Porch topped up my basic mechanical knowledge of the Dodge. Thank you. West Dubbo never dies.

Sometimes when you have to phone a business, corporation or government dept, it can be frustrating. The Australian Broadcasting Corporation, known as Auntie, is brilliant. Bang, straight through to the copyright department, and yes, you can use information. No photos though, no direct quotes, but other than that away you go. Zoe Kean's article on eels was electrifying. Not even Friday yet. Eels are incredible creatures and their journey to breed is an outstanding story.
Thank you Zoe Kean and ABC.
Eels-https://www.abc.net.au/news/science/2022-01-09/eels-australia-most-hardcore-animal/100572614

Bees. Bel Smith spoke with a couple of experts about the social lives of bees on Radio National, Australian Broadcasting Corporation 25/5/2019. Excellent information. Thank you.
https://www.abc.net.au/radionational/programs/scienceshow/high-drama-in-the-lives-of-honey-bees/11147578

The ABC again. Dragonflies and damselflies: Why these vividly coloured, mosquito-eating predators are 'underrated' insects, by Gavin McGrath.

Australia's stinging trees pack a punch you don't want to experience. Thank you Tony Mlynarik, Conservation Partnerships Officer, Brisbane City Council, for permission to use your information in a Land for Wildlife article.

Thank you Lisa Palermo, director of Ellpee, for permission to quote, in-directly it seems, a couple of lines from Brian Cadd's 'Don't You Know it's Magic?' in a not musical context. I was referring to the unknown bird who calls at first light in winter. Plus The Creek itself. Both have a magic that is not trickery, or shallow, but a life-giving and life-sustaining force. Just like Brian Cadd.